The SECRET OF JI 3:
SHADOW OF THE ANCIENTS

Also available in The Secret of Ji series:
Six Heirs
The Orphan's Promise

Forthcoming:
The Eternal Master

The SECRET OF JI 3:
SHADOW OF THE ANCIENTS

PIERRE GRIMBERT

TRANSLATED BY
MATT ROSS

This is a work of fiction. Names, characters, organizations, places, events, and incidents are either products of the author's imagination or are used fictitiously.

Text copyright © 2013 by Pierre Grimbert
English translation copyright © 2014 by Matt Ross

All rights reserved.

No part of this book may be reproduced, or stored in a retrieval system, or transmitted in any form or by any means, electronic, mechanical, photocopying, recording, or otherwise, without express written permission of the publisher.

The Secret of Ji 3: Shadow of the Ancients was first published in 1998 by Les éditions Mnémos as *Le Secret de Ji, volume 3: L'Ombre des anciens.* Translated from the French by Matt Ross.

Published by AmazonCrossing, Seattle

www.apub.com

Amazon, the Amazon logo, and AmazonCrossing are trademarks of Amazon.com, Inc., or its affiliates.

ISBN-13: 9781477825013
ISBN-10: 1477825010

Cover design by Kerrie Robertson

Library of Congress Control Number: 2014905665

Printed in the United States of America

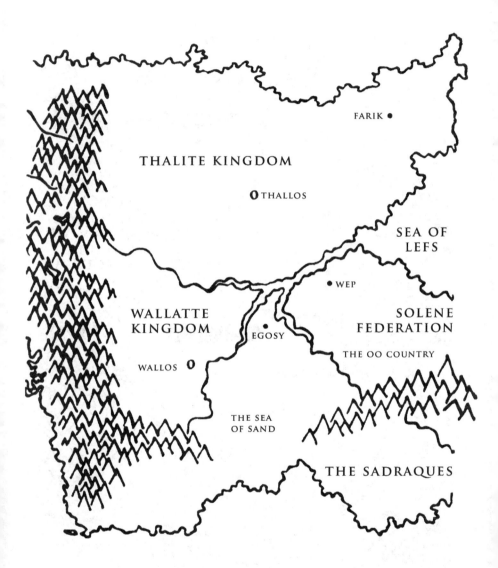

AUTHOR'S NOTE

At the end of the book, the reader will find a "Short Anecdotal Encyclopedia of the Known World," a glossary that defines certain terms used by the narrator and provides supplementary details that don't appear in the story, without giving the story away, of course—far from it!

Therefore, the reading of the "Short Anecdotal Encyclopedia" can be done in parallel with the story, at moments the reader finds opportune.

CONTENTS

Prologue 1

Book V: The Old Country 1

Book VI: Pilgrims 85

Book VII: To the Memory of Men 171

Short Anecdotal Encyclopedia
of the Known World 243

PROLOGUE

A Zü reveals his name only to his peers . . . and his dying victims.

My name is Judge Zamerine, leader of Zuïa's messengers in the Upper Kingdoms. My power stretches across the six wealthiest kingdoms of the known world. I control four hundred devoted men ready to sacrifice themselves. Each and every one carries the sacred hati. Four hundred elite soldiers, feared even in the smallest, most remote villages.

The greatest kings dare not defy me. They fear Zuïa's judgment. They fear me. I once considered myself to be the most powerful person north of the Median Sea. I was wrong.

I believe my master to be a god.

Or, at least, an incarnation of one. A servant god of Zuïa, even if my master jeers at the idea. Perhaps he does not know, but he is serving the goddess's plan, just as I am. I am sure of it.

I should be sure of it.

My newfound vulnerability is heavy and difficult to bear. My master can rid himself of any threat. He is invulnerable. He reads minds. He controls the bodies of others. He can kill with a caress, or a look.

This is not legend. I have seen him do it.

He could have made me his slave, just another miserable soul pacing among the many tens of thousands in his encampment. But I preferred to become his ally.

I put my intelligence at his service. My influence in the Upper Kingdoms is useful to him, and my presence at his side reinforces his hold over the barbarian horde that makes up his army. Our army.

I proved myself to him, and he has recognized my worth. He has granted me a personal guard while we wait for my assistant to return with better men. Soon a hundred of my messengers will gather at my side, while the others await my command. I have never seen anything like it, not since the arenas of Lus'an.

My master gave me a thousand slaves, and I tried to make them live according to Zuïa's law. It was an interesting experiment. Six hundred of them remain.

My master has a grand project planned, one that exceeds mortal ambitions. He takes no half measures. If he attacks a village, he burns it to the ground. If he punishes a traitor, he will torture the man on the rack for several dékades. Everything my master attempts, he achieves. No hesitation. No weakness.

My master knows exactly what he wants, though he speaks of it to no one. He is the most secretive of men. Even I do not know his face. All I know is his name: Saat.

The king of the Guoris did not have the reputation of an easygoing man. Ossrok, the northerner who commanded the mercenary fleet for the Land of Beauty, stood in front of the king, who did nothing to change this reputation.

"I can hardly congratulate you!" the king shouted. "Yet again, you let some oblivious travelers land on the Sacred Island. And this, despite your supposed vigilance!"

"Usul's island has not been under surveillance for more than two moons," the mercenary objected. "Following your orders, Majesty."

"I never ordered you to stop patrolling it!" the indignant king responded, his face darkening with rage. "I simply asked you to show some discretion. I dare you to say otherwise!"

Ossrok knew, despite his employer's dishonesty, to hold his tongue. The original idea was to let the Sacred Island fall away into memory. To do this, he had to pull all of their boats away from her coast. A single, lonely frigate passed by each day to ensure that all was in order and to feed the monsters that guarded the accursed place. However, today the frigate's crew had found traces of a secret foray onto the island, and now Ossrok was at the mercy of the king's tirade.

"Most of them must be dead," the mercenary announced, in a tone he hoped was reassuring. "With luck, only one escaped, which would explain why we didn't find their boat. My men didn't venture to the island's center, of course, but I am willing to bet they would have found several corpses."

"You don't understand anything then! I don't want these people to die," the king responded.

Ossrok thought about this before responding. Indeed, he didn't understand.

"Majesty," he began slowly. "Excuse my audacity, but the rats of Farik are not tame animals. They are fierce enough that the Eastians use them on the field of battle, as you know. A simple bite can be fatal if the animal carries the sickness. And several of the creatures we released on the island were pregnant, I am sure of it. And now . . . now, you're telling me you didn't want them dead?"

"No, of course not," the king whispered, truly dismayed. "The rats were only supposed to scare them."

"The fate of these foreigners will serve as an example then," the mercenary replied. "You can count on my men to tell this story to anyone who will listen."

The king slowly nodded his head. His anger dissipated, and in its place bitterness, regret, and guilt pooled. He dismissed the commander with a gesture.

"Majesty," Ossrok stubbornly continued. "Why are you so worried? It was just a few foreigners, foreigners who deliberately transgressed one of the most important taboos in the Land of Beauty. Don't you think they deserved their fate?"

"The rats are nothing, Ossrok. Maybe it will be better for those who die from the sickness. If they saw Usul and survived, their agony has only just begun. I am crying because I couldn't stop that. I am crying . . . with compassion."

The commander finally left the king, shaking his head. The Guoris were a very strange people.

I remember the arenas on Lus'an. I had just turned eleven, already a responsible man. Smart enough, anyway, to understand that there was no real way for the bastard son of a slave to serve Zuïa.

One day, a messenger brought Zuïa's sentence to my mother, at the request of my presumed father. I did nothing to stop him.

I already had a deep faith in the goddess, and, as I have said, I was a responsible man. I asked the messenger to bring me to one of the temples. I had only one desire: to be like my father, to become a priest of Zuïa, to be among the elite.

At the time, I didn't know that I would have to confront death. I hardly worried about the death of others, which was as natural to me then as it is now, but I also had no thought for my own, inevitable end, which hovered nearby as if behind a dark veil, or on a horizon too distant for me to see.

My stay in the novices' temple was very short. During my time there, I worked with other men of my age, completing the various tasks needed on a farm. More than anything else, though, I learned about suspicion and intrigue. Eventually I learned to be cunning, and I formed several of my own alliances with the most powerful boys there. Some volunteered, others were forced. It was a great skill I developed in the temple, one that I still work to improve, and without which I would most likely not be alive today.

One day, all of the novices walked the road to Lus'an. We went by foot, under an oppressive sun, shouting Zuïa's laws over and over again. This was the custom of the temple, and under the bright sun we yelled our creed so loudly that the messengers couldn't hear the sound of their own horses.

The journey took four days. Six boys died from exhaustion and thirst. They were too weak to begin with. After we began, no amount of water or rest could have saved them. Had they completed the march, they would have died a few days later anyhow. It was better for them to die as they had.

Two others tried to run away, but we had already entered Lus'an, and no one can leave that land except the messengers. The two who tried to run lost their right to be novices and, as a result, became our slaves. I think the second one survived eleven days.

As for me, I made sure to use the journey to strengthen my alliances. Promises for the gullible ones, threats for the weak, extortion for those who gave me the opportunity. I encouraged rivalries, always taking the winner's side. I flattered the receptive ones, bought the greedy, and swore fidelity to the fools. I played the game so well that when we arrived, of the sixty-seven novices remaining, twelve were fully loyal only to me, and they became my guard. Twenty-one others were indebted to me, and they became my people. Another twenty or so were scared of me, and they became my slaves. The dozen remaining represented the small dissenting faction of enemies, an inevitability. Even the most virtuous of men can't help but have enemies.

None of us had heard about the arenas. At nightfall on the fourth day of the march, we reached Lus'an. In the mythical temple of the Great Work, they put us in separate cells. This was the first step in our training.

That the cells were locked was not strange to me; the temples were always built that way. But why separate us? I wondered. And why exempt us from our daily chores?

They suggested we sleep, so I dutifully applied myself to the task. Actually, it wasn't hard; the long trip had exhausted me, the same as everyone else. The prospect of tomorrow's trials loomed over me.

As I drifted to sleep, I could hear some novices talking with their neighbors through the bars of their cells. I absentmindedly listened, always on the lookout for some way to blackmail or control them. Eventually sleep overtook me, by the goddess's good grace. I was going to need all my energy.

We were prisoners in our cells until midday. The messengers let us out only to bring us directly to the arenas. Never in my life had I seen so many priests in one place. We all gathered there, from lowly novices to the Supreme Judges, adorned in the goddess's most coveted decorations, the kind you can only see in Lus'an. We all had congregated, paying homage to tradition.

I didn't bother to study the gathered priests with more than a cursory look. I had already figured out what was going to happen. The sixty-seven novices were in a walled-in circle. A sea of red Züu covered the tiered benches of the arena. On the walls hung thirty hati, placed at regular intervals.

Zuïa was choosing her messengers.

I gathered my guard to my side and looked for a signal from the Judges. But it never came. Instead I took the initiative and sent my men toward a portion of the wall. We had grabbed thirteen hati before the others even moved.

Soon they followed my lead, and a scramble exploded across the arena. The novices fought each other, grabbing at daggers, murder in their eyes. A few among my own "people" approached us, searching for protection, but we gave them none. The fools had hesitated and earned no quarter from me. I chased them down, screaming in their faces, demanding that they return with a hati. Some turned and joined the fray. Others continued to plead for *protection. With a solemn nod I had my guard slaughter those who failed me. Mayhem engulfed the arena.*

When three of my men fell, I immediately recruited those who had slain them. The victors had been my slaves. Two I kept, but the third, an enemy from the beginning, I stabbed as soon as his back was turned.

Supreme in my power, I now had two hati in my hands. I gave one to the strongest unarmed novice, earning his gratitude and loyalty as the blade passed from hand to hand. He thanked me by cutting the throats of my two remaining enemies.

The fight was over. Twenty-six novices remained. Of them, only fifteen were unharmed. The hati were not poisoned, of course, but the victory was easy all the same.

Through the blood of others I earned the praise of the Supreme Judges. Zuïa recognized me as one of her best servants. Never had I been so happy. It was a joy that remained unmatched until I met my new master. He will spread the arenas to all the kingdoms in the world.

Emaz Drékin walked down a crudely carved stone staircase. Few people had ever walked this path. It was a privilege for those few who had earned the title Emaz. Drékin himself hadn't walked it for nearly thirty years, not since Lana's birth.

He concentrated on his feet and the stone beneath them. Though the stairs were wide, some were covered in a thick, slippery dust, others by rubble, others still by the bones of animals that had made this underground their home. In the dancing light of his torch, the descent felt even more dangerous. Emaz Drékin had only one desire: to be done with this.

When he finally reached the bottom of the stairs, he walked hastily across an immense, deserted room. It was empty and abandoned, like all the others. He took the first passageway on his right, then a second to the left, which ended at a locked door. The Emaz stuck his key in the hole and jiggled the lock.

For a moment he feared that the lock would be too rusted over, but with an effort, the key turned, and the door opened with a groan, which resonated noisily in the man-made cave.

Beyond the door lay another room, just as big and empty as the one before. Drékin ignored the barren shelves and walked straight toward one of the marble columns, behind which he squatted down. He pressed on a hidden mechanism and a trap-door opened at his feet. Drékin carefully placed his foot on the first rung of the ladder below, hoping that the years hadn't eaten away the wood. As he made his way down, the light from his torch swept away the shadowy darkness.

Nothing had changed. The hidden room was exactly as he had left it twenty-eight years earlier. He slowly finished his descent, taking care to not miss a step, or let his torch fall. The room was filled with notebooks, ancient texts, and parchment. Should the torch slip from his fingers, a fire would engulf him before he could make his escape.

Maybe fire was the solution . . . The thought turned over in his mind for a long moment.

He thought about the little space, hardly more than a closet, and imagined flames licking at the dry paper. For centuries the Maz had filled it with dangerous writings. Stacks of texts had been loosely tossed into this nook, as if it were the trash heap of the Temple's archives. Drékin needed but one text, and he knew exactly where it was.

He found what he sought, a little volume placed at the top of the nearest pile. The priest gently swept away the dust on the cover. A title and a name emerged from the dark leather. *To the Memory of Men. Maz A. d'Algonde.*

Drékin sighed. He opened the book and scanned a few lines before slamming its secrets closed, horrified.

Lana was no longer in Mestèbe. Had she been killed? Had she fled? He had no idea. But he couldn't live with this weight on his mind. He couldn't risk anyone discovering this journal one day.

He had to act, even if it went against all the principles he had been teaching his whole life.

My master is powerful, and not only in his own right. He has a gift of surrounding himself with extraordinary men. Men like me.

His power is equal to a god's, and he chooses his own priests. We are his allies, his captains, his cursed souls—as the slaves call us.

My master is skilled at so many things that he has no real need for us captains. Our army, far from struggling, grows by the day.

To call it an army is misleading, though; it's more like a horde. They are barbarian warriors who speak in strange tongues; they are primitive and violent brutes, cruel to their enemies and their allies alike. They have no guiding principles, no code or civility. Though they are vile and repugnant creatures, their overwhelming power intoxicates me.

My master is a peerless strategist. His only fault is that he pays no mind to our losses. Though our troops seem inexhaustible, I am loath to give our adversaries even the slightest hint of victory by wastefully sacrificing even a few hundred men.

Sometimes my master condescends to hear my advice. When he does, we are rewarded with sensational victories. The conquered, so impressed and scared, choose to join our ranks as soldiers rather than as slaves. I am proud of these victories and the soldiers they bring. As a reward for joining, the conquered soldiers are permitted to bring with them their oldest sons. The others—women, old men, children, the sick and crippled—my master deals with according to his mood. Our Great Work feeds no useless mouths.

Perhaps that's what it is. Perhaps the Great Work is ridding the world of unproductive souls—the inept, the weak, the inferior people that plague us. My master must be an incarnation of Zuïa.

I said he surrounds himself with extraordinary men, and he does, though I should clarify that not all of these men are my friends, nor do I approve of them all. Two that are particularly contemptible are his war chiefs.

The first remains a stranger to me, except for his bizarre letters. His scribblings are circular and unpredictable; they make me question his sanity. The second war chief I have no doubts about. He is a brute above all else, with a skull as thick as an oak tree and empty as Aluen's tomb.

His full name is Gors'a'min Lu Wallos, but everyone calls him Gor, or, when his back is turned, Gor the Gentle. Not because he ever showed tenderness, but because he so thoroughly enjoys torture.

Gor is the biggest human I have ever seen. He is larger than the Arque who broke Dyree's nose in the Small Palace, and much stronger too. I saw him defeat three horses, which were being whipped bloody, in a match of tug-of-war. After he had pulled them ten steps, the beasts collapsed, their exhausted bodies tangling together in a pile of hooves and manes.

I can't stand his stupidity, his drunkenness, his frequent rages. More than anything else, I hate the disrespect he shows me. I admit he can make any soldier obey his command—they're made out of the same mud, after all—but his arrogance plagues me unrelentingly.

Dyree will soon join us. My assistant is the only novice to have ever escaped the arenas of Lus'an with twelve hati. Not content only to protect his own blade, he killed the other boys to take their trophies. He might have collected them all had I not intervened. I was overseeing the rite, and eventually ended the carnage Dyree was inflicting. He is the best warrior I have ever seen. Even without a hati, he might be able to beat Gor the Gentle.

Unfortunately, my assistant can't be bothered to become a full messenger, to become Zadyree. I doubt his faith in Zuïa. Even so, his place at my side makes him a messenger among messengers, the tracker of traitors. It is a difficult task, and one that he deeply enjoys. He likes the dangerous prey, he likes to best another, he likes to kill. He will be with us soon.

Upon his arrival, I will put Dyree in charge of the slaves, who are far too numerous to be managed by a single captain. I still have no idea what my master plans to do with them. I doubt he wants to sell them, given his immense wealth. Maybe he wants them to work? But for what project? What new stone will he have them place for the Great Work?

Up until now, the only task given to the slaves is to pray. They have no choice, but this simple faith is all they have left, so they take to it with the passion that only the hopeless can muster.

My master ordained a certain Emaz Chebree as the grand priestess of the god Somber. I don't know if this name, Somber, is a real one or not, or if its constant use has overwhelmed the original. I have never heard of such a god, but it is the name that Chebree shouts, invokes, prays to, and makes her subjects fear and adore. Somber, the god chosen by my master.

Many of our warriors have converted to this new cult. Somber has become He Who Vanquishes, and this idea pleases the warriors greatly. My master is quite satisfied with the rapid expansion of his new religion.

Of course, I am still loyal to Zuïa, despite Chebree, who can be quite convincing. As far as being an Emaz, I would be surprised if she had ever even seen the Holy City of Ith. But she is a passionate and calculating woman who has earned my respect. She is also ambitious, and along with my esteem comes suspicion.

The last of the priests is none other than my master's son. At least, we think he is the master's son, and neither of them corrects us. He is a large, well-built young man, but he doesn't have any of the Goranese traits that one would expect.

I don't know what his talents are. He sleeps a lot, and remains motionless most other times. He seems to not see or hear us. Only my master can wake him from his listless state.

His eyes. I can't stand his gaze. An empty, haunting gaze. A somber gaze.

BOOK V:
THE OLD COUNTRY

The tavern door swung open, letting in the wind and rain, and, worst of all, two unusual characters. Worja Standing-Drinker had been a barkeep for thirty-five years, and he had owned the shoddy tavern in Three-Banks, at the mouth of the river Rochane, for the last ten years. As he leveled his gaze on the two figures in the entryway, all of his experience told him two things. The first was that the new customers weren't Rominian, and the second was that they weren't in his bar to drink or eat. He glanced under the counter to make sure that his dagger was in reach.

The taller stranger was unquestionably an Arque, although his skin was noticeably darker than that of an average northerner. But the color of his skin was a minor detail, one that Worja noticed only after he was able to take in the sheer size of the giant. The stranger was as hairy as a bear and looked to be at least twice as strong. A mace dangled ominously from his side.

The origins of the smaller stranger were harder to guess; he might have been Lorelien, or Kaulien. Like his companion, he carried a weapon. Not a mace, but a rapier instead, and it clanked against his thigh as he walked. Both men wore fresh wounds and sullen expressions, and from his post behind the bar, Worja could see the strangers were nothing but trouble.

The two strangers approached the bar with heavy footsteps, and as they walked, the innkeeper's eyes silently pleaded to his patrons for help. To his dismay, he saw that his five possible rescuers kept their noses firmly in their goblets. Rominians didn't like strangers, especially armed and surly ones.

"We're looking for a healer," the Lorelien announced, his voice weary. "We were told that you know one."

Worja cursed the idiot who had directed these strangers to his door. It must have been a Presdanian. *May the god Phiras bring wrath upon the Presdanians*, he thought.

"Whoever told you that is a liar, good sirs. There is no one in all of Three-Banks who could claim to be a healer. I'm afraid you'll have to continue on to Mestèbe," Worja answered quietly.

The Lorelien translated the exchange for the Arque, who shook his head, his eyes wide with emotion. The answer seemed not to suit the strangers. Worja should have guessed as much.

The Lorelien didn't let up. "Unfortunately, we're short on time, barkeep. Who cares for your wounded in Three-Banks? Surely there must be someone in this town capable of providing basic care. Do I have to bribe his name out of you?"

"That won't be necessary, sir. Like I already said, there's no one here who can help you. I suggest that you go on your way immediately, if you're in such a hurry."

When will these strangers get the hint that they aren't wanted here, Worja wondered as he tightened his grip on the dagger, his hands trembling.

The Lorelien sighed and leaned his back against the counter, looking resigned. Suddenly, in one fluid movement, he spun around and hopped over to the opposite side of the bar. A moment later the barkeep had his hands in the air and a blade at his throat.

"Right, then!" the stranger announced. "I guess my friend and I haven't made ourselves clear. We didn't come here to burn this place down, although personally I'm starting to feel the temptation. We're just looking for a healer, and if we don't receive this simple bit of information by the end of the night, I can tell you one thing: we will not be the only ones in need of the healer's services!"

Not a single one of the Rominians, bewildered and stunned by the sudden outburst of violence, moved a muscle. The Lorelien continued his menacing tirade, his hands tightly holding Worja, whose legs were quivering.

"My friend Bowbaq here sank an entire pirate ship this past dékade. Don't you think it might not be such a good idea to upset him?" They all looked at Bowbaq fearfully.

"Look mean, Bowbaq," Rey ordered, and though the giant hadn't understood a single word of the actor's speech in Rominian, this he understood.

The giant bared his teeth and contorted his face to look like Mir the lion. Then, feeling ridiculous, he decided to simply cross his arms and stand in front of the door. Rey tried hard not to laugh, though the giant's expression produced the desired effect.

"What business do you want with a healer?" piped up one of the hostages, finally.

"Hmm, I don't know, we want to buy a fishing net? By all the gods and their whores, what do you think we want? We have a friend who needs a healer as soon as possible. I'll give a golden terce to anyone who gives us a chance to save him."

"Lorelien money is worthless here," the drunkard grumbled.

"It's a golden terce or a private meeting with my friend Bowbaq. I can guarantee it will be a real lively meeting. Now, do I have any volunteers?"

After a moment of tense silence, a Rominian stepped forward. "The healer is my brother, Vi'at," he admitted reluctantly. "I'll take you there for a golden terce. But I can't make any promises that he'll agree to help you. He's a thoroughbred Hélanian like me. He refuses to talk to Presdanians, much less strangers."

"I can be quite convincing," responded Rey with a sneer as he released the innkeeper. "My arguments aren't the kind you can easily deny."

The *Othenor* danced slowly on the clear water at the mouth of the Rochane, its wooden beams groaning slightly as if it were resting after the thousands of leagues covered since the last moon. The boat mirrored the state of its passengers: exhausted, empty, and despondent.

Yan had been watching over Grigán since they had reached Three-Banks, giving Corenn a chance to rest. Yan had sailed the *Othenor* to the continent at exceptional speed: their incursion onto the Sacred Island of the Guoris had been just the night before, and the young man had not slept since then.

Maz Lana stopped praying briefly to observe the young Kaulien. Yan had seen Usul. He had spoken with a god, and after, he had not said more than ten words. Grigán's wound tortured him, as it did all of them, but was there something else? What did Yan know? What had he kept hidden from them?

Grace called for Lana to worry first about the warrior, before thinking about their quest, but Lana still prayed to Eurydis to relieve Yan from his pains. *A young man shouldn't have to bear such torments.*

The captain's cabin door opened and Léti stepped in. She had cried most of the voyage, but had no tears left. Her face was without expression, or rather, it looked the same as always: furrowed brow, pursed lips, and searching gaze. Scorning the injustice and indignant at her powerlessness.

"They're coming," she said in a weary voice. "They found someone."

Lana left to wake Corenn, which was easy enough, since the Mother hadn't been able to fall asleep. Bowbaq, Rey, and a small, plump Rominian soon joined them next to Grigán, who was laid out on the floor.

"What happened to your face?" Corenn asked the stranger. "Rey, did you hit him?"

"He fell," Rey assured her. "Right, Vi'at, my friend?"

"It's true," the man mumbled as he rubbed his chin. "I took a false step and fell."

The Mother shot a disapproving glare at Rey, who acted like he hadn't seen it. Then she shifted her gaze to Bowbaq, who blushed from ear to ear. She promised herself she would figure out what had happened soon, but for now there were more pressing matters.

After the healer took a glance at Grigán, he asked simply, "What bit him?"

"Rats," Corenn responded, seeing no reason to lie. "Dozens of them."

"Like the ones you find on the islands of the Guoris, maybe?"

Rey interjected, "Don't take another false step, Vi'at, my friend."

"Nothing to worry about. Your story isn't mine. Guoris or Loreliens, you are all foreigners. What matters is the ten golden terces you promised me. I want to see them."

The Rominian, emboldened by Corenn's presence, was gaining confidence. Léti approached him to protest, but the Mother counted out ten coins onto the healer's outstretched hand.

"I will give you another ten if you can save him, Master Vi'at," said Corenn as she left the room. And if he didn't?

"I don't want anyone stepping on my toes," the man practically shouted. "Everyone leave. I only need one person to help."

"Me," Yan said in a choked voice.

The others turned toward him. He hadn't spoken for several decidays. After such a long silence, no one wanted to oppose him.

"Good, then the others can leave," said the healer.

After a long look at their prostrate friend, the heirs left the cabin one by one. They were leaving Grigán's fate up to a stranger, but they had no other choice.

Before leaving, Léti leaned over to the Rominian and whispered in a thick voice, "If he dies, it will be your fault."

The man closed the door behind her and swallowed noisily. As he turned to face his patient, he pushed the laconic Kaulienne's strange, vaguely menacing expression out of his mind.

Then he got to work, shivering and cursing these strangers and their . . . strangeness.

Corenn tried hard to keep her mind off of what was happening below deck, so she concentrated on something else: the only other thing that could preoccupy any of them.

Yan hadn't said a word about his meeting with the god, with Usul. He had revealed a name, nothing more. The name of the Accuser. The name of the man who had sent the Züu killers after the heirs. The name of their enemy. Saat. His Excellency Saat the Treasurer, wise emissary representing the Grand Empire of Goran.

Saat had never returned from the fated voyage to the island of Ji, 118 years ago. He wasn't one of the survivors, or so they had thought. But how could he—already an old man at the time—possibly be alive a century later?

Perhaps Ssa-Vez and Vanamel, among the supposed dead, survived as well. Perhaps even Nol the Strange. The Mother thought back to the three-century-old manuscript they had found in Zarbone's library: it had mentioned another man named Nol. Was it the same Nol who had dragged their ancestors into this adventure? It had to be, she thought. Was he immortal? Was Saat?

Where did Ji's portal lead? The questions swirled in her mind.

Corenn hoped that Yan would be able to answer at least a few of the countless questions that haunted her. Then she remembered Grigán's miserable state, and her face hardened.

They hadn't made much progress. Corenn had guessed that their enemy was one of their own, an heir, and she'd been almost correct. Yet though she held troves of information on the current generation of heirs, she had no idea where Saat might be hiding. She had no idea how to foil his plans, and, in truth, had no idea what his plans might be. Assuming that he hadn't died on the other side of the portal, and that he had found his way back to this world, why had he attacked the heirs? Revenge? Protecting a secret? Fear? And where did his powers come from?

Corenn shuddered, remembering the possessed soothsayer declaring threats at the assembly of barons in the Small Kingdoms. And even more chilling, the demon's attack on the Broken Castle, and Séhane's murder. The Mother had never heard of such powerful magic. Were these events acts of divine intervention? Had the heirs provoked the wrath of the gods?

Yan warily observed the Rominian at work. Up to this point, Vi'at had seemed corrupt, contemptuous, and intolerant, but as Yan watched him conscientiously examine Grigán's wounds, the young man started to hope that he might also be competent.

The Kaulien didn't know Rominian dress or custom, but Vi'at's clothes were certainly unique. Atop his head he wore a small, flat hat, a simple piece of fabric folded in half and stitched together, which stayed on his head with the help of a thin cord tied under his chin. The cap didn't protect him from the rain, since he was drenched. The healer untied it and set it on a bench, along with his outer green robe, embroidered with a rose pattern.

Yan was surprised to see that the rest of his clothes were covered in the same rose pattern. Apparently Rominians cultivated an eccentric fashion. Questions bubbled up from his curious mind to his lips, but the questions died in his mouth. None of that was important now. Yan wanted only one thing from Vi'at: to save Grigán.

"How long has he been unconscious?" the healer asked.

"Since last night," Yan responded, his voice catching in his throat. "He stirred in his sleep a few times, but never for long. It has been several decidays since the last stirring."

"I see."

The healer examined the warrior's bandages, which he hadn't yet touched. In fact, he hadn't touched anything in the heavy bag he had dragged to the *Othenor*. Yan's hope drained as time passed and the healer continued to merely observe.

"Do you think it's serious?" he finally asked.

"That depends," the healer responded, with no effort to be tactful. "I have heard of the Guoris' rats. They are the rats of Farik. They come from the other side of the Curtain. It's said that some of these animals bear a strange sickness. For some moons, the disease turns the beasts into savage, bloodthirsty creatures, which allows them to dominate their brethren. Because of this savagery, they gain control of the colony's food, females, and anything else of worth. In the end, though, the disease always kills them."

Yan waited patiently for the rest of the story, but it never came. Vi'at had already dived back into studying Grigán's exposed wounds, his disgust apparent. Still the healer hadn't dared to touch Grigán, and Yan grew impatient.

"So?" Yan asked. "Do you think the rats can transmit this disease to humans?"

"Oh! They can, yes. But as far as figuring out if it's deadly, that's what I don't know. I've never healed anything like it. Cleaning his wounds, dimming his pain, lightening his sleep, those are my powers. For the rest, hmmph!" he finished with a scornful expression.

"Well, do what you can already," Yan begged. *Help him, please,* he thought. "What can I do?"

"First, we are going to remove these bandages. I brought a variety of ointments that we can apply to the wounds to keep down the swelling and prevent infection, if we're not already too late."

With that, Yan and Vi'at got to work.

Though she hadn't slept in two days, sleep continued to elude Corenn. So she had volunteered to watch over Grigán, despite Yan's pleas. That young man needed rest more than anyone.

The healer had done his best. Now all they could do was wait and hope. Alone in the dark, listening to the rhythmic breathing of their sick friend, Corenn again let her mind wander.

It was the fifth day in the dékade of the Hearth: the Day of Women. In the Kaul Matriarchy, tonight was always spent in celebration, a final night before the Season of the Earth arrived and the cold set in.

Corenn had always enjoyed the simple pleasures of a full cellar, a solid roof overhead, and a stack of dry wood. For many years, she had spent her winters comfortably in the Grand House, where no one lacked for supplies. As the Mother charged with Tradition, and a member of the permanent Council, she had always fought to assure that the same was true for all of the Matriarchy's citizens, with considerable success.

Someone else had to fill that role now that she was gone. It had already been five dékades since she had left Kaul, too long for anyone at home to sustain any hope that she was still alive. They might already have emptied out her study in the Grand House, and maybe even her old living quarters.

The dékade of the Hearth . . . She didn't have a home anymore, and she wouldn't, ever again, as long as Saat kept hounding them with the brothers of the Guild, Züu killers, and demons. She would have no home until they finished their quest. What chance did they have without Grigán? What was the point without Grigán?

The Mother took the warrior's hand and held it tightly in her own. She never would have let the others see her do such a thing. Even after all they had been through, she had to portray herself as strong and confident in front of them. She placed her fingers in his calloused palm. Now, more than ever before, she needed reassurance.

"Don't leave us, Master Grigán," she whispered. "We need you. *I* need you."

The warrior's thumb gently caressed her fingers. The movement startled her, and she gripped his hand tightly. The Mother couldn't know if it was a simple reflex or if he had heard her, but she remained completely still for a long time after.

Stumbling toward the *Othenor*'s common room, Yan banged his head twice and fell on the steps. The night had been excruciating. Though he had never been drunk enough to feel sick, he imagined it would feel like this.

He pushed open the door leading to the small room. The laughter he had been hearing since he rolled out of his hammock suddenly stopped. He knew he must look horrible, but not so bad as to shock his friends, who were seated around the table for lunch. Yet each one stared at him. Yan could still feel the omniscient god permeating his mind with predictions about the end of the world, and could hardly understand what they were saying.

"Yan, your hair!"

"What happened to you?"

"It's white!"

The young man repeated their words to himself a few times before he realized what they were telling him. He needed to see a mirror. Laughter followed him out of the room. Harsh laughter, he thought.

He remembered seeing a mirror in the captain's quarters, and he headed that way, feeling uneasy. Entering the quarters where Grigán healed, he found the mirror and stared at his own face. The hair running across his forehead had lost all its color, leaving behind a bright white streak. He clumsily set the mirror back down. The phenomenon hadn't disfigured him in the least; he didn't give a margolin's ass about it. He had other problems to worry about, much more serious problems.

He turned toward the bed where Grigán lay, and what he saw astonished him. After another glance at the warrior, Yan knew that he would not stumble on his next trip to the common room. No, he would enter not as a spectacle, but as an afterthought. Grigán the warrior was healed, and it would be his task to guide him back to his friends. Yan embraced him.

"You're healed! You're healed!" Yan kept repeating, his eyes full of tears.

"To be honest, I'm in agony. Please don't squeeze so hard." The warrior's tone was acerbic, as always, but his face showed joy. Together, Yan and Grigán hurried to their friends.

Yan watched as they gathered around the table. All seven heirs. Not a single one had died. As long as they were all there, they could handle anything. Anything.

"Did he turn your hair white because you shaved off his mustache?" Rey asked, setting off a new round of laughter.

"It was to heal the wounds on his face," explained an annoyed Yan.

"What!" Grigán played along. "You're the reason I must bear this insult! Léti, go find my blade right away."

"You won't miss it," Corenn said when the laughter subsided. "You look less serious this way."

"But he is too serious!" Rey shouted.

They continued to exchange pleasantries for a while, and amid the laughter, the tension of the previous days lifted. Grigán ended the conversation by confessing to an overwhelming fatigue and returning to his quarters. Without his blade and leather outfit, covered in bandages and wounds, the warrior looked precisely what he was: an exhausted veteran, fatigued by twenty years of living as a fugitive.

Yan insisted on accompanying him, despite the convalescent's protests. It was the right decision. As the exhausted warrior laid down to rest, he suddenly remembered that he had an important question to ask.

"Yan, do you know who our enemy is?"

The young man wondered if it was the best time to tell him, but the warrior refused to rest until he knew.

"It's Saat. Goran's emissary. He is still alive," Yan confessed.

Grigán's mouth opened to ask another question, but he hesitated. His eyes fell on the white streak of hair falling across Yan's forehead, and he came to a decision.

"And Usul's supposed curse? The curse of a god's knowledge?"

Yan looked at the warrior's tired wrinkles, his bruised skin, and saw Grigán's ever-present worry for the other heirs, when it was actually he who was in the worst situation. Usul had foretold that Grigán would die before the year's end.

"No curse," Yan pronounced with a false joy. "Everything is fine. We will find Saat, right?"

"You can count on me," the warrior responded simply, with a wink and fierce smile.

He turned his back and quickly fell asleep. Yan walked back to the common room and listened to his friends' joy. If, up until now, he had found this adventure to be freeing and exciting, it had now become something more akin to what the others must have felt all along: a painful, endless ordeal.

Grigán's weakened state prevented him from walking, so they decided to head to Romine by boat, following the coastline of Hélanie province to the mouth of the Urae. From there they would sail up the river into the Old Country's capital. The voyage wouldn't take more than three days.

Corenn's hope, and therefore the whole group's, was to discover something in the Imperial Eclectic Library of Romine. It was an ancient library, known better as the Deep Tower Library, and many believed it to be a haunted place. It was also purported to house all of human knowledge. If there were any place that held the secret to Ji's portal, the Great Sohonne Arch, or the other portals that must exist elsewhere, it would be there. Nol, the other world, and the Mog'lur demon were other mysteries the heirs hoped would be revealed in the ancient library.

Grigán woke a little after midday. He took to the deck, and with the sun on his face, he found himself happy to see the *Othenor* on open water. With Grigán on his feet, the heirs reminded Yan of his promise to recount his experience with Usul. The young man couldn't think of an excuse to delay any longer, and he reluctantly began his tale.

Bowbaq trembled when he realized how close Yan had come to drowning. Léti shivered, imagining the shark circling him. Lana was enthralled by the idea of a god conversing with the young man. She, who had given everything in her life to Eurydis, without any proof of the goddess's existence other than her own faith, was deeply affected by his experience.

Yan told them that Usul had revealed the hiding place of Maz Achem's journal. The object was in Ith, in the Grand Temple's secret archives. When she heard this news, Lana wanted to cry. The journal existed, here was proof, and there would be many answers in its pages. And while she felt a joy knowing that the book existed, she also felt a pang of regret knowing that it had been under her feet for years. Tears welled in her eyes, but she wouldn't let them fall. To do so would be unbecoming of a Maz.

Or so she thought.

Yan's revelation that the world behind the portal was Jal'karu overwhelmed her, and tears streaked down her cheeks.

"The black gods," the Maz said through her tears. "Wise Eurydis! Our ancestors were taken to the black gods. May their spirits rest in peace."

Rey put an arm around the priestess's shoulders, but she kindly pushed it off. She was a Maz. She shouldn't inspire pity. She should be an example, spreading the three virtues of the Wise One. Knowledge. Tolerance. Peace.

"He also said Jal'dara," Yan added, hoping to comfort Lana. "Does that mean anything to you?"

"No," the priestess apologized, rubbing her eyes. "I have never heard the name. Surely it means the same thing."

Corenn interrupted, "Maybe not."

"Of course it is the same thing," Rey responded. "He tells us that behind the portal is Jal'karu—the place where demons grow, if we interpret Lana's words correctly. It can't be anything else."

"Jal'dara could represent another form . . . another spiritual interpretation," said the Mother.

"How can a place be two things at once?" Bowbaq asked.

No one responded to the giant. Their theories were based on nothing, yet the possible consequences were staggering. Only Lana could understand what Corenn was suggesting, but it was useless to discuss it. The truth would remain shrouded until they reached the Deep Tower and the archives within.

"Since we know what's waiting for us, why should we go all the way to Romine?" Rey asked the group. "The more logical choice would be to go straight to Ith and find Achem's journal."

"Romine is only two days away. Ith is more than two dékades, without taking into account that we won't get much more out of this sloop. We would have to change ships anyhow, so we might as well make it to Romine. We're so close," said the Mother.

"All right, Corenn. Once again you're right. Any other good news, Yan?"

Yan's heart was heavy after telling his story. Usul had told him that Grigán would die. The god had foretold a deadly war, with the Upper Kingdoms losing the most. It would be the annihilation of the greatest civilization in the known world, and all before the year's end.

But Usul was playing with the future. By revealing these events, he scrambled the possibilities. Yan could influence anything the god had pronounced by trying to escape it, or by altering an event that the god was hoping to cause. Either way, the future was uncertain. Usul had found a way to amuse himself, but the god's play caused Yan suffering, a suffering he wouldn't soon shake.

The god had also foretold his Union with Léti. The young man wanted that with all his heart, but what should he do now? From the moment he had emerged from that well, he had been guarding his words, acting cautiously. Trying to act as if nothing had changed. Was that the best solution? What should he do? Try his best to change the future, at the risk of exacerbating the problem? Or try to escape the responsibility, in the hope that things would work themselves out? Usul was right. *Not doing anything is still doing something.*

"Yan, did you hear me?"

"I have nothing else to say, Rey. You know as much as I do."

Only one thing seemed clear to him. Handing this curse over to his friends wouldn't help anyone. He had to fight his own demons, alone.

The two days of the crossing passed quickly. To avoid gnawing on his problems, Yan used the time to exercise his Will. Making a coin fall was a small task to him now, laughably easy. His next task was to stand it back up again, before knocking it over once more. He would knock it over, and stand it up again, down and up, down and up, using only his mind. At the end of the two days, his record was fourteen consecutive times. He stopped only because he feared the returning shock: the *languor*, Corenn called it, the dizziness that seized magicians after they had cast a spell.

Yan had to train alone, as the Mother spent most of her time at Grigán's side. He was improving, though, spending more time on his feet above deck than lying down below. The warrior acted as if he were perfectly healed; he had even begun to wear his black leather again. He was obviously embarrassed when he learned that Corenn had patched and stitched together his shoddy armor. Grigán wasn't used to people doing things for him, and the Mother's kindness troubled him deeply, to Léti's great amusement.

The young woman and Bowbaq spent the two days playing with the cat, Frog. With his *erjak* powers, the giant was weaving an unusually strong bond between Léti and the animal, a bond like those he had with his lion and mountain pony. It was a long and delicate operation, which required, above all else, the animal's trust. The dwarf cat, already an adult and hardly accustomed to humans, had to be persuaded over and over to even pay them any attention. It got to be so difficult, Bowbaq warned Léti that he might not be able to keep his promise.

At Reyan's request, Lana began to explain to the actor the great values of the Moral of Eurydis. But the student didn't care much for religion; his newfound interest was no more than a pretext, a way to spend time with the Maz. In fact, he paid little attention to the priestess's words—only enough to make a joke or two, or to ask personal questions. The actor's ruse held for a day. On the second day, Lana put her religious mask back on. *Rey should be interested in Eurydis, not her priestesses*, thought Lana as she went back to spurning the eager actor.

"Lana, I think you should remove the mask," Grigán warned as they made their way up the Urae. "You must know that the

Rominians hold the Ithare in contempt; they have ever since the era of the Two Empires. It is the same today."

"I never had any problems in Mestèbe," the Maz said, with genuine surprise.

"Mestèbe is in Presdanie, which is worlds away from Romine in Uranie. We are essentially going into a new kingdom, Lana. The last eon's provincial wars are still fresh in their memory. Romine's people have their own identity, and they all fight for their independence."

"This country is too old," Rey commented. "Too big. Too jagged. Have you ever met a Jérusnian? They have nothing on Manive's merchants, I can assure you. In my humble opinion, the Upper Kingdoms will have five more kingdoms in the next generation, and one less."

The next generation, Yan reflected wistfully. Who ever said the Upper Kingdoms would survive a year, let alone a generation?

Grigán continued, "The Rominians are quite eccentric and, more often than not, suspicious. Keep your eyes off them and hope we avoid trouble."

"You could be from Romine, then," Rey said.

"You don't know how right you are. Their justice is famous for its speed. And they don't like Loreliens either," said Grigán.

"What ingratitude. To attack me like that, after all I've done for you. If it weren't for the horrendous stench that rises from this thing the locals dare to call a river, I would immediately leave this boat in protest."

Léti grimaced, imagining the dive into the water. Everyone knew the Urae was the dirtiest stretch of river in the world. A brief silence had fallen over the group, and in that moment, the carcass of a dead creature thudded softly on the hull of the *Othenor*. They cast their eyes out over the filthy water, full of trash, excrement, and more carcasses. Beyond the water was the depressing countryside. They looked upon it, as they had on the Ubese in the Baronies, and their eyes ached for the rich, colorful landscape of the Lower Kingdoms. No matter how long they stared, they found no solace in the expansive brown wasteland.

Romine was a sprawling city, and the *Othenor* began to cross the first of the city's districts a full deciday before reaching the city itself. The view was limited to a succession of motley buildings, from luxurious family mansions to dilapidated shacks with foundations covered in mud stains.

The farther the boat advanced, the closer the buildings advanced toward the water's edge, first to the shore and then beyond it. Ramshackle homes clung desperately to pilings, and Yan struggled to navigate the crowded and putrid waters. Outside of a few smaller boats, the *Othenor* was the only vessel on the water. The other boatmen stared in surprise and anger at the sloop, their angry looks revealing to the heirs that such a large boat was not customary on the river. One came to Romine on foot, or not at all.

They passed under two bridges that had been fortified centuries ago. One was half-destroyed and seemed poised to collapse at any moment. Finally, after sailing another league along the sinuous river between rotting houses, Yan was forced to stop the sloop in front of an abandoned, decrepit lock.

"And here we are!" Grigán said. "We'll finish on foot."

The heirs got to work readying for departure, a process held up by the actor, who didn't know what to do with his treasure. After considerable thought and grimacing, he decided to bury it under a tree at the edge of the water.

"If only I had a horse," he grumbled to himself as he dug. "Or an ass, just a simple ass. Grigán, are you busy?"

"What?" the warrior asked.

"No, nothing," the actor said, smiling to himself.

With that done, they set off. Behind them was the abandoned *Othenor*, run aground in a muddy river. The sight of it in the mud stirred up melancholy in Léti's chest. After all the days they had spent on her decks, to be left behind, she thought, and she sighed as she turned her back on the sloop. Again, their numbers were diminished.

In the form of a ten-foot-long electric eel, the god Usul circled tirelessly in his cave. His eternal prison. He stirred, though not out of boredom or desperation. For the first time in longer than he could recall, he was enjoying himself. He was thinking about the mortals.

His last visitor had been one of the more interesting ones he had ever met, and their meeting had muddled the future like never before. From his cave, Usul watched and listened, silently following each of the major actors who would shape the future. As he watched, he pondered, gambled, and imagined the thousands of constantly evolving possible futures.

Little by little, Usul discerned a few constants. No matter what these people did now, the Upper Kingdoms' story was already written. That much seemed certain. Arriving at this end pained Usul—he did not want his game to end so quickly, and he wondered if he could intervene somehow. He was the master of his domain; inside his cave he was He Who Knows. Beyond his walls, though, he was powerless. He pondered his situation over in his mind for a moment before abandoning it.

No matter, he thought. He still had many destinies to watch over, and every one was as consequential as the fate of the Upper Kingdoms. He was impatient to see the forces clash. Even if the overwhelming probability suggested that the victor was already crowned, Usul's encounter with the visitor had woken his curiosity, and now the question loomed large in his mind: What could humans hope to accomplish against immortals?

Though the roads in Romine were crowded and busy, the heirs were unable to slip through the crowd unnoticed. In the capital of the Old Country, the Rominians stared at the interlopers with obvious scorn. Following Grigán's advice, the heirs kept themselves from responding to these muted threats. Except for Rey, who let slip a string of insults on the strange way people dressed in the city.

The Rominians' dress seemed to mix that of all the other kingdoms: Kaulien tunics, Junian robes, Lorelien shirts, Goranese coats, and capes, furs, woolen vests, and other clothes were thrown together in a complete cacophony of styles. And though the styles were strange, they were nothing compared to the colors.

Though they used every possible type of clothing, each Rominian wore only one color at a time: red, yellow, blue, green, or any of a myriad of other shades. Often these garments were weighed down with embroidered patterns and excessively large brooches, which looked surprisingly like butterflies, Manive roses, Gyole dolphins, crowned eagles, or the cross of Jérus.

"Those are the symbols of each province," Grigán explained. "Romine's and Uranie's symbols are both the crowned eagle. You'll see how, based on these symbols, the Rominians will ignore anyone who doesn't bear a matching symbol."

"What's the point of the colors?" Yan asked.

"No point, at least that I know of," said Grigán.

"They reveal affiliation with certain military castes," Lana answered. "I suppose the tradition has been passed down in some families, and that others are content to imitate the nobles."

The Maz had studied the Old Country's history when she had studied Ithare's own history. The two nations had been enemies for centuries. Now that she was in the capital, Lana realized how different their cultures were. And noticing the hostile glances directed at her robes, she knew it had been a good idea to follow Grigán's advice regarding her mask.

Léti, who had also seen the way the Rominians looked at Lana, asked, "Which gods do the Rominians pray to? Not Eurydis, I imagine."

"Unfortunately, no. Odrel, I think, has the most followers here."

"That doesn't surprise me," Rey commented, without further explanation.

The small line of foreigners followed a progression toward the neighborhood said to be the old imperial city, where Zarbone's friend lived. He was their key to entering the Deep Tower. In this section of the city, even the houses were painted in bright colors matching their owner's affiliation. All were adorned with at least one crowned eagle.

At the front of the group, Yan and Bowbaq turned each corner with the curiosity of children. Lana moved ahead torn between two attitudes: one where she did her best to hide her profession as Maz of Eurydis, and the other where she proudly displayed it—though neither was acceptable according to the Moral. Rey, who could see her uneasiness, teased her by exaggerating how important it was to display herself correctly. Léti, Corenn, and Grigán guided the group from the back, following the directions Zarbone had given them.

The warrior tried in vain to hide his fatigue. The walk from the lock to the imperial city hadn't been far, but he was out of breath, and waves of vertigo periodically washed over him. In front of an enormous five-storied building, encircled by a sprawling park protected by an outer wall, Grigán stopped and put his hands on his knees.

"Here we are," he announced to the group, between breaths. "At least, this place fits the description."

Reyan whistled in admiration, giving voice to the emotion they all shared. Zarbone had described his friend as being wealthier than he. To own a place like the one standing before them, he must be. Maintenance of the park alone would require three full-time gardeners, working every day of the year. The lawns were manicured, and the hedges perfectly sculpted. Not a single flower was out of place. No unwanted sprout troubled the perfect alignment of the moon-grass imported from the Baronies. No rebellious branch deformed the magnificent sculpted shrubs, which, of course, were all cut in the image of a crowned eagle.

"Let's enter," Rey proposed. "I can't stand these eccentrics staring at us anymore."

"We can't just walk in on someone's home like that!" Bowbaq objected, clearly offended. "That would be deeply impolite."

In Arkary, the word *impolite* had a much stronger meaning than in any other kingdom, Yan remembered, amused. And a stronger meaning for Bowbaq than for any other Arque.

"There's no bell," Corenn noted.

"Let's go. Enter!" the actor decided, putting action to words as he walked through the garden's entrance toward the entry door. "We are already unwanted in Lorelia, Junine, and the Land of Beauty. Personally, I'm not too worried about the Rominians."

The others followed Rey as he led them to the mansion's doors.

"If the gate to the gardens wasn't locked, maybe this one isn't either," Rey suggested, with a knowing smile.

"Perhaps we should—" Grigán started to say, still gasping for air.

The sentence died in the warrior's throat. His eyes rolled back in his head, and he collapsed heavily. Only by the grace of Bowbaq's quick hands did Grigán avoid smacking his head on the stone pathway. Corenn rushed to his side, putting a hand on his chest. Under her fingers she felt his heart still beating, and she breathed a heavy sigh of relief.

Rey opened the door and offered to drag Grigán inside, but before anyone could protest, two men appeared in the doorway and drew their swords. The guards swung wildly at Rey, who survived thanks only to his attackers' clumsiness. The heavy swords breezed through the air, catching nothing but the heavy wooden door, where they stuck with a thud. The actor swore and jumped straight at them, knocking both guardsmen on their backs. An instant later, he had his knife at the throat of one, while Léti subdued the other with the point of her rapier. The two men were dressed in red, but they weren't Züu. They were Rominian.

"Get out, thieves!" a quavering voice yelled from the hallway. "Or I'll pierce your hide!"

A tall, skinny, balding man stood in the hallway several feet away. From where the heirs stood, he didn't seem that impressive. But he was pointing a crossbow at Léti, and that was enough to make him an enemy.

Without thinking, Yan launched his Will. The crossbow's cord snapped, and the Rominian shouted as the cord whipped across his hand. But the languor for this impromptu spell was so strong that Yan felt his legs quiver. For a moment he lost his grip on reality. His eyes went dark, and the sound of Léti screaming for Bowbaq to grab the final fugitive drowned in his ears.

"Bandits! Thieves! Marauders!" the newcomer moaned, when the giant gingerly pulled him toward the group. "This is why we are suspicious of foreigners."

"We are not thieves," Corenn assured him. "We are Zarbone's friends, Zarbone of the Land of Beauty. You must be Lord Sapone?" She handed him their recommendation letter.

The Rominian ripped the letter open and glanced at it sideways. Even if it were all true, he wouldn't be happy about it.

"Which one of you is Grigán?" he asked, when he had finished.

"He is," said Lana, who was supporting their sick leader.

"You're lying! It says here that Grigán has a mustache. And yet, this man has no such thing!"

Trying to avoid an angry quip, Corenn took a deep breath. She, who had a reputation for being as impassive as stone, wanted to ruthlessly humiliate this straitlaced Rominian. She was fine with stupidity, but since she was often called to arbitrate Council disputes, she couldn't stand bad faith.

"Lord Sapone. We are not your enemies. We need your help to get into the Deep Tower."

"I don't—" the Rominian started to yell.

"We are ready to pay for it," the Mother interrupted him.

Sapone regained his calm, and made it look like he was thinking it over. Then he peeked outside, verifying that no one had seen the strangers enter. Satisfied, he closed the door behind them.

Yan meditated at Grigán's side while Corenn and the others planned with their host how they would penetrate the greatest library in the known world. As his comrades planned for the future, Yan silently wondered if there would even be one.

Grigán's rapid return to health had made him hope, but now only disappointed him even more bitterly. The warrior's wounds had mostly healed, the deep gashes in his skin closed and scabbed over, but Yan knew that a deeper, more sinister evil had penetrated his friend. The sickness was clear to him, horribly clear.

Usul had predicted Grigán's coming death, knowing full well that by speaking the future he might change it. The future could be molded by He Who Knows, and by He Who Asked. Yan knew Grigán's fate; what remained a mystery was whether he could save his friend. Doubt clouded his mind. Even if he warned Grigán, the warrior couldn't do anything against the illness that assailed him.

Yan saw only one way to change this future. A dangerous way. A way that was just as likely to kill his friend as it was to save him. Usul was right. Yan was reacting exactly as predicted. The young man cursed the omniscient god.

The only way to heal Grigán was to work with magic. Water magic. A specialty he had never practiced, nor even studied.

Water is life, Corenn had said. *The indispensable element that gives movement to your body, and allows your mind to reason. To* heal the warrior, Yan would have to work on the water element of his being. He must activate, protect, and reinforce it.

At least that was the theory. The young magician had touched only the earth element, and he had no idea if water worked in the same way.

He decided to do a test, to simply brush by this part of Grigán. If he could feel the water in him, surely he could heal it.

Slowly, calmly, carefully, he began to concentrate his Will. One by one he lost his senses: taste first, then smell, touch, hearing, and, finally, vision. The world fell away, and all that was not Grigán disappeared. With great care, Yan focused on the warrior's essence.

The complexity of elements that made up a human intoxicated him. Up to that point, he had used magic only on inanimate objects. But for the first time, he focused his Will on a living being. He could see earth, the first element he had learned to recognize, but somewhere at the edge of his understanding, he could also see the other elements.

He could see water, and he immediately realized that he would fail. Though it was only a spiritual representation, he saw it as a stream of pure water flowing over a sculpture made of ice. The image frightened him, and he vowed to never use his Will on something so fragile. Not, at least, until he learned more.

He could see the devouring fire. Fire, the tendency in all things to become something other. Caterpillars into butterflies. Babies into adults. The living to the dead.

Grigán's fire was melting his water, and Yan thought perhaps he could blow back the fire. Perhaps he could keep it at bay, maybe even extinguish it altogether. But what would happen if he did? Yan had no idea. Surely such an action would permanently alter his friend. Yan would never dare take on such a responsibility. Corenn's warnings reared up in him: the study of fire was the most dangerous, even though it seemed like it would be the easiest to master. It was black magic.

Finally, he saw the wind. Grigán's spirit. He saw the warrior's soul, his dreams, his emotions. Though fire was the most dangerous of the disciplines, it was wind that was the most complex. Yan perceived it as a fog surrounding the ice sculpture. Despite his fears, he couldn't resist the desire to touch it. As soon as he did, a string of images and feelings invaded his own mind. Contact was a revelation.

Something distracted him, and reality violently imposed itself. Yan realized he had let his Will grow throughout the entire exercise. He had no choice but to unleash the accumulated force against a wall and wait for the languor to follow.

The horrible feeling settled over him. It wasn't exactly painful; though regaining his senses was always a brutal moment, it never lasted very long. Cold and weakness seized him, becoming his inevitable masters. The feeling was so strong he thought he might die.

Some time passed, though he couldn't be sure how much. His body fought a long battle with the rest of the world, until the two came to an equilibrium and the turmoil passed.

Lana was at the room's entrance, her face ashen. Her eyes drifted to a gaping hole in the wall, then to the young man, pale and crumpled on his armchair. For her, the whole thing had passed in an instant, but for Yan it had been among the most grueling trials of his life.

"The Eclectic Library is forbidden to foreigners," announced Sapone, who was comfortably settled in an armchair large enough for three people. "I can already see that this kind of argument doesn't mean much to you, as you didn't hesitate to break into my home. But that's no longer a problem."

"In our strange kingdoms," Rey retorted, "it's customary to open the door for visitors who stand in front of it."

"In Romine, Mr. *Adventurer*, it's customary to not visit someone until you have been invited to do so," Sapone responded, clearly not amused. "As such, everyone stays at their own home, and we all abide by this decorum."

"Forget about our intrusion, if you would," Corenn interjected. "How do you do it? How do you get in?"

"Oh! Me, I've never been. The place is *truly* haunted, you know. I've already lost one librarian in there; I would never personally risk going inside. The librarian who works for me now has been there for ten years. I see no reason to expose myself to the ghosts."

"Could we meet this man?"

Sapone stared at Corenn with a strange grimace. They all could see the greed plain on his face, as if the word itself were tattooed there.

"Not before we come to an agreement," said the Rominian. "I need to know exactly what you plan to do down there."

"Buy some fishing line, of course," Rey said, mockingly. "Our healer just ran out."

Corenn ignored the actor's quip and answered seriously. "Research. How does it concern you?"

"Currently, less than twelve people enjoy the royal privilege to visit the Deep Tower. As you know, it is normally forbidden to everyone, and has been so ever since the ghosts invaded its halls. It was sealed off for more than a hundred and fifty years.

"That is, until our good sovereign, who needed gold to protect the kingdom's provinces, had the idea to sell it. Of course, he never wanted to sell the whole tower. No one could amass a sum massive enough to buy the entire library. Instead, he sold it floor by floor.

"He only found eight takers," continued Sapone. "For my part, I own the entire eleventh floor of the Tower, and all its contents. I paid dearly for the privilege. Three times more than I paid for this manor. For this reason, you must assure me you won't degrade the property in any way."

He finished his last sentence with a hostile stare at Frog, who was playing with the fringes of a rug. Léti realized what he was looking at and shooed the cat, who fled into another room.

"You have my word, Lord Sapone," Corenn assured him. "Now, could we meet your man?"

"All in good time," he responded. "First, though, I would like to speak a little business." And with that the negotiations were under way.

Seeing the spectacle of the Rominian merchant distractedly bartering with the Mother, then more violently with Rey, Léti thought to herself that if Loreliens were specialists in commerce, the Rominians had them beat for venality. Finally, when they had agreed, Sapone led them through his labyrinthine halls to his personal librarian.

"Of course, our deal holds only if he agrees to escort you," the Rominian clarified.

"But . . . isn't he in your service?" Corenn asked.

"He is, this is true, but he has a particular personality," responded Sapone. "I put up with it because, other than that one fault, he is very competent."

Sapone had been leading them while he spoke, but with these final words, he stopped in front of a tall door engraved with the customary crowned eagle. "Master Hulsidor?" he called out, while gently tapping the wood. "Could I disturb your peace for a moment?"

"What do you need now?" someone yelled. Then, as he opened the door, "Who are these foreigners?"

Corenn, Léti, Rey, and Bowbaq looked at each other, astonished. The way it looked now, Hulsidor could have been the master of the house, and Sapone his valet.

The librarian was a small, bent man, with a deformity on his face that made him look menacing. His gray hair was cut very short, in stark contrast to his long, pointy beard, where a piece of torn parchment clung. The man shamelessly wore the symbol of the Gyole dolphin, showing his loyalty to the Presdanians—those who were most hostile to the Uranians. For Sapone to put up with his considerable oddities, Hulsidor must be very competent indeed.

Sapone repeated his question. "Can we come in for a moment?"

The librarian stepped aside, grumbling that if Sapone kept interrupting him, none of his work would get done.

The heirs followed their host into his personal library. It might not have been as impressive as Zarbone's, but it was much better maintained. The volumes were perfectly aligned on impeccable shelves. A worktable was covered in bookbinding and cleaning tools, which indicated that Hulsidor was working on refurbishing some new acquisitions.

Sapone explained the situation with all the tact he could muster, imploring his employee to wait until he had finished talking to answer, but Hulsidor's response was quite clear.

"No! It's too dangerous. The phantoms are more active than ever. Last time, a *strangler* almost got me. Your presence will make them even more excited."

"We won't give you any trouble, Master Hulsidor," Corenn said. "We will follow your advice perfectly."

"And worse, they are foreigners! Brulin would never let them pass."

"Who's that?" Rey asked.

"He is the Tower's only guard, and he's only there during the day," Sapone assured them.

"What!" The librarian jumped out of his seat. "You're not about to suggest that we go in at night? You're crazy!"

"I negotiated a deposit for you," the Rominian said, trying to reassure him. "If you die, Lady Corenn here will owe me twenty-five monarchs."

"Good for you! Take a torch and go ahead then! There is no way I will go down there at night."

Léti walked up to the man and tenderly took his hand, her face composed into a suppliant mask.

"Master Hulsidor . . . please," she said softly.

The man feigned disinterest for a long moment while everyone else stayed quiet. Finally he gave in.

"All right, all right," he said regretfully. "I'll take advantage of the opportunity to have a look at the ninth floor. A colleague has forbidden me to see it. But I will guide the entire operation."

Léti gave the man a kiss on the cheek and walked out of the room, Frog at her heels. The others stared after her, admiringly.

Rey opened his mouth to make a joke, then thought better of it. Instead, he went to find Maz Lana.

When Lana had walked into Grigán's room and discovered Yan silently crying, she called out to him, but he couldn't hear her. An instant later, he realized she was there and looked at her with a terrified expression. Then he turned his gaze to the wall and a hole appeared, just as he fell unconscious.

By the time she reached his side, he had awoken. Weak, and with a glazed expression, but conscious.

"Yan, you were crying," she said, for no reason.

The young man nodded. He had realized, when he came back to reality, that he had made an error that could have been fatal. Corenn had warned him: *Never call upon your Will under the influence of rage, suffering, or liquor.* Now he understood why. In his emotional state, he had lost all reservations and pushed too much force through his body. If Lana hadn't accidentally interrupted his concentration, Yan might not have survived the shock that returned to him.

He stared at the hole he had made in the wall and blushed in confusion. Not a single brick had fallen, and there had been no explosion. But a few bricks had clearly just disappeared. There was no way he could hide the damage before someone else would notice. Though he would have confessed his error to Corenn either way.

He approached Lana, who was already praying. The Maz had not asked him a single question, and for her discretion, Yan was sincerely appreciative. After a brief hesitation, he sat next to her on the floor and prayed with her. He had not prayed to Eurydis since Norine had died, but after confronting Usul, his faith had been reinforced. The gods existed, as real as stone. And they listened to people.

"He is not in danger, Yan," Lana said after meditating. "In Ith, we had a few cases of Farik sickness. I never heard of anyone dying from it directly."

The young man nodded sadly. The Maz was sincere and was trying to reassure him. Yan knew that Grigán suffered from worse than a bite, though, and he wasn't sure what to believe.

"Usul, he foretold . . . some things," he finally admitted, his heart pounding. "Mostly terrible things. That's what it is, the curse of *inhuman* knowledge. I know the future, and I don't know what to do to change it. By trying to stop it, I could instead cause it."

The Maz took a deep breath and reflected. Yan needed her. He needed Eurydis. He needed peace.

"One of the poems in *The Book* finishes with this: *The idiot is happy, the sage lives long.* I have debated this passage with my students for many decidays, but we can avoid this long discussion because I know the lesson that we can learn from it," she began. "Everyone is looking for happiness, Yan, but if the idiot is happy, it's because he doesn't understand the world. He is satisfied with his own lot in life, as miserable as that may be. He doesn't fight it. He accepts all the pain and sadness so readily that he doesn't suffer much from it. He doesn't understand the implications, and he forgets quickly. The idiot leaves the world young, because he doesn't know when to fight for his own life. He went through life with a smile, but he leaves no trace of his existence.

"The sage is also looking for happiness," she continued. "But his happiness is more complex; he understands the lives of his friends, his family, his people, even of all humanity. His happiness is more difficult to attain, but oh so much more pleasant. He rarely feels this happiness completely, but each victory fills him with a joy a hundred times more powerful than the idiot's pleasant acquiescence. Because the sage fights for himself, Yan. He works. He fights for his ideals and never succumbs to fatalism.

"Yan," she said, "don't be a sage living like an idiot. We can't change the past, but the future? That is yet to be decided. Will you rest prisoner to a future that only you know?"

Yan stood up and walked over to Grigán's bed, a grave expression on his face. The Maz had troubled him.

"Where are we?" Grigán said in a thick voice. He tried to sit up. "Where are the others?"

Yan smiled at Lana and ran into the hallway. He wanted to announce the good news. He wanted to act. He wanted to fight.

He wanted, more than anything, to talk to Bowbaq. What he had seen in Grigán needed clarification. If Yan was right, he was about to study a new magical specialty.

Zamerine waited for his master in the officers' tent. The Zü had once again challenged a strategic decision made by Gor the Gentle, the chief of the barbarian army. This convocation probably had nothing to do with it, but Zamerine had to calm himself when he imagined Saat's rage. He never wanted to face that anger again.

He took a few nervous steps, caressing the handle of his hati, knowing full well that the poisoned dagger was worthless against his master. Saat no longer suffered wounds. It was as if nothing hurt him. Fatigue too seemed an affliction that never ailed him—Zamerine had never seen him sleep. This was in stark contrast to the master's son, who left his sleeping quarters only on rare occasions.

Outside, Zamerine could hear the slaves chanting, singing of the glory and power of the god Saat had forced on them. The barbarian queen Chebree had written the songs, following Saat's will. Hearing the words, it was hard to believe a woman had written them. Somber was He Who Vanquishes, He Who Conquers, He Who Rules. Not a compassionate god.

Rumor had it that Chebree had become Saat's mistress, though Zamerine had ordered anyone who repeated these rumors to be punished. Even if they were true, it didn't much matter. The Judge might have ordered the gag rule in jealousy, for he had never been much interested in the pleasures of the flesh, and Chebree was the first woman he had ever met who merited his interest. Saat already had so many concubines. Couldn't he have left her alone?

The master finally appeared, and the Zü stiffened. As always, Saat was wearing a thick mail coat, as well as a Goranese helm girded with a black band. Zamerine had never seen him wear anything else. His master's face was hidden behind his customary helm. All who had ever tried to look upon the master's visage had been killed on the rack, or buried alive, depending on Saat's whims.

The Zü had seen only his hand, and that only rarely. Upon it ran deep wrinkles, and it was spotted with age. It was the hand of a centenarian, but as vigorous as that of a man at the peak of his powers. It was a dead hand that held a firm grip on life.

"My loyal Zamerine," Saat began with obvious scorn. "You will send fifteen of your men to Ith. We will have some work for them soon."

"Fifteen?" the Zü exclaimed before he could stop himself. He tried to recover. "Yes, master," he said dutifully.

The Judge knew it was a misstep, but it wouldn't prove to be a fatal one. Saat seemed to be in a pleasant mood. Maybe now was a good time to learn more of his plan.

"What counsel should I give them?"

"None. They will wait for our signal, which you will give once I have decided. We are finally going to get rid of the last fugitives," he added, his voice tense.

"Master," Zamerine insisted. "How do you know they will go to Ith? Where do you get this information?"

The Zü examined the finely wrought helm, only two feet from his face. What expression did Saat have on underneath his iron mask? Was he contemptuous? Amused? Wrathful?

Zamerine took an unconscious step backward, though he knew it was useless. At any instant Saat could take control of his body and force him to stab his hati through his own chest.

"I do not know if they will go to Ith," the High Diarch corrected him. "I only know that for now, they intend to go there. In fact, they are currently in Romine, but the Old Country is too far to send your little red men in time."

"You can . . . you can . . . read their minds at such a distance?" the Zü stammered, stupefied.

Saat put his hands on his hips and stared at his subordinate. Though his master's face was shielded, Zamerine understood that he should leave, and that he would never, ever betray his master.

Hulsidor categorically refused to start their descent into the Deep Tower that same night, so the adventure would be put off until the next day. Corenn hoped that he wasn't stalling and that they would, in fact, leave tomorrow night. The librarian's reason for hesitation reeked of superstition rather than reason.

According to him, the specters that haunted the library were most dangerous on the eighth day of each dékade. Harping on about this superstition, he managed to scare off the gullible Bowbaq and the fearful Lana. Even Corenn had to admit that she had lost her confidence. The others, if they felt strongly either way, kept it to themselves.

The heirs discussed their plans in Grigán's room, where the rapidly healed warrior paced, his impatience boiling over. A slave to his habits, he often brought his hand to his face as if to caress his mustache, before he realized it was no longer there. Each time he did this, he would resume his vigorous pacing.

Corenn listened to the conversations while her gaze shifted between Yan and the fissured wall. She looked at once disapproving and dismayed. The young man knew he was about to get a lecture. He wondered if it would be worth it to explain the whole story.

"So you are saying that we are going to lose another day," Grigán grumbled. "I'd prefer it if we could pass as Rominians and enter the library by ourselves."

His friends silently nodded. They had already discussed it, and had come to the same conclusion. They needed a guide, if for nothing more than to simply show them to the most fruitful bookshelves.

"I hope that we'll at least get something out of this," said the warrior. "I don't know anything about libraries, but it would surprise me if we could learn more in one night about Nol, the portals, and Jal'karu than our ancestors gathered in a century."

"The Deep Tower has been closed for more than a century," Corenn reminded him gently. "And it's the largest library in the world. Imagine what a treasure trove of knowledge must be hidden there. There are works that predate Romine itself!"

"Hmm, I guess," conceded Grigán, struggling to share the Mother's interest.

After his long period of rest, an uncommon luxury for him, Grigán felt a great need to act. His fever had passed, his weakness had disappeared. He felt fully recovered. He tried to think of something to pass the time, and his eyes fell on Léti.

"Should we get back to work, Mistress Léti?"

The young woman jumped to her feet and led Grigán into the hallway. Just before exiting, the warrior froze, in front of Yan. Grigán seemed to remember, when he was sleeping, a presence...

The young man returned Grigán's stare, looking surprised. The warrior shook his head, embarrassed, and followed his student out the door.

Yan and Bowbaq hid themselves in the mansion for the rest of the day, so well that Corenn never had the chance to ask what had cut through the brick wall, though she suspected a mistaken spell. There was a chance that Sapone, who was already trying hard to ignore his visitors, hadn't yet heard of the destruction. If he had, he probably would have thrown them into the street after rightly demanding compensation.

It wasn't in the Mother's nature to scold her student, and she had no intention of doing so. She simply wanted to understand what had happened, and, if needed, explain certain principles of Will that Yan had not yet mastered.

She never got her chance to sit with the young magician, though. The next day, Yan and Bowbaq disappeared again without any explanation, both seeming quite excited. The heirs, who had not seen Yan smile since he had confronted Usul, chose to leave their friends alone to work on their secret project.

The rest of the group did their best to keep occupied until nightfall. Grigán advised them all to rest before the coming sleepless night, but he had no intention of following his own advice. In fact, as the warrior recovered, his energy seemed to redouble, and in an attempt to do something to pass the time, he cleaned, sharpened, and oiled all of their weapons and then checked the equipment. Finally, too impatient to suffer the waiting, he decided to travel to town, to prepare for their voyage to Ith. Since he barely spoke Romine, Rey offered to accompany him, and Léti joined the group.

Maz Lana spent several decidays discussing theology with Sapone. His patience was hardly commendable. Even though the priestess consciously listened to his stories praising Odrel, He Who Cries, the Rominian made no effort to even listen to the principles of Eurydis's Moral. Quietly the Maz remembered her teachings—*A seed in the wind sometimes becomes a tree*—and she held out hope that the Rominian might reflect on her words. It was a distant hope, but she thought perhaps, after many days, he might at least follow one of her three virtues—knowledge, tolerance, peace—even if he never became a devout follower.

She remembered that her ancestor, Maz Achem, had contested this theory upon his return from Ji. The priests should launch a crusade of massive conversions, he had counseled. And annihilate the demonist cults, with force if necessary.

Of course, he had just seen Jal'karu.

Alone, Corenn decided to fill out her journal. The exercise allowed her to sort out the multiple threads that wove together to form their quest. They knew their enemy, but that only brought up more questions. How could Saat possibly still be alive? Why such a relentless desire to exterminate them? Where did he get his powers? What were their limits?

It seemed to her that the only way to pierce through the layers of secrets would be to solve the mystery of the portals. And that they might accomplish at nightfall, in the Deep Tower.

Corenn then asked after Hulsidor; learning more about the library might help them organize their search. But the man had barricaded his study, refusing to see anyone. He claimed his preparation was long and difficult, and that he needed to be left in peace, gods be damned! The Mother did not insist.

Grigán, Léti, and Rey returned toward the end of the day, looking smug. The actor had met one of his old partners, a poor artist who loved his art, and therefore someone they could fully trust. His troupe of street performers would leave in two days, headed for Pont, in Lorelia, for the Day of the Earth festivals. The troupe immediately accepted Grigán's offer to accompany them after the heirs' business in the Deep Tower was complete. The route from the Wet Valley through the Murky Mountains was not the safest, so Léti's and Grigán's swords would be reassuring. The rest of the heirs could travel inconspicuously in a mixed troupe of musicians, jugglers, and comedians.

Rey had also brought Lana a change of clothes. The Maz's robe, covered in Eurydian symbols, was much too visible in the Old Country's capital. The actor, with his newfound fortune, had bought her a brand-new traveling outfit.

Lana was embarrassed by the gift. First, because she wasn't used to gifts, and second, because the new clothes seemed horribly revealing. She never knew that without Grigán's and Léti's vigorous objections, Rey would have chosen an even shorter outfit. She thanked him sincerely, but didn't go so far as to try on the new clothes.

Night fell, and the heirs gathered around a table in the service quarters. Sapone, as lord of the manor, would never share his own table with foreigners, whose presence he could barely stand, and whose persons he would already have thrown in prison if it weren't for their lucrative agreement. Yan and Bowbaq skipped dinner, as did Hulsidor, who was still locked up in his study. There was a strange mood at the table that night.

After dinner, Yan finally came to find Corenn, a knowing gleam in his eye. The Mother followed him, filled with curiosity. She had imagined many ways this encounter might go, but she had never dreamed that her student would teach her a lesson in magic.

Bowbaq couldn't help but blush as he watched Corenn take her place across from him. He was convinced that last night's discussion between himself and Yan had been very impolite.

Corenn had been hoping that she would find the room where they had been hiding out, but this one had no special or unique furnishings, other than the cat, Frog. Bowbaq and Yan hadn't spent all that time just talking, had they? What could they possibly talk about for an entire day?

The young man confessed to the Mother that he had let his mind focus on Grigán's, without explaining his reasoning. It was best he kept that explanation secret, because the Mother was sufficiently shocked by the first part of the story.

"That was stupid and thoughtless, Yan," she said, without anger. "What were you playing at? If you had tried to manipulate his spirit, even just temporarily, you could have killed him! You have so much to learn . . . And, you tried to perform magic on a human, something even I have never tried!"

"I'm sorry. I regret it," the young man confessed sincerely. "I know I was wrong, but don't we say that mistakes lead to discoveries, and the mad make history? Well, I discovered something," he said with a smile.

The Mother held back the rest of her lecture, saving it for later. For now, she wanted to listen to his story so she could better choose her words at the end.

"As I was concentrating, I saw something," Yan said. "It was no longer Grigán, or rather, it was him, but in symbolic form. It's a bit difficult to explain. Until now, when I trained with a coin, I perceived a shapeless mass, like a pile of sand I could modify at will. With Grigán, it was much more complex. You could almost say it was a . . . a kind of sphere."

Astonished, the Mother stood up. If she hadn't known Yan so well, she would have thought he was lying. "What are you saying?" she asked.

"Um . . . yeah, a kind of transparent sphere. Did I do something wrong?" The young man's face showed a genuine fear.

"What was in this sphere? What did you see?"

Yan hesitated before responding. He couldn't tell if his story was making Corenn angry or joyous. The sphere was only the introduction to his revelation!

"It's a bit bizarre. I think I must have imagined most of it. There was a kind of pyramid, made of ice on sand. Flames leapt from the sand and were melting the ice, which created a fog at the top of the sphere. I thought I must have been seeing the four elements. Or, rather, my interpretation of the elements."

"And the sphere represented the *recept*, the degree to which any object will receive magic," the Mother exclaimed with a smile. "You are exactly right. You saw the Sublime Essence!"

Yan breathed a sigh of relief. Luckily, he hadn't been speaking nonsense. The exact opposite, in fact; it seemed like excellent news.

The Mother paced around the table to calm herself and gather her thoughts. Yan could tell she was disturbed.

"What does it mean? You never brought it up before," he asked.

"I would have in some future lesson, but it wasn't anything pressing. It is only a theory. Some of the greatest mages of ages past described the Sublime Essence exactly as you just have. It took them their entire lives to reach this spiritual level. Their entire lives, Yan."

The young man opened his eyes in surprise. It hadn't seemed that difficult to him. What would Corenn say next?

"The Sublime Essence is only a mystical interpretation, with no logic to the average person. But for the rare magicians who perceive it, all describe it in the same way, which speaks to its importance. It's the greatest proof of the power in your Will, Yan," the Mother said with clear admiration.

The two magicians stared at each other for a moment, each one feeling gratitude, hope, and some fear at such power.

"Sorry, I didn't understand all of that," Bowbaq interjected. "So, is Yan erjak or not?"

"What!" exclaimed Corenn.

"I tried to explain to him how I do it," the giant explained. "And I tried to explain how he uses his magic. But neither of us dared to try it. Do you think it's possible, Corenn?"

"What are you talking about!" the Mother cried, not ready to believe it.

Yan responded, "About Will, of course. Bowbaq, in his own way, is a wind specialist. You could certainly teach him how to work with earth, and he can equally teach us how read minds and spirits!"

Corenn looked at the young man's face, then sat trying to concentrate. Yan had just disrupted all of her understanding of magic, her domain.

"I had the idea when I brushed Grigán's Sublime Essence," her student continued. "It seemed to me that I touched his mind. If I had gone any further, I could have seen his thoughts. I could have traveled in his dreams."

"He asked me to explain how I work. It was very difficult for me to find the right words, but Yan said that he had done something similar. Corenn, do you think he is an erjak?" asked Bowbaq.

The Mother's gaze flitted from one to the other. They looked like two oblivious children, playing with a new toy.

"Do you even realize that you may have just revolutionized magic?" she responded, smiling.

Bowbaq worried that it might be impolite, that it would bring him misfortune. Yan, confident, waited to hear his teacher's words.

"The element of wind has always been the least understood. It is the most complex discipline. Who would boast to understand human emotions, the soul, the wandering spirit, dreams, death? Until now, most magicians claiming to be masters of the wind have been illusionists. They interfere with the mind to temporarily deform perceptions. At this small feat, they excel. I was going to teach you how to accomplish this small task, Yan. But you, you have gone much further. You saw the Sublime Essence. You are strong enough to completely grasp the mind in its entirety. So, by logical extension, you must be an erjak," Corenn said.

"I don't know or see any of those things," Bowbaq reminded her, "and yet my power works just the same."

"Yan's is infinitely stronger," Corenn explained, her tone turning serious. "In theory, he could do much more than read minds. He could control them."

A heavy silence followed the Mother's response. The idea hardly filled Yan with enthusiasm. *Magic doesn't put you above others*, Corenn had told him; *it makes you responsible for them*. On the heels of this revelation, his responsibility had just grown immeasurably.

"This means that you also can become a magician, Bowbaq," the Mother noted. "I can teach you, if you would like."

"Do I have to?" the giant asked shyly.

"No, of course not!"

"Well, I would prefer not to, friend Corenn. I'm scared I wouldn't understand it. And it seems far too dangerous."

His companions didn't need to lie to him. With even half of Yan's power, any error could be fatal.

The door swung open suddenly. Hulsidor stuck his head into the room and rudely warned that anyone not outside in two millidays would stay in the mansion tonight.

The heirs gathered their things and left the room. Sapone's hospitality would extend no further. Nonetheless, Corenn took the time to counsel her student. "So much power brings an equal amount of risk, Yan. Promise me, you won't try something like that again without me?"

"Don't worry, Corenn, I've learned my lesson."

"Another thing, did you actually read anything in Grigán's mind? Or did you just think you could do it?"

He hated to lie. But despite his youthful naïveté, he knew it would be a bad idea to reveal Grigán's thoughts.

That he had been thinking of a woman. Not Corenn, but a Ramgrith.

The librarian had scribbled intricate, mysterious symbols all over his face, hands, and arms. He wore the upper half of a mail coat under his clothes, along with a steel cap held on his head with a chain. Lastly, he strapped to his back a broadsword nearly twice as long as Grigán's scimitar.

"Do you really think you'll need that thing?" Rey asked, letting his scorn show.

"Of course I will," Hulsidor responded seriously. "How do you propose a librarian get any serious work done without a long sword?"

"Of course," the actor said, trying to take him seriously.

The librarian shrugged his shoulders and left the manor out the back door, as Sapone had asked him to. The heirs followed.

"This Rominian is crazy," a smiling Rey whispered in Lana's ear.

The Maz couldn't understand why this so amused her friend. She checked to make sure the belts on her clothes were firmly tightened. It was the first time in fifteen years that she had worn anything other than her priestess's robes.

"It's foggy," Hulsidor mumbled to himself, as he waded through the rising mist. "It will be easier to get through the city, but the scare-shouters will love it."

"Are those ghosts?" Bowbaq asked, already fearful.

"One type only. There are also the stranglers, the moonshiners, the skull-crunchers. Oh, and the screamers. I hate the screamers. Try not to disturb one."

The giant wanted to offer to watch the door. Human adversaries, he had learned how to deal with, even the Züu, but to face ghosts—that was another thing entirely. The murky air enveloping Romine did nothing to comfort him. The same was true for his companions, who were speaking loudly to hide their fears.

"But why do the dead gather there?" Rey inquired, trying to lighten the mood. "They have nothing better to do?"

"Why don't you ask them?" spat the librarian. "It's said that they infested the library when my ancestral colleagues dug so deep into the Deep Tower that they found the old Romerij library. When they first opened the old library, they were joyous, and crowds tried to enter. Shortly thereafter, people started to go missing. Bodies vaporized in the hallways. If you ask my opinion, that's when they should have closed off the cursed hole. Instead, they waited two years and had to wall off the entire building."

Grigán and Corenn shared a knowing glance. *All of human knowledge . . .*

Lana asked timidly, "Are these ghosts actually dangerous?"

Hulsidor stopped and stared at her for a moment. "If you don't believe me, we will not go down. The Tower is not a library like any other, you know. We're not taking a leisurely stroll down there. We might even have to fight."

"Really?" Grigán couldn't stop himself from saying it, before he diplomatically assured Hulsidor, "We will do our best to stay out of your way, Master Librarian."

The Rominian started to walk again, sulking; he wanted to keep arguing but was smart enough not to try a Ramgrith warrior.

"What can a weapon possibly do to a ghost?" Yan asked. "Since they are already dead."

"It does enough damage to keep them at bay," said Hulsidor. "It's usually fine if you keep an eye peeled for them. Except for the leeches, of course. You better hear them early enough to flee. On the fifteenth floor they've already lost three men. And the farther down you go, the higher you have to climb to escape. Sometimes I envy my first-floor colleagues, but their books are useless."

"What does this 'leech' look like?"

"I have no idea. You only have to hear them scream to form an image of their fangs. If I order you to run, trust me, and run to the exit without looking back. Some curiosities are best left unexplored."

Yan nodded thoughtfully at this wise advice. He had been thinking about it a lot recently.

The young master woke. The soldiers called him Young Diarch, though none of them understood the word. Their ignorance was no matter to him. All they needed to understand was that Gor the Gentle bowed to him, which was enough to command their respect, their admiration, and a certain bit of superstitious fear.

They said he must be the High Diarch's son. Some thought that he and the High Diarch could very well be the same person, as one was always cloistered in his tent—or in his chariot, when the army was marching—and the other never removed his helm. Those who spread such rumors learned to regret it when they were bound to the wheel. The High Diarch heard all rumors.

The young master stood and slowly walked toward the concubine encampment. His friend was calling him. There was no need to send a messenger. They spoke as they always had—mind to mind. Despite the distance, a single voice rose above the din of thousands more.

Two *gladores* of his elite guard followed him at a respectful distance, having learned long ago to stay out of his way. Speaking to the young master was forbidden, and he returned their silence in kind. It was best for the gladores to make themselves as scarce as possible, erasing themselves almost entirely. Their presence was useless—no one would dream of attacking the Young Diarch. The gladores were there only to lend him an air of prestige.

The bodyguards became aware of their destination only as they arrived, and they watched silently as the young master entered one of the last buildings left standing after the army's most recent attack. A new set of slaves were housed inside. Some would be added to the ranks of the High Diarch's concubines. The others could only rejoice. As slaves, they could hope to survive many more moons, with any luck from the gods, whereas most of the concubines killed themselves after a dékade or two.

The atmosphere was heavy with sweat and fear. Inside the chamber, six women were huddled along the farthest wall. Two had already died, while a third lay on her side, her eyes frozen in place, drool running down her cheek. Their rape was as much mental as physical.

The High Diarch, Saat, stood in the center of the room, ignoring the women's pain, insensitive to their shattered lives. He was simply waiting for his creature's judgment. So the young master probed the survivors' bodies. It only took an instant. And he shook his head. No.

Saat lost his temper and unleashed it on the madwoman, who died instantly. The High Diarch had only pointed his finger, but that was all he needed to extinguish her spirit forever.

Violence alone was not enough to appease Saat, and he handed the other women to his creature, the Young Diarch, who prolonged their agony for more than a deciday. The gladores saw three slaves writhing in agony under the young man's gaze. Saat admired the power seething from his creature, power already ten times stronger than his own.

He shivered in delight at how its power grew—and that it was completely under his control.

"We're here," the librarian announced, to no one in particular. "Try not to make too much noise."

"Why? Do you think the ghosts are sleeping?" Rey said tauntingly.

"The ghosts? I'm not sure, but definitely the guard," an irritated Hulsidor responded. "We are about to walk right in front of his house, so be quiet!"

The heirs crept past the guard's dark and quiet abode without a word, each step drawing them closer to the Deep Tower. On the horizon they could see the structure. Only five stories tall and in a state of neglect, it was hard to distinguish from all of the other fog-engulfed buildings in the neighborhood.

Yan watched closely as the librarian approached the library. The Rominian kept his eyes fixed on the walled-in windows and seemed ready to flee at the slightest sound.

"Can the ghosts come out of the Tower?" the young man asked.

"I have no idea, actually," Hulsidor admitted. "They have never done so during the day, but does that prove anything? At night, they are bolder. Maybe a leech is waiting for us, right behind that door!"

Corenn asked, "How do you know they become bolder at night?"

"They throw my floor into chaos. They can throw around more books in a night than I could put back in a dékade," said the librarian, a hint of scorn in his trembling voice.

"Well, won't that be great for our research," Rey commented.

The main door was decorated with the crowned eagle of Romine. Hulsidor stepped to the right of this entrance and led the heirs to another door, less imposing and more discreet.

"The grand entry is completely blocked off," he explained. "Even if someone found the key, I'm not sure they would be able to open it."

The other entryway was more practical. It was a simple wooden door with a small stair, leading directly to the floors below and the Deep Tower's caves.

"It's an entry meant only for librarians," Hulsidor clarified. "I mean to say, that it used to be, before."

"What's written on the door?" Lana asked.

Even though the script was perfectly written, the Maz had a hard time with the complicated Rominian alphabet, as did most visitors to the Old Country. Hulsidor translated for her without looking at the text.

"What do you think it says? It's a ban, by royal order, doubling as a warning. I suppose that, despite this, you won't change your mind?" he asked, with little hope.

Corenn shook her head after looking at the script. She knew enough Romine to confirm their guide's translation.

"Too bad. Then we will descend," he said. "I will go first, but you won't want to block my exit. Think of the ghosts as a pack of wolves: If you show them your fear, they will attack. If you are aggressive, they will attack. Don't speak, whisper. Don't run, walk calmly. Avoid them if you can, but don't look away if they catch your eye. If one is bothering you, walk away slowly. If they continue, come find me and then come back up. If they start to sing, or if there is a funny odor, it's because they are hungry. Watch your back while you are in the Tower. They sing to signal a group attack."

"Maybe I'll just stay here, Corenn," Bowbaq said in a shaky voice. "I don't know how to read; I won't be much help."

"Not possible!" the librarian interrupted. "You should have thought of that before. Anyone could see you out here, and I would lose my head."

Grigán agreed. "It would be best if we stuck together, Bowbaq. Remember Junine."

The giant shivered, thinking of the Mog'lur that had attacked them in Séhane's palace. He had no desire to be locked down there with ghosts, but it might be worse to stand alone, waiting in the foggy gloom for his friends to return. He griped his battle mace and nodded.

Hulsidor checked that the symbols he had drawn all over his skin hadn't been erased. He took a deep breath, produced a feather and ink from his sack, and drew a complicated pattern on Léti's hand, offering no explanation. The young woman obediently watched him draw. The man then put away his materials without any movement toward the others.

"Now be quiet," he said, practically spitting the words. "And do exactly as I tell you."

The librarian jostled a key in the lock and slowly pushed the door open, ready to close it at a moment's notice. The interior was, of course, completely black. He grabbed his sword and swung the door open wide.

Two piles of manuscripts fell noisily to the ground, making them all jump. A whitish form slipped away with a malevolent giggle.

"They love to leave us little traps behind the door," the Rominian explained. "Nothing too dangerous, once you get used to it, but be careful in the stacks."

The heirs followed him inside, exchanging nervous glances. For the rest of the Upper Kingdoms, the ghosts of the Deep Tower were only a legend, right up there with the Bird of Truth, the Trusset Fountain, and the Halfblood-Moon. This didn't feel like a legend, though. This was all too real.

The Rominian lit a few more lamps, handing one to each of the heirs. Gradually the entry chamber filled with light. The room had no walls, and the light from their lamps stretched the length of the Tower. The first floor held few books, acting more as an antechamber to the floors below.

The librarian sniffed the air like an animal, but said nothing. Grigán held his curved blade; Reyan and Léti held their rapiers.

Yan thought about grabbing his own sword, but preferred to scan the rest of the room, letting his curiosity win out.

"It would be best to leave our bags here," Grigán suggested. "And the cat too."

Frog meowed from within his basket, as if he had understood. He was so small and discreet that it was easy to forget he was there at all. Bowbaq, who was in charge of the little cat, was guilty of just that.

"I'll wait here then," said Léti, who didn't want to leave her animal. "With Bowbaq, if you don't mind."

"Yes!" The giant couldn't agree fast enough.

"Fine," Hulsidor said. "Don't leave. And don't touch anything either. Everyone else, follow me."

The librarian took a small, serpentine stairway, which made its way along the Tower's wall. Yan, Grigán, Corenn, Rey, and Lana followed the small man down the stone stairs.

Alone with Bowbaq, Léti let Frog go. He hastened to attack a Goranese navigation map already crumbling with age.

Hidden in the shadows, a white form sniggered, knowing it would be an entertaining night.

The steps in the Tower shone, worn slick from millions of footfalls over the centuries. This, along with the fact that three of the heirs held a weapon in one hand and a lantern in the other, made the descent itself quite dangerous. By some architect's fantasy, the stairwell was walled off from the library itself. The heirs had made their way down six full floors before ever laying eyes on a single manuscript.

Between the sixth and seventh floor, a wall of books blocked the stairwell entirely. Hulsidor cursed, giving rise to a bout of jeering from behind the obstacle, which only served to anger the librarian further.

"It's not funny! Not at all! You hear me? This is completely idiotic!" he yelled at the tricksters.

"I thought we weren't supposed to provoke them," Rey reminded everyone.

"Those aren't dangerous," the Rominian explained, still irate. "The moonshiners merely amuse themselves at our expense. What annoys me is that they take the material for their tricks from *my floor*. All of these works are mine!"

Rey couldn't help but laugh at the ghosts' prank. They shared his sense of humor.

The stairway was quickly cleared, the books carefully piled along the walls, which left even less room on the narrow stairwell. Finished cleaning, they continued to descend.

At great speed, a milky form rushed from the shadows. Hulsidor shouted, "Protect your lamps!" but too late, and three of the lanterns fell dark. The ghost disappeared as quickly as it had come, mischievous laughter following in its wake.

"I didn't even have time to see its face," Yan said regretfully as he relit Grigán's lamp.

"You didn't miss much. They are horribly ugly," the librarian said loudly. He wore an alarmed look on his face, and his brow furrowed at the pace of the attacks.

"Do you not want to go into the ninth floor?" Lana asked as they passed the ninth-floor platform.

"Another time," said the librarian. "Have you seen how active the moonshiners are? I imagine the others must be equally aggressive tonight. I will do you the honor of our planned visit and then we will climb back up. Only this, nothing more."

"We're not here for a simple visit, Master Hulsidor," Corenn reminded him. "We need to do some research."

"Are you joking? You can't actually be serious! After everything you've seen already!" hissed Hulsidor.

Grigán responded, "We have seen far worse dangers than a pile of books and extinguished lanterns."

"Very well, as you wish! After all, I only promised to bring you to the eleventh floor. Not to keep you alive," responded Hulsidor.

No one said a word until they reached the door in front of the eleventh-floor stacks. Hulsidor unlocked the door and entered.

"Careful!" he yelled, suddenly panicked, as he saw a vaporous form detach itself from a wall.

Léti repeatedly walked over to the top of the stairwell, staring into the dark and listening to the silence. She knew that her friends had descended deep into the Tower, and that their research would take time. Several decidays, even. The waiting was unbearable, though.

Now she regretted not having accompanied them. She wasn't worried about the cat, who seemed fine without her. The same could not be true for her friends, especially if there was a fight. Despite appearances, Grigán was still healing, and any conflict would quickly tire him. Rey was the only one who could effectively defend Corenn, Lana, and Yan, who had little idea what to do with the sword he carried.

She distractedly caressed the medallion Yan had given her. The words engraved within were still a mystery to her. At times Yan was gentle and attentive, but that might just mean he was a good friend. He could also be terse, as he had been since seeing Usul. Worst of all, even as they confronted an endless string of dangers, with each day possibly being their last, Yan had never asked for her Promise.

And yet, right under her feet, he was risking his life for her. As were Grigán, Corenn, and the others. She couldn't just wait here, helpless. The cat could watch after himself just fine. She should have been where she was needed.

She approached Bowbaq to tell him she was going down. She was nearly close enough to touch him when she froze. The giant was immobile, bewitched by a feminine figure.

Léti squatted behind a heap of old parchments. Tears came to her face, but she cut them off as rage replaced fear. She was alone, and Bowbaq couldn't have been entranced for very long; she couldn't leave him to whatever agony he was facing. She would never again retreat from danger. She had to do something. She just needed to figure out what.

Grigán rushed inside the library's eleventh floor, Rey at his heels. A white form rose up in front of Hulsidor like a cobra, and from their vantage they could vaguely discern two arms that ended with long talons, and a face that was marked with three gaping holes: two for eyes, and another, much larger, for a set of enormous fangs.

"Whatever you do, don't move," the librarian whispered. "We surprised it, but it might leave on his own."

The heirs stood immobile in front of the menacing ghost. Its form varied, seeming to dance in the air, growing and shrinking, but always larger than a man.

Suddenly, Yan smelled a strong, spicy odor. He remembered the librarian's advice and stiffened. The ghost jumped at the weaponless Lana. It screamed like a bat as it attacked. Rey's hands were too quick for it, though, slicing through the specter before it reached its target. The ghost fell underneath the actor's blow, but as Rey drew back his arms, the heirs could see the deep cuts its talons had left behind.

The ghost gathered itself in the stairwell behind them, spitting like a cat. It hung in the air for a beat, considering if it was hungry enough to fight through all those blades. Eventually it recoiled and slithered deeper into the Tower, like a tadpole hiding in the mud.

"So they are vulnerable," Grigán whispered. "They become flesh when they attack! That's how we can fight them off."

"And you wanted to take your time doing research," Hulsidor, still pale, mumbled. "That there was a skinner. We named them that after we found one of our colleagues' body on the fifteenth floor. This is the first time they've made it to my level."

Rey pulled up his bloody sleeve and whistled quietly in admiration. The ghost had lacerated his arm with six talons, and the gashes ran from wrist to elbow. Grigán examined the injury and announced that it was nothing serious, which partially relieved Lana. The Maz felt responsible and insisted that she make Rey a bandage. The actor let her dote on him without objection.

Yan and Corenn started to explore the floor. Apart from the moonshiners' tricks, the stacks were perfectly arranged, the books having been placed with care and dusted off regularly. The only discordant note was the piles of books that reached the ceiling. They created walls and dark corners in the already-foreboding labyrinth. Yan felt like a ghost would jump out at any second, and he advanced with caution and sword in hand.

"It must have taken centuries to gather all these books," the young man commented.

"You're right," Hulsidor answered. "There was an ancient rule that anyone could visit the Eclectic Library if they donated at least one work not yet in its halls. In the last few years, that became impossible."

"So there must be a kind of directory," Corenn said hopefully. "A more or less comprehensive list."

"The registers," Hulsidor confirmed bluntly. "The moonshiners stole those long ago, long before Sapone hired me. What exactly is it that you are looking for?"

"Anything about a place called Jal'karu. Does that mean anything to you?" asked the Mother.

"No. My floor has mostly financial, commercial, and trade records. The only reason Sapone invested here."

"That's what I was starting to wonder," Corenn said, sighing. "We won't find anything we need here. We must descend farther."

"Have you lost your mind!" shouted the librarian, his anger briefly overcoming his fear. "Or are you just idiots in the first place? You'll get yourself killed!"

"Lady Corenn is a Mother of Kaul's Permanent Council," Grigán said through gritted teeth. "I suggest you give her the respect that title warrants."

The librarian glared at the fierce-looking Ramgrith and swallowed loudly. Grigán had become incensed at their cantankerous and superstitious guide. He saw now that he would have to take control of the operation.

"Do you know each floor's specialty?" Corenn asked politely.

"No," the Rominian said. "The first fifteen only. No one has ever gone below the fifteenth. I mean, no one who has delved that deeply has ever returned."

"Do you know where we could find history and theology?"

"History is on the third floor," the man said confidently. "We can go there right now; the door is never locked."

"And theology?" asked Corenn, her voice still calm in the face of the librarian's vitriol.

He shook his head, confessing his ignorance. Theology must be lower than the fifteenth. That far down, the ghosts multiplied and grew in strength, and aggression.

Grigán said, "We will have to be quick then. We won't have time to search more than one floor. We should split up into groups."

The Mother agreed. Though the idea of diminishing their numbers further did not please her, she knew it was their best chance at finding anything.

"I'll go down," she decided. "Lana, I would like it if you would accompany me. Your knowledge will be helpful. Master Hulsidor, could you show Yan the third floor and help him search?"

"With pleasure," the Rominian assured her, happy to have gotten an easy task.

Predictably, Grigán and Rey decided to accompany Corenn and Lana, to ensure their protection. Yan didn't complain about his task: Corenn would hate to put him in danger again. She preferred that he stay closer to Léti.

They were about to separate when Hulsidor gave them a final recommendation: "Some ghosts will try to speak with you. Don't listen to them. They are the sirens. They will bring you straight to the leech."

"We have the same thing in Lorelia, but we call them barmaids," Rey joked.

No one was in a mood to laugh. The parties split up, Yan and Hulsidor turning to rise through the levels again, while the rest continued their descent into the unknown. For those who marched deeper into the library, a strong, spicy odor followed their every footstep.

The third floor, dedicated to studying history, was in much worse shape than Hulsidor's level. As proof, hundreds of books were simply thrown in piles that stretched from the entryway to the back wall, sowing anarchy in the room.

"We'll never find anything in this mess," Yan noted. "Or at least, we have very little chance."

"I told you so," the Rominian replied, happy to recover some of his battered honor.

Nonetheless, they got to work, Yan with much more vigor than the librarian. They were trying to find anything on Nol the Strange and his visits to the kingdoms' royalty. The task wasn't easy. To begin with, there was no classification system to follow. Secondly, the subject was so refined that it was hard to think of a general theme where it might be found. And lastly, Yan could only read Ithare. Little by little, their confidence eroded.

Hulsidor gave up first. Instead of searching, he started to draw more of the mysterious patterns on his hands.

Yan couldn't help but ask, "Where did you learn about those symbols?"

"In a book, of course. *The Exorcism Manual*, by Jéron the Tender. It's a rare work."

"I suppose that it is some kind of protection?"

"It's exactly that. These are *magical* runes," he said, as he stared at the young man.

Yan stopped to more accurately examine the jumble of dots and lines that the Rominian had scribbled all over himself. Corenn hadn't yet taught him anything like it. They could be real, for all he knew. Taking note of the intricate patterns, Yan began to see Hulsidor in a new light.

"I am Yan the Curious, specialist of the earth," he announced after a moment, using the formal title that magicians used when presenting themselves.

The Rominian looked perplexed. Yan wondered if had made an error in assuming the librarian was a magician, which Hulsidor confirmed. "What do I care? I have no use for a farmer! What a strange thing to say!"

Yan blushed in confusion and buried his face in a book. He was relieved that no one else had seen the episode. Then he remembered that his friends were heading into mortal peril, and his shame burned a little hotter.

Bowbaq seemed hypnotized by the ghost that was dancing in front of him like a flame devouring a candle. It didn't seem to be aggressive, but Léti knew she had to act, and soon.

This ghost's features were more precise than the others'. It had a human form, a woman's body, which many would describe as beautiful. The only obvious illusion was her hair, which floated above her head as if she were suspended underwater in a calm wave.

The ghost moved her lips, but Léti could not hear anything. As discreetly as possible, she leaned in, hoping to be near enough to make out what was being said. She drew closer, but still no sound could be heard. If the ghost were speaking at all, it was directly to Bowbaq's spirit.

The giant shook, and the young woman hoped he was waking. Her flicker of hope faded when she looked into the face of her friend. His eyes were dead, frozen over, and he seemed to twitch rather than move. From this alone she knew the specter still had him under her control. Bowbaq continued to stir, his feet now coming to life and forcing him into a few awkward steps toward a heavy, oaken wardrobe. His arms moved next, lurching forward unnaturally as he rifled through the wardrobe, emptying its contents on the floor. A small pile of dry papers pooled at his feet.

Léti grasped what was about to happen. Terrified, she knew she had no more time to calculate risks or make other plans. She jumped out from her hiding place and ran straight at the ghost.

She swiped at it three times with her rapier, but the milky shape had no consistency, and Léti's blade cut only air. The spirit turned toward her with an evil smile. She felt it trying to penetrate her mind, but Léti rejected the intrusion with rage.

The ghost smiled, with a victorious expression, and Léti hesitated. It was her undoing.

She felt a violent blow to her back and fell to her knees, crying out in pain. Grigán's training was the only thing that could save her now, and she rolled to her feet to face her new enemy.

A nine-foot-tall ghost menaced her with talons as sharp as knives. He spit and started to sing, a doleful song, not unlike wind whipping through an open plain.

Léti took four steps back into a wall. The two ghosts slithered toward her like snakes. Behind them, a bewitched Bowbaq lowered his torch to the pile of papers. The flames leapt from the lantern and breathed life into a small, dangerous fire.

How spiders could survive in such an environment was an unsolvable mystery, thought Grigán. He led the way, and he was forced to rip apart countless webs as they descended.

The heirs paused at the fifteenth floor's landing. The next descent would take them to depths from which no human had returned. *A bed of serpents*, Corenn thought, *and we are trying to steal their eggs.*

Grigán questioned her with a look, and the Mother nodded. They continued their descent cautiously. *From the forge to the fire*, thought the warrior.

"How many floors do you think there are?" Lana asked.

"Hulsidor himself wasn't sure," Corenn responded. "He figured that the ancient Romerij library starts at the twenty-sixth."

Grigán shook his head, trying to remember why he had agreed to this trip in the first place. What were they doing there, exploring a haunted ruin in Romine, while all the answers they searched for waited for them in Ith, on the other side of the continent?

Because they weren't sure, he reminded himself. It was possible that Achem had said nothing more in his journal than Corenn had in hers. Perhaps he simply kept notes on his daily activities, never mentioning why Saat had become their enemy.

Saat, one of the wise emissaries sent to Ji. A man declared dead more than a century ago. Their only chance to escape him was to unravel their ancestors' secrets. And for that, they would have to resolve the mystery of the portals.

"I feel like the ghosts are calmer down here," Rey commented. "It worries me. Especially considering that odor."

"We have entered their domain, their lair," Grigán explained, as he kept a lookout. "They are surprised, but it won't be long before they react. Violently, I would guess."

As if they were listening to him, three forms materialized in front of the warrior. They would have cut him to pieces if his blade hadn't been at the ready. One was monstrously tall, and another fidgeted his talons frantically. The third slowly reached out his fingers toward the blade, grasping to separate the warrior from his weapon. Grigán was ready and attacked the ghost with a simple jab from his scimitar. The phantom lurched back and began to sing.

"Don't turn around, Grigán," Rey said calmly. "But I have just as many on my side."

Two skinners were blocking the stairway, cutting off their only escape. Grigán tried, in vain, to force his adversaries backward. Rey had no better luck. The ghosts seemed to be coordinating to block their escape.

Lana cried out in pain and looked down at the floor, just fast enough to see two talons disappear into the stone. They had left a few bloody creases on the priestess's calves.

Other hands suddenly appeared, along with gaping maws filled with fangs. These ghosts had nothing in common with the moonshiners from the first floor. They were dark souls, hungry for human flesh.

"Stomp them!" Grigán yelled. "Keep them from climbing!"

Corenn and Lana obeyed, but Corenn cried out in pain only moments later, when a set of talons clawed her leg. A similar attack befell Rey and Grigán. The battle grew desperate, with talons at their feet and skinners in their faces.

More milky talons appeared through the interior wall, swiping at the heirs' faces and trying to grab their hands and weapons.

Grigán shouted, "Follow me!"

He threw his lantern down the stairwell and pulled a dagger from his belt. With a weapon in each hand, he pushed the ghosts back long enough to open up the passage. He rushed down the stairs, jumping over the lantern. His friends followed suit. A few steps below, they ran into a sealed door, which the warrior smashed open with a kick. With great haste, the others followed him into the room, leaving behind fifteen ghosts suspended in the wall where the heirs had just been.

Their talons no longer caught any victims, and that seemed to enrage them. But their prey had let themselves in.

Grigán cleared away a table and flung it between the heirs and the ghosts. Lana watched, petrified, as the ghosts turned and swam toward them.

Rey jumped out from their absurdly inadequate barricade, where Corenn and Grigán were already crouching. He practically threw the priestess over the table, before jumping over it himself.

The ghosts surrounded them, and several began to sing. Their spicy odor was unbearable.

This time, we went too far, Corenn thought to herself, in resignation.

Yan felt like his effort was pointless. In the short time he had, he would barely be able to determine what epoch and which kingdom each book came from. To simply fall upon a page where Nol or Ji were mentioned, he would need uncommon luck.

For his part, Hulsidor had completely abandoned the project. The librarian focused his attention on a nervous examination of the surroundings and on trying to convince Yan to climb back up to the top of the tower.

"Corenn will get us when she comes by," the young man repeated, distractedly, for the third time.

"But they won't come back up! I know that's hard to hear, but it is what it is. Forget your research, and let's go!"

Yan ignored his warning. Hulsidor approached him, taking Yan's silence as the start of a turnaround.

"What are you looking for anyhow? Let's stop wasting our time. We might as well wait up top rather than risk ourselves down here for no reason. My colleague does such a poor job organizing his floor that I regularly steal books from him without his knowledge."

"From what pile did you take the books that Sapone sends to Zarbone?" Yan asked, inspired by an idea.

The Rominian sighed and indicated a stack that was a little smaller than the others. The books weren't placed haphazardly, but rather were stacked perfectly one atop the other.

"In there. He has been working for eight years to organize Jezeba's history. As you can tell, he's not very efficient," said the librarian.

Yan rushed to the books. What good fortune! Two times the Jez sultans had sent their war chief with the other emissaries to follow Nol: three hundred years ago, and again two centuries after that. With a bit of luck, the same thing had happened five centuries earlier.

All he had to do was find a manuscript from around that epoch, written in Ithare. Yan searched through thirty or so manuscripts before he found one that fit the description. He began to eagerly flip through it, not noticing the smoke or the burning smell starting to trickle down from the first floor.

Grigán and Rey were exhausted from fighting off the ghosts' attacks, and greatly relieved to see them stop. Though they couldn't be killed, the ghosts still feared steel and the strange pain it caused them. Or at least that seemed to be the case. The two hoped this would keep the ghosts at bay, but doubt clung to them.

Corenn struggled to think of a way out, but nothing came to mind other than the dim hope that the ghosts would stop and let them pass. It was a probability so remote she didn't dare waste another thought on it. The ghosts who left never did so for long, or they were replaced by a new one. The room was filled with spirits.

Were it not for their individual fear of the blades, the ghosts could have easily overwhelmed the heirs with a simultaneous assault. Luckily, they seemed incapable of working together on a strategy. They simply appeared and then disappeared, teasing their prey. The sound of their song echoed off the walls. Hulsidor's skinners, the scare-shouters, the stranglers, the skull-crunchers, and the moonshiners all drifted in and out of the room, Corenn recognizing each as they appeared. A few of the ghosts pushed their singing into a strident cry, and when they did, she recognized them as screamers.

"Enough!" Lana cried out in desperation, her hands covering her ears. "By Eurydis, enough!"

A heavy silence gathered around the ghosts, and the nearest ones pulled away from the clustered humans. The priestess slowly stood, not ready to believe in the miracle.

"Blessed be Eurydis!" she said, her tone that of shocked surprise.

A few ghosts spit; others chattered their claws and teeth. If invoking the goddess seemed to keep them at a distance, it did nothing to their angry hatred. Yet to see what happened when she said it louder . . .

"Eurydis! Eurydis!" the heirs shouted together, each time louder than before.

Without thinking about it, taken with enthusiasm, Corenn joined her Will to her cries. The ghosts skittered away with angry screams. Encouraged by this success, the heirs jumped out from behind the table and headed for the door, invoking the goddess. Perhaps this way they could escape.

Three new ghosts took form in front of them, blocking the way. The others gathered behind in frustration, like wolves forced to leave their prey to a bear. These newcomers, who had earned their brethren's respect, looked vaguely human. They looked feminine, actually, and the name of the goddess seemed to have no effect.

Grigán remembered their names. "Sirens! The Rominian warned us. Don't listen to them!"

One of them let her gaze fall on Grigán and smiled. A smile that she let grow just wide enough to reveal her teeth, which had two abnormally long canines.

Welcome, mortals, the siren purred directly in the heirs' minds. *What are you doing here?*

Grigán moved in front of his friends and threatened the ghosts with his scimitar. Somewhere behind him, Lana chanted the goddess's name, which kept back the seething mass of angry phantoms.

Corenn couldn't ignore the question, even if she were walking into a worse trap than Lord Dorn-Ton's.

"We aren't enemies," she said, after a long silence.

And yet, you are well-armed, the specter taunted. *All these naked blades, are they really necessary?*

Rey shouted, "Come closer and I will show you."

Come now, come now. We aren't your enemies either. Threatening us, really? Why do such a thing?

"So we can leave, then?" Grigán asked,

The warrior already knew the response. He had no illusions on the subject. The ghost chose to completely ignore the question.

If you don't come here as enemies, you must be searching for knowledge, the siren said, revealing her canines as she did. *How can we help you?*

"By hanging yourselves," Rey said. "If it pleases you, madam."

Suspicious, Corenn asked, "What would be the price of your help? Human flesh, I imagine?"

The ghosts shuddered and clapped their teeth, and it looked as if they were salivating. The leading siren tried to hide her hunger and swallowed noisily before addressing Corenn directly.

I can offer you a deal, she said excitedly. *I will take you to the works you wish to see. In exchange, you leave me one of your servants.*

The stunned heirs didn't know how to respond. The ghosts' intentions had lost all possible ambiguity. Facing such a horrible situation, even Rey was quiet. With a subtle nod, Grigán suggested to Corenn that they could try to fight their way through. The Mother responded by shaking her head, to the warrior's great surprise.

"I have a counteroffer for you," she finally said. "You guide us as you said. In exchange, I will give you a book that you have never seen."

The siren spit in frustration. She seemed to be arguing with her peers for a moment. Grigán used the time to question the Mother.

"What are you talking about?" he whispered. "What made you think this could work?"

"I don't know. I just had a feeling. These ghosts are more or less the library's guardians, right? I had to try."

Corenn didn't get a chance to respond. The sirens had finished their discussion.

We accept your offer. But beware, mortals: we will hold nothing back if you betray us.

"Nor shall we," Grigán responded, pointing his blade at each of the sirens.

Despite this bravado, the warrior knew he was in no position to threaten them. The sirens held no superstitious fear of Eurydis; if they attacked in anger, the other ghosts would immediately follow, and the heirs would have no chance to escape.

What is the subject of your quest then?

"Jal'karu," Corenn responded confidently. "And the portals that take us there."

The siren smiled a cruel smile, showing even more of her beastly canines. Lana thought they might have grown.

You won't be disappointed, the siren said enigmatically. *Follow me.*

Léti fought hard against her two adversaries. The feminine form was not the most dangerous, and seemed to be more concerned with disarming Léti than attacking her directly. This was untrue of the other ghost, which struck at her as fast as a serpent and as strong as a bear.

"Bowbaq! Bowbaq, help me!" she called out repeatedly.

The bewitched giant could not hear her, though. Bowbaq, stumbling like a drunk, fed his fire with the manuscripts, and the fire grew, the flames lapping up toward the ceiling. In a centiday, the entire room would be in flames.

Firm footing, steady hand, Léti repeated to herself. But these adversaries were different, and Grigán's lessons wouldn't save her. If she struck too early, they did not materialize and her blade encountered only air. If she attacked too late, well, she feared the cost of striking too late.

The clawed ghost had already cut open her cheek and side, focusing its attacks on Léti's vitals. She knew that it wouldn't stop until she was dead.

Léti understood that she would never get the upper hand if they kept at it this way. She was tiring, while they seemed indefatigable. She was injured, while her strongest blows appeared to merely agitate her attackers.

She quickly considered another approach and trained her eyes on the two spirits, waiting for just the right moment for her dangerous plan. It finally came when the two ghosts were both on the defensive. Seeing her opportunity, Léti leapt through their vaporous bodies and made a mad dash to Bowbaq.

She had only enough time to kick him violently in the shin before she had to fight the ghosts off once again. Bowbaq cried in pain and looked around the room, dazed, as if he had just discovered it.

The feminine form approached him and disappeared into his body. Bowbaq stiffened and stumbled before reaching for a heavy pile of books and throwing them into the fire.

Seeing her friend possessed filled Léti with hopelessness that was quickly replaced with rage. She would not let the ghost control Bowbaq. Blood pounded in her veins, and a determined expression settled on her face.

Her adversary materialized and tried to rip out her throat, as it had already attempted twenty times. Léti let her rapier fall to the ground and grabbed what she thought were its wrists. The supernatural ghost "skin" was terribly cold, but her fingers remained tightly wrapped around it. She gathered all her strength in her legs and spun the heavy form into the flames. *Sharp mind.*

The specter cried out in pain and was instantly consumed, its form burning up as quickly as dry leaves.

The young woman turned to Bowbaq, hoping another brilliant idea would come to her. She never had the time to find one.

A piece of wood from the burning ceiling crumbled and fell on her shoulders, and she lost consciousness.

All around her, the flames kept growing.

Yan rejoiced. He had been right. Corenn had been right. The visit to the Deep Tower in Romine was worth it. Finally they had learned something about the portals. It was there, written in black and white in front of his eyes. A ray of hope.

The history of Jezeba was fairly boring. The last dynasty had maintained their power with an iron fist, so the chroniclers had no coup d'état to describe, no rebellion or conspiracy to cite. As a result, they were interested in the smallest details of the sultan's court. One such detail involved a certain secret diplomatic mission from five centuries earlier.

And it wasn't mentioned in just some small paragraph either; the subject took up the greater part of a three-inch-thick volume! It was surely the last copy in the world, but its contents were vital for the heirs.

The text told of a strange madness that overtook one of the sultan's counselors upon his return from a distant voyage with a stranger named Nol. The man kept repeating an inspiring tale of a marvelous land, strange children, and dangerous caves. For his part, the sultan threw the madman to the bottom of his dungeon and ended the incident. This was all interesting, and it confirmed what the heirs already knew, but there were more mysteries revealed still.

The distant voyage hadn't been to Ji, but to Sola, in the Oo country, toward the center of the Eastian Kingdoms on the other side of the Curtain Mountains.

With this text in hand, Yan knew where they could find the next portal!

Yan thought about ripping out the page, but the idea of destroying a book, and particularly this one, which had made it through centuries undamaged, revolted him. It was out of this same respect that he chose not to steal the entire book. Even with all the best excuses, it would still be stealing. As best he could, he etched the details in his mind.

He reached hopefully for a few more books when Hulsidor interrupted him. "Do you smell something funny?" he asked.

Yan stood up and tried to remember where he had put his sword, thinking the librarian had smelled the spicy odor particular to hungry ghosts. It was something else, though, which worried Yan all the same.

Hulsidor walked over to the half-open door and pulled it wide on its hinges. A heavy white mist slipped into the room, carrying with it the thick smell of smoke.

"Fire!" the Rominian shouted. "We have to leave right away!"

Yan glanced into the stairwell and grew pale. This was no false alarm. Somewhere above them a fire raged. Somewhere above them was Léti. The faint hint of heat brushed his face, but it was nothing to what burned in his chest.

He looked around, searching for an idea. Hulsidor had already chosen his path. He wouldn't wait for the young magician, and he ran out of the room, climbing the stairs four at a time. Yan didn't mind. He was going to go up soon as well, if only to check on Léti, but first he had to warn the others.

There was no time to descend to their level, plus he would be alone and exposed to any attack. He also had no idea what level they were on.

The smoke burned his eyes and scratched his throat, but he finally found an object that could serve his plan: a lustrous glass globe, made to house candles. Yan filled it with bits of paper found among the mountains of books. He wrapped the whole thing in a large cloth and doused it in oil from his lamp. Finally, he lit his ball of flame and threw it down the stairs. As he watched it fly from his fingers, he hoped it wouldn't break on the first step and that Corenn would understand the message.

Yan turned and rushed up the steps toward the first level. That's where he would be most helpful now. He would help Léti and Bowbaq put down the fire. If he wasn't already too late.

The higher he climbed, the more the stairs filled with smoke. Black cinders stung his eyes and throat. The stone steps shuddered with a resounding shock. Yan sprinted up the last few stairs, not worrying about flames, ghosts, or falling stones. He was too focused on what might have made the sound.

Rightly so. The exit to the first floor was blocked by a heavy wardrobe. Hulsidor braced himself against the steps, trying to lift it, but it didn't budge.

"It's your giant friend," he spat when he saw Yan. "He blocked our passage! I saw him do it!"

The young man could respond only by coughing. Usul had warned him that Grigán would die, which was hard enough to handle. What the god hadn't told him was that Grigán might not be the only heir to fall.

Corenn, Rey, Grigán, and Lana followed the three sirens, escorted by a myriad of other ghosts, less subtle but equally dangerous. This mass stayed well away from the mortals, even without Lana chanting to Eurydis. It appeared that the pact they had made with the sirens gave them protection from the other spirits.

The heirs had lost track of what precise floor they were on, though it was beyond the twentieth, surely. The floors became less regular as they descended, the landings were undefined, and the architecture fell into worse states of abandonment. All around them on crumbling bookshelves were thousand-year-old books covered in dust and rubble. Corenn lusted after such a trove of knowledge, but they had no time to spare.

The lower caste of ghosts grew in number at their backs. Grigán feared that they would decide to attack anyhow, that the growing depths and growing horde would give them too much confidence. Strangely, though, when the heirs began down a new stairway, the ghosts stopped cleanly at the one that preceded it. They couldn't, or perhaps wouldn't, descend any farther. Only the sirens escorted the heirs now.

The last few floors were more blocked than any before. The books and hallways were mixed with excavation materials covered in centuries of dust. More sirens hurried to their sisters' sides and joined the escort. Corenn wondered if they were approaching the ancestral Romerij library. Would they really get to the bottom of the Tower?

They soon had their response. Their progress stopped at an obstacle created by human hands, or ghosts' talons. An impressive pile of dirt, beams, and rubble completely barred the way. This was the passage to Romerij, the Mother guessed.

Wait for me here, their guide said, before disappearing behind the obstacle.

Grigán complained, to no one in particular, "As if we had any choice."

The lead siren's departure left them ill at ease. She seemed to possess a certain control over the others. Enough, at least, to have prevented any attack until now. The heirs counted each breath while they waited.

"This place is cursed," a terrified Lana murmured.

"You think?" Rey couldn't help himself.

"I mean ... I can feel it. As if evil were an odor," said the Maz. "And it is seeping from behind that wall."

They stared at the obstacle nervously. What secrets, what mysteries were hidden behind the mountain of rubble?

"Eurydis, Eurydis!" Rey cried out suddenly. His rapier danced agitatedly in the air.

"What happened? Did they attack?" Grigán asked as he took a fighting stance.

"They tried to—to enter my mind," the actor explained angrily. "Treacherous bitches! I wouldn't want you even after I die! Phiras take you!"

The sirens bore the insults calmly, carnivorous smiles growing on their faces.

"It's not a good idea to invoke He Who Is Night," Lana scolded. "Never, and especially not in anger."

Rey mumbled, "They're already damned, anyway."

The actor would not let his guard down again, and as they waited for the siren's return, they grew more nervous. Then the highest part of the obstacle began to move, and the heirs took a step back. A gap opened, releasing a breeze smelling of fetid vapor. A book appeared in the gap, and then the siren walked across the pile.

Here you will find what you seek, she said as she handed Corenn the book.

The Mother grabbed it, filled with emotion. She had waited for this moment for so long, she could hardly believe it was happening. The manuscript was heavy, thick, and in excellent condition, considering it came from before the Rominian Empire. Its cover bore no title, so Corenn opened it to a random page, as Rey and Grigán surveyed the waiting sirens.

Corenn glanced at one page, then another, then switched to a separate section. Her friends simmered with impatience.

"It's illegible," she announced with great disappointment. "The text is written in Ethèque. No one can translate it."

"You lied to us!" Grigán shouted.

I did no such thing, the siren responded with a malevolent smile. *This book discusses Jal'karu and its portals at length, as I know from reading it. How is it my fault if you are incapable of reading it?*

Corenn contemplated the book's pages sadly. She had never felt so frustrated. The secret of Ji . . . Everything they wanted to know was right under her eyes, and completely out of reach at the same time.

"If we could take the book with us," Lana said, "we could try to—"

It is forbidden! The siren sprang into their minds with fury at the mention of such a sacrilege. *It's our treasure. These books must never see the light of day. Never.*

"Lana," Corenn said softly, "look."

The Mother handed her a loose sheet found stuck between two pages. It seemed like the text was the start of a translation.

"It's in Ancient Ithare!" the Maz exclaimed. "It looks almost like a poem, or a prayer. I recognize this word... and that one... I would need some time, but I could translate it!"

Nothing will leave here, the specter said as she grabbed the sheet. *Ever. Now you must hold up your end of the bargain. If you can, I will let you study this document at length.*

The heirs turned to Corenn, worried. The Mother rustled in her pockets and pulled out a little journal. Her journal.

The siren ripped it from her hands and glanced at its pages with interest before stopping and smiling cruelly.

This kind of work is not famous, she said, victorious. *You did not keep your part of the bargain!*

"May I?" the Mother asked, sticking out her hand. "I haven't yet given this volume a title."

The ghost reluctantly handed it to Corenn, who wrote a few words on its cover with her traveling pen.

"'*A History of Kaul's Permanent Council,*'" she read out loud. "'By the Mother of Tradition.' You will see that the majority of this journal looks nothing like a diary."

The siren grabbed the book back with a hostile whistle. She read through it again, frowning. A law unknown to mortals kept her from bias on this subject.

Very well, she said after a moment. *You respected the deal you made with me. Regretfully, I must leave you to my sisters!*

Lana jumped and snatched the piece of paper from the ghost's hands. She never would have thought she possessed the courage, but her motivation—to find answers—was stronger than her fears.

The sirens crept toward them slowly, still fearful of Grigán's and Rey's blades. Their smiles had disappeared, along with the polite demeanor and gracious faces. The heirs were now facing sharp talons and sharp teeth.

Rey asked, "Anyone have an idea how to get out of here?"

Lana invoked Eurydis over and over, but this had no effect on their intelligent foes. Quickly, the sirens organized themselves for a coordinated attack, one the heirs would be unable to withstand. The ghosts bore down on them, and Corenn realized with horror that Grigán was practically on his knees. So soon after his illness, the warrior had pushed himself too far.

"We can't force our way through!" Rey shouted, even though they all already knew. "We have to take refuge somewhere."

The actor tried his best to accomplish the task. His shirt and cape, already covered in blood from the previous attacks, was quickly torn to shreds. At this rate, they wouldn't survive much longer. They had come so close.

Then a panicked movement shuddered through the sirens, and some fled into the Romerij library. The heirs looked around for the unexpected help, but discovered only another threat. The smell of smoke crept into the room.

They didn't waste any time, but used the confusion to escape to the stairs, pushing back the disoriented and isolated sirens. A fire raged in the stairwell. What strange phenomenon could have lit a fire in the bottom of the Tower? It was a question they didn't bother to ask. Instead, they found the least dangerous path and climbed with reckless speed.

A crack reverberated from the room they had just left, followed by a powerful howl that froze their blood. The heirs didn't bother to discuss it. They all knew what had happened. Fear quickened their steps. The fire had angered the leech.

Together, Yan and Hulsidor tried to move the wardrobe blocking the doorway, but in vain. It was impossible to move it, and their blades barely dented the oak wood. They needed an axe and enough space to use it; they had neither.

Yan worried about what had happened to Léti and Bowbaq. Their silence didn't help. Had they fled? Were they injured? Worse?

He couldn't believe that Bowbaq would betray them; there must have been some other explanation. Hulsidor had seen an illusion in the smoke, that was all, Yan concluded, unwilling to consider any other possibility. Either way, they had bigger problems to confront. The rest would clear itself up later, or never.

They were both sweating profusely, from the effort and the heat. Doubt washed over them. They were wasting their energy. They would never get through this way.

Yan had an idea. He told the librarian to step back, which both intrigued and angered the man. Then the magician cast his Will against the wardrobe.

The magic cracked the wood, and a two-foot-long fissure appeared. Hulsidor cried out in surprise and backed away from Yan fearfully.

The young man took a moment to rest then; the languor was stronger than he had expected. Corenn said it was easier to destroy than to create. Yes, but this wood had a very weak recept, and it had strongly resisted his Will.

He gathered his thoughts, hoping to perceive this new thing Corenn had called the Sublime Essence. The wardrobe's was a sphere full of sand—the earth element, a little bit of fire, and infinitesimally small quantities of water and wind. It was a simple, solid object with no spirit and a tiny amount of life that had been slowly devoured by time.

The sphere itself symbolized the sensitivity of the object to magic. Yan couldn't figure out what element it was made of, as the sphere was only a spiritual interpretation of reality. He saw it as glass.

From practice comes greatness, Corenn said, and practice had taught him that the thickness of the sphere's walls was proportional to the object's resistance to magic. The wardrobe's sphere wall was quite thick.

Magic seemed like their only chance, though, so Yan steadied himself and tried again. He slowly concentrated on the fractured heart of the wardrobe and let his Will grow to its limits. He focused solely on concentrating his Will, and then he unleashed it with all the force in his body.

One of the planks exploded noisily, showering them in a rain of splinters. The other planks hadn't moved an inch. There was now a hole in the wardrobe, but it was still too narrow for passage.

The languor that hit Yan was so strong it knocked him to the floor. The young man passed out, falling heavily to the ground, weak and icy to the touch, despite the fire's heat.

"Help!" Hulsidor cried desperately through the hole.

The Rominian cursed the carpenter who had made this wardrobe with two-inch-thick planks.

Something was following them up the stairs, and Lana had no desire to learn what it was. She was running faster than she ever had in her life, but the inhuman snarling that pursued her only seemed to get closer. It was a horrifying sound, coming from a single throat. It sounded powerful. It sounded hungry.

"You can go faster!" Corenn shouted, struggling for breath. "Don't wait up for me."

Grigán swore and grabbed Rey's lantern. He let the Mother pass in front of him and threw the object down the stairs, lighting a small fire on a landing below. The warrior had no belief that the small fire would do anything to slow down their pursuer, but he had to try.

"You two, run!" the warrior ordered. "I will stay with Corenn."

Lana protested, but Rey grabbed her hand and forced her to follow him. With their youthful strength, they quickly disappeared from view.

"Grigán, climb!" Corenn implored him. "I'm exhausted. Leave me now! And remember me well."

"What are you talking about?" the warrior managed to whisper between breaths. "I'm in no better state than you. And I won't abandon you, Corenn. I will never abandon anyone again, ever." He said this last to himself.

They hadn't climbed up even half the steps. Behind them, the king of ghosts pursued, talons squealing on the centuries-old stone. Ever closer.

Léti was woken more by a strange instinct to survive than by the fire or Hulsidor's racket. She was intelligent enough to realize she had to slowly crawl out from the rubble to stay hidden, but what she saw distressed her.

The entire floor was in flames. If the center of the room hadn't been empty, the fire would have already washed over her. Crackling came from the floors above, indicating the fire's spread. Would the Rominians try to save the building?

Her memory came back to her piece by piece, and as it did, she peered through the smoke, searching for Bowbaq. The giant was on his feet, not far from her, and was doing a strange dance in the middle of the fire. He was still possessed. Before anything else, she had to bring him back to himself.

An idea formed clearly in her mind, and Léti didn't bother looking for her rapier, but instead grabbed a long piece of burning wood. With flame in her hand, she cautiously approached her friend.

It was a strange spectacle, watching the bearded giant, covered in ashes, dancing like a drunk. Bowbaq's destructive strength was terrifying, especially with his mind being controlled by an evil spirit.

Léti thought she was close enough and sprinted the last few yards. She pushed the burning wood into her friend's calf and jumped back anxiously to see his reaction.

Bowbaq jumped reflexively, and the ghost left his body like a panicked fish. The giant immediately grabbed at it with his immense hands.

"Come back here!" he growled like a bear, as the ghost slid away. "Come back and fight!"

Léti couldn't believe her ears. Was this really the peaceable Bowbaq?

The ghost didn't respond to his threats, but dove into the ground, laughing. She had no idea she was heading directly for another fire.

Bowbaq massaged his temples and mumbled in frustration. Léti didn't waste any time explaining. She rushed to the exit, before remembering that Hulsidor had locked it behind them. She turned on her heels and ran to the stairwell, only to discover that the passage was blocked.

That was why the librarian kept screaming for help. She stuck her head through the hole and saw Yan's inanimate body on the stairs.

"Is he injured?" she said, panic rising in her voice.

"Only exhausted. Help us!" the Romine implored as he coughed.

The smoke burned their eyes and mouths as the intolerable heat encircled them. If the floors above were as badly damaged as theirs, it wouldn't be long before the entire tower collapsed on top of them.

"Where are the others?" she asked fearfully.

"They are below! Help us, quick!"

A heavy hand lightly brushed Léti aside. Bowbaq had recovered enough to take action, and he grasped his battle mace with a single hand, knowing exactly what to do with it.

"Don't stand so close," he said, simply.

Hulsidor took two steps back before the first blow fell, and four more steps back after. Bowbaq swung again and again. After the fifth strike, the giant had opened a hole large enough that even he could pass through it.

The Rominian dove through and ran to the door without so much as a thank you. He unlocked it and rushed outside, followed by Frog, who was equally loyal to his friends.

Léti jumped down the stairs and picked Yan up, enough so that Bowbaq could pull him through the opening. Sounds of running rose from the lower levels, reverberating on the stone walls. Léti climbed back up, and they waited anxiously for their missing friends.

Only Lana and Reyan appeared. The fire and wardrobe surprised them only slightly, their focus remained on the more immediate danger behind them.

"It's following us," Rey warned as he stationed himself above the hole in the wardrobe, with his rapier drawn. "Behind Corenn and Grigán. It's enormous."

Léti went to find her weapon and tried to imitate the actor's position, but the wardrobe's placement made their positions difficult to maneuver.

"This won't work," Rey decided. "We'll just cut each other up."

"Let me do it," Bowbaq said in a deep voice. "I *want* to do it."

The actor moved out of the way, leaving space for the giant, who stood above the opening and closed his eyes. He listened for the smallest sound coming from the stairs . . . and let his anger brew.

He was erjak, so when the spirit had contacted his own spirit, he had let it in. The next moment, the visiting spirit invaded him. By then it was too late. Bowbaq hadn't been ready, and he had fallen under the ghost's control.

He had watched, powerless, as his body built the fire, threw the wardrobe over the stairwell, and danced on the flames. The entire time he had fought it, but in vain.

"Were they very far behind you?" Léti asked, worried.

"I don't know," Rey responded. "Maybe."

Bowbaq had suffered through the experience like torture, and he had endured so much pain that even the violence he wanted to commit didn't bother him. The episode with the Gyole dolphin hadn't revolted him as much as being possessed. He was ready to fight.

"Yan is waking," Lana announced.

"I think I can hear something," Rey said. "They're coming."

Bowbaq had heard them as well. He raised his weapon over his head and took a deep breath.

"As soon as they get here, we have to leave immediately," Rey urged. "The Tower could crumble at any moment."

His friends didn't move, and he had to push Léti, Yan, and Lana toward the exterior, thinking that, for once, he was the only one being reasonable.

Bowbaq alone heard his friends running up the stairs. He could hear them gasping for air. They were close, and the giant expected their pace to slow, but the opposite seemed to be true. Something was pushing them, and they ran faster than ever.

The giant opened his eyes and saw the light of a lantern approaching. A few seconds later his friends finally appeared. Grigán shamelessly pushed Corenn through the hole and dove through after her. They were red, breathless, terrified.

"Bowbaq, outside, now!" Grigán ordered.

The warrior dragged himself and the Mother to the door as fast as he could.

But the giant ignored Grigán's advice; he had never been so sure of himself. Something enormous emerged from the darkness, and Bowbaq struck.

The Rominians watched the Deep Tower's destruction in satisfaction. Some even laughed as it burned and then crumbled. Someone suggested they dance, and they circled around it joyously.

The Eclectic Library was, for the less informed, an ancient symbol of royal tyranny. For the more well educated, it was a phantom's lair that they should have destroyed long ago. No one understood that Romine lost one of its great treasures that night; no one dreamed that this treasure represented thousands of years of human knowledge. Of course, it didn't all burn; most of the lower floors were simply buried in the rubble—just as the Romerij library had been before. How many centuries would it stay buried this time?

Hulsidor disappeared in the crowd. The heirs were cheered when they fled the burning tower. For the moment, no one cared that they were foreigners. The usual xenophobia was forgotten as the Rominians treated the strangers like liberating heroes.

The heirs gathered at a distance, and Grigán made sure no one approached them. They heard a dreadful crash, followed by loud applause. The second floor had just collapsed.

"Bowbaq!" Léti cried, running toward the tower.

The entire building crumbled with a resounding crash. The heirs contemplated the disaster in silence, hardly hearing the Rominian degenerates' cries of joy.

A pile of debris at the edge of the rubble suddenly moved, and Bowbaq—his hair in disarray, covered in ashes and dust—looked around, stupefied. He began to cautiously search through the rubble, ready to strike anything that moved. The heirs nimbly pulled him away.

They ended the night in the *Othenor*'s quarters, their last welcoming retreat before leaving for the Holy City of Ith.

Apart from Yan, they all had serious wounds. Bowbaq had bruises all over his body and a few burns, one of which, he learned, came from Léti. All were exhausted and in a piteous state.

They had lost nearly all of their equipment: Corenn, her journal; Rey, the antidote for the Züu's poison; Lana, her Eurydian robes. And their cat, Frog. Once again, their group had shrunk. If Rey hadn't hidden part of the stolen treasure from the Small Palace, they would have been completely ruined.

With his veteran expertise, Grigán gave advice on treating the different wounds they had sustained. Their equipment room became a dispensary where the healers worked on their friends first, and then tried to heal themselves.

Since returning, they hadn't spoken much. When they were sure that everyone was all right, they relaxed a little and told their stories.

Bowbaq confirmed that the "leech" resembled a giant urblek, but no one else had ever seen one, and the Arque failed to describe it any other way. Eventually, frustrated, they stopped pushing him. After being chased for more than twenty floors, Corenn would have liked to learn a little more.

Yan recounted his own story, telling them of another portal that led to Jal'dara. In Sola, in the Oo kingdom, Nol had appeared five centuries earlier with a group of wise emissaries, as he had done on Ji with the heirs' ancestors.

"Well, that brings the number to four, at least," Corenn summarized. "We know Ji's portal, the one in Jérusnie has never been found, and the Great Sohonne Arch in Arkary has never seemed to work. Maybe the one in Sola . . ."

Grigán caught the Mother's gaze and understood what she meant.

"That's lunacy, Corenn," he said. "The voyage would take more than five dékades alone, with a significant part in the middle of the Eastian Kingdoms. Surely we have better options!"

"Once we reach Ith, we will already have covered half the distance," the Mother argued. "There is a chance that the portal in Sola still works. We have to consider—"

She stopped herself when Lana rejoined the group with a serious expression. The Maz had just finished her translation of the stolen page. She read to her stunned companions:

Child neither good nor evil
Man or god, same naïveté
One is himself from his first breath
The other is only a god that men make

Mortal only exists in flesh
Eternal survives on spirits
Warm water of Dara's valley
Somber mud of Karu's pits

Promised day when gods will hear the voices
Open the portals, bind the guardians
Banish the unjust, make the virtuous kings
When the highest break their chains

A long silence followed her reading. The Maz acknowledged that she had finished by letting her hands fall to her sides. The heirs contemplated the meaning with growing alarm.

Vaguely unnerved, Bowbaq asked, "What does that all mean?"

Lana took her time to choose her words. The poem had been sown with hidden meaning and mystical references, which no other Maz would have understood without knowing the heirs' secrets. But for her friends, she had to be as clear as possible.

"It means, dear Bowbaq, that the children behind the portal are different. Very *different*," she added, emphasizing the word. "And that Jal'dara is much more than a paradise. It's the birthplace of gods."

They sat with this overwhelming knowledge for a moment, long enough to grasp its implications. One of them immediately came to mind.

If Jal'dara was the birthplace of gods, it was also the birthplace of demons.

They started to understand what their ancestors might have seen, and from whence came Saat's power. It was terrifying, and they had thought their situation couldn't be worse.

Their enemy had immortals on his side.

BOOK VI: PILGRIMS

The heirs had been in Romine for only two days, but they couldn't wait to leave the inhospitable city where they had skirted death.

They were at the end of the Hearth's dékade. It was the Day of Bread, as Lana taught them, as they prepared for their voyage to the Holy City. The day was a short one, as most of the heirs slept until well after the sun rose to recover from their sleepless night, and there was so much to do that they had almost no time to discuss their discoveries. Each of them wanted time to gather their own thoughts before suggesting anything to the group.

Their pilgrimage to Ith would be by land, as Grigán and Corenn had agreed. The warrior thought it would be faster to go through the Wet Valley and the Murky Mountains toward Pont in Lorelia, even though the coming Season of the Earth would slow down the effort. They would then continue to Lermian, traversing to the south of the Grand Empire, and finally they would take the Alt to the Holy City. By sea, the voyage would take three dékades, without allowing for damage to the boat or any storms they might encounter. Grigán hoped to reach Ith in less than twenty days on horseback.

They didn't have time to find a buyer for the *Othenor*, and were forced to abandon the sloop in the waters of the Urae. Before turning their backs on the vessel, the heirs scrabbled together the last of their equipment. Yan looked at his sword, Lorelien clothes, and Junian socks, and laughed to think of the harpoon and fishing lines he had brought with him when he left Eza only five dékades earlier. It might as well have been a century ago, so much had happened since.

They planned to pass the first leg of their newest voyage with Rey's friend's troupe of street performers. The artists gained an escort to Pont, while the heirs got a cover story and the easy passage between kingdoms that was always given to entertainers. This would be especially important in Semilia, and when passing through Pont.

The heirs next had to find themselves mounts and wagons. They decided to take only two wagons, but those were large enough to shelter them all from the Murky Mountains' frequently bad weather. Lana approved of the choice, as did Yan, Bowbaq, and Rey. Compared to Grigán or Corenn, they all struggled to ride, and the idea of traveling on horseback for twenty days straight didn't please them much. Nonetheless, the Mother suggested they each get a mount as well, in case of emergency.

Still using the stolen treasure for funds, the heirs replaced the equipment they had lost in the Deep Tower. Food and potable water, of course, but also candles, matches, blankets, and warm clothes were secured. Who would have thought their quest would take them all the way to the cold season?

Finally ready, the heirs joined the street performers, a well-traveled troupe that didn't much care about their travel companions' strange origins. Introductions were done quickly and without any real enthusiasm. Only Rey's friend, the Lorelien juggler with the strange name of Gallop, paid them any attention. The fifteen other traveling artists, Rominian for the most part, hardly turned to greet the newcomers.

The heirs couldn't ask for any better treatment than being left to themselves on their last night in Romine. They wanted to speak alone, and they piled into the largest wagon for a serious discussion.

Grigán carefully looked around the wagons before joining the others, but the area where they were staying the night was a calm and rarely visited abandoned neighborhood. In contrast, Gallop and the others were headed to one of the busiest streets in Romine for a final performance. Yan realized that he had no idea what their show even looked like, before burying the thought. He would have other opportunities to see it.

The heirs began by talking about everything except what was most pressing in their minds. There was fear among them too, as if by simply mentioning their names, gods, demons, or ghosts would materialize out of the mist that covered the city for the second night. But Rey's jokes made them slowly relax, enough that they were soon ready to discuss serious matters. Saat and Jal'dara, the gravest of topics, were the first to be addressed.

"We are facing something," Corenn commented to herself, "that goes beyond just our own destinies..."

They all turned to face her and hear what the Mother had to say. Corenn woke from her daydream and noticed their attention, each waiting to see what their leader would say about the most recent events. Perhaps she would indicate how they should move forward. The Mother forced herself to take charge.

"Our enemy is no longer a simple mortal. He has survived beyond his natural limits for more than a century. He knows the place where gods grow. We can guess that he went there, when our ancestors did, and from there stole a great power, something strong enough to control demons and maybe other things we don't yet know."

Though no one had interrupted her, Corenn paused. The Mother couldn't help but use her powers of persuasion, even though her audience already agreed.

"Saat is easily the most powerful human in any kingdom, if we can even call him human. And, unquestionably, he is evil. The implications of our quest are now bigger than any of us. Saat surely has the power to influence thousands of lives. The power, and the intent."

"But how?" Léti asked. "And why?"

"I don't know. Maybe for the same reasons he exterminated the heirs," said Corenn.

Rey interjected, "A thousand apologies, Lady Corenn, but that is a lot of maybes."

"*Maybe* you are smarter than all of us; can you come up with a solution?" Grigán said, glaring at Rey.

"Let's summarize what we know for sure," the Mother responded. "I think no one here will doubt Usul's words? Our enemy is Saat the Treasurer, ambassador of the Grand Empire of Goran to Ji more than a century ago. He is still alive, against all logic. Outside of that, the portals all lead to the same place, a place called Jal'karu or Jal'dara. And it, according to the text we found in the Deep Tower and Lana's translation, is the birthplace of gods. As extraordinary as it seems.

"Moreover, Saat commanded that all the heirs be assassinated, but he has no apparent reason to hate them. To hate us. We can only guess that he fears us, which reveals him to be evil, for only an evil man kills those he fears. So the questions we have to ask are: What is he trying to accomplish? And how can we oppose him?"

No one had a response. Corenn had just exposed their deepest fears to a cold, pale light. And though everything was clearer now, the problem seemed no less insurmountable.

Yan thought about Usul's prophecy. The Upper Kingdoms would soon lose thousands to a deadly war. It wasn't simply a possibility, it was the future as foretold to him by a god. Could Yan really influence the course of history and avoid a war whose players he did not yet know? He saw no way he could, just as he saw no way to help his companions. Grigán's illness, his own relationship with Léti, the darkening cloud of war—it all seemed too much. Yan's head sagged under the burden.

"We at least know a partial answer," Lana said. "As you already noted, Corenn, Saat killed only the heirs born after the emissaries returned."

The Maz stopped her explanation there. In fact, she didn't know how to use this information. There were too many possibilities.

"I don't understand," Bowbaq announced. "What does this all mean?"

"It means that Saat is scared of us," Rey responded with a frown. "But we don't know why."

"Our ancestors must have known," Grigán intervened. "Maz Achem must have known. Maybe he wrote about it in his journal?"

"And maybe not," Rey said before trailing off.

"We won't know until we get to Ith," Corenn concluded, disappointed that they couldn't figure anything out before then.

Yan felt worse than ever. Only he knew part of the response, but what help would it be to add more troubles to the fears that weighed down his friends?

All they could do was wait, reach the Holy City as fast as possible, and hope. Hope that they wouldn't face opposition along the way, hope that the journal would still be there, and hope that its contents would help them.

But time was their enemy.

Gallop was a little shorter than Reyan, and a little younger, but no less talkative—and just as arrogant as any Lorelien. The acrobat was a juggler by trade; he and Rey had met for the first time when the actor was trying to master the difficult art of knife-throwing. That memory brought up another for Gallop, a much more amusing one, since the juggler couldn't stop laughing when he recounted why Rey had quit that profession. The actor very seriously commanded Gallop to stop his story, and his friend agreed reluctantly, though his laughter never stopped. The heirs never learned the truth, but they found that they liked the small Lorelien right from the beginning.

He was the only acrobat who spoke to them. The others, either because they were impressed or because, like most of their Rominian brethren, they just didn't open up easily to foreigners, showed them nothing more than indifference.

The small group had sixteen people. Apart from Gallop, the heirs only met a few others. There was a giant, and two clowning dwarves who never removed their makeup. In addition to those three, there was a "master of wolves" and a "master of monkeys." The first had only one animal, which was so old and so accustomed to humans that the "master" didn't even bother chaining him up. Likewise, the wolf only moved to take naps away from the bustling camp, or to beg for treats like a common dog.

The master of monkeys, Tonk, was fat and, as the heirs later witnessed, violent. He had two pairs of mimastins, smallish monkeys from the Lower Kingdoms. Bowbaq saw burn marks and bruises on their furry little bodies. The giant stared at them for a long time with his fists clenched, contemplating how painfully the tiny monkeys were tortured. Grigán, seeing the anguish on his friend's face, forced the giant away from the cage, warning him that Tonk was watching them.

The giant, not Gallop, was the chief of the little troupe. He was a massive man who went by the name Nakapan and periodically stared at Bowbaq's muscular body jealously. Nakapan's wife was a fire-breather, his son an acrobat, and his two daughters horsewomen. The only words he spared for the heirs was a warning he gave while looking at Rey: they should always be respectful to his daughters. As Nakapan walked away, Grigán repeated the recommendation to the actor, who feigned anger at the lack of trust.

The troupe had six average-sized wagons of their own, so in addition to the two that belonged to the heirs, eight carriages set off on the Day of the Tanner for a voyage to Pont in Lorelia. Yan, Corenn, and Bowbaq sat in the larger wagon, leaving Rey and Lana alone in the smaller one, to the actor's great joy. Grigán and Léti preferred to ride at the convoy's side. The warrior enjoyed this position because it allowed him more freedom of movement. Léti, on the other hand, chose to ride alongside the warrior out of respect for the title of bodyguard, a role she took very seriously. She imitated the master-at-arms as often as she could.

For his part, Yan was thinking of Kaul, and of Eza and Norine's home where he had grown up with Léti. Everyone felt emotional ties to their homes, but reason seemed to be pulling them farther away.

Yan told Corenn how he had fainted after casting his Will against the wardrobe. The languor had knocked him unconscious, even though he had thought he could withstand it. The Mother listened to the story attentively, and had no trouble explaining what had happened.

"You were almost certainly strong enough *before* you unleashed your Will," she assured him, "but too weak afterward. Don't forget that your mind uses the same energy as your body. You have to account for that when you are trying to anticipate the languor. You have to anticipate your weakness."

Yan nodded; magic was not easy. Even for him, a natural-born student.

"I know several exercises," Corenn continued, "a few tricks—ways to enhance your concentration. I had intended to teach you all of them once you understood the theory. That seems ridiculous now, since you have already advanced so much in your magic. You've already seen the Sublime Essence!"

"I don't feel that skilled," Yan replied seriously. "On the contrary," he said, sulking, "I can't control anything."

"*Even kings must breathe*," Corenn recited with a smile. "Since you have no problem concentrating, I think it would be a good idea to teach you how to use forces outside of your own body, to diminish the languor. This should help you master your power."

"Didn't you tell me that this technique is quite dangerous?" asked Yan.

"Of course. All magical techniques are dangerous, Yan. That's why we don't teach them to idiots," said Corenn.

Bowbaq, who was driving the wagon and listening intently, said jovially, "Another reason I should stay out of it."

They laughed, happy to finally be free of any immediate danger, but the moment was short-lived. Bowbaq's comment reminded Corenn of their recent discovery, that all erjaks were magicians. She had never thought to understand their abilities in this way, but if she revealed their powers as magic, half of them would be killed in a single moon. The Arques were a superstitious people. It was best she kept the idea quiet, thought the Mother.

Inversely, all magicians would be powerful erjaks if, like Yan, they could see an entity's entire spirit. While erjaks acted without method, instead using a power they could not explain, magicians immediately ascribed this power to having an innate understanding of the wind element. Erjaks acted instinctively, but the Arques had many established rules and taboos to prevent any erjak from abusing power. Though a magician would have to work to attain the instinctive power native to erjaks, no such taboos or rules would hold her back from abusing the power. The idea that her fellow magicians could use their Will on people's souls and minds as if they were miserable guinea pigs froze Corenn with fear. For this reason, she thought it best to keep the knowledge a secret. Then she realized that this same discovery could have been made hundreds of times, and at each occasion, people could have made the same decision to protect other magicians and erjaks from the truth. Thus, the secret remained.

How many similar secrets were closed away in ancient books, centuries-old temples, forgotten ruins? Corenn had always believed in the supernatural, which, though unexplainable, still existed. But what they were confronting now went well beyond her prior beliefs. Immortals, children gods. So many questions and no responses. Yet...

"How does this technique work?" Yan asked, unknowingly pulling the Mother out of her reverie.

It only took Corenn an instant to recover and answer, "With serenity. You must be in complete control of yourself to draw energy from a foreign body, to manipulate it, and to unleash it on another object. It more than triples the difficulty in a typical spell, but if you master it, you can avoid the languor."

"And what part of that is dangerous?"

"All that power in your hands is difficult to handle, even for the most prudent magician. The power is intoxicating. We always have a tendency to accumulate too much force, since it seems inexhaustible. It isn't, though. Eventually there comes a moment when the object providing the force shatters. If this happens, the languor will overcome you with twice the force."

Yan swallowed nervously. He could hardly imagine the effects of such a powerful shock. It would be a violent and painful death.

All this talk both kindled his curiosity and made him nervous, as all things magic did. He took a moment to gather his courage, and then finally asked Corenn a more pressing question.

"Bowbaq can teach me to be an erjak," he said in a shaky voice. "I am curious... if you agree... I mean, could I..."

"Why do you want this power?" Corenn asked gravely.

Yan dropped his eyes and looked out on the countryside, until he saw Léti riding next to Grigán. He followed her with his eyes for a moment.

"Knowledge," he finally responded. "I am curious what Bowbaq sees and feels, when he 'speaks' to his lion. Aren't you?"

Corenn eyed him with a light smile, before letting out a frank laugh.

"All right, all right," she conceded. "For knowledge. It's only that, right? You will study a new discipline of magic with another teacher. Wind requires little force, but rather an expansion of your mind. It can't hurt you. It is out of the question to stop *our* lessons, though. Those will continue regardless of your *curiosity*," she said, falsely scolding.

"Oh, no!" Yan assured her candidly. "I would never dream of it."

"And above all else," the Mother said, serious again, "never try, never test your powers on a human again. The mind is a fragile thing, Yan. Bowbaq can read it, so much the better. You can *alter* it, though, Yan. That is much too serious a thing to be playing with."

Yan nodded his head slowly. It was the first time Corenn had forbidden him from doing anything. He swore he would respect her command.

Soothed by the wagon's irregular rocking, Lana gazed at the dreary countryside surrounding Romine. Like her friends, she was wondering how she had arrived here, so far from her home, her daily chores, her entire life. Previously a Maz of the Grand Temple, she was now a simple mortal thrown out on the street, another unknown future twisting in the wind.

Two moons earlier, the only life she had ever known was in the Holy City and a small part of the Grand Empire. Since leaving, she had passed through the Baronies, the Land of Beauty, and the Old Country. Now she was crossing the Wet Valley, with its sinister reputation, in a troupe of Rominian entertainers hostile to Eurydis. How strange all this was. How sad.

Lana tried to pull herself together, not wanting to fall into self-pity. It was a feeling that contrasted sharply with the three morals of the sage goddess Eurydis: knowledge, tolerance, peace.

She forced herself to find the manifestations of those three morals in her own journey. Eurydis had allowed her to survive the Zü's blades, and the goddess had given her friends for her journey: the proud Grigán, Corenn, Léti, Yan, sweet Bowbaq, and finally, the libertine Rey. The goddess had, up until now, kept them all from irreparable harm. And, despite the difficulties they had faced, their quest continued, progressed, and now was finally starting to make sense.

Wasn't that a sign?

Lana was no theoretician, and didn't pretend to interpret divine signs, but in her heart of hearts, she felt that Eurydis guided their way, that the goddess wanted them to succeed. The Maz attached herself to this idea, finding in it the courage to continue.

"Look over there." Rey pointed. "Red pigs!"

Lana watched a drove of thirty or so pigs sleeping, shaded by a copse of cadenettes, the thin yellow-leaved trees that pocked the landscape. Insects hovered about the animals, making a cloud that hung over them, visible from fifty yards away.

"The Rominians eat the flesh of those disgusting animals?" she asked ingenuously.

"Not always," Rey responded. "Sometimes it's the opposite. I suggest you don't get down right now; they would devour you in an instant."

Lana looked back at the wild pigs with a frightened expression, and the actor couldn't help but push the sham a bit further. "I've seen a group smaller than that one completely destroy a convoy like ours. Look, I think they're starting to move . . ."

"Reyan, you're lying to me!" the Maz realized. She continued, amused, "I am certainly a believer, but not *that* gullible."

"But I'm not lying," Rey insisted, acting offended. "And I would prefer it if you called me Rey. Reyan sounds much too fourteenth century."

"But it's the name of your ancestor!" Lana exclaimed. "Aren't you proud . . ."

She let the sentence die in her throat. One might able to explain the other. Anyway, it was much too personal a subject for her to give her opinion.

Rey kept quiet and the conversation stopped for a moment, leaving them both with a forced smile.

"Tell me," the actor suddenly broke the silence. "How is it that someone as beautiful as you is not married to an old, grumpy, bearded Emaz?"

"Reyan . . . Rey . . . I am a widow," Lana said, not trying to hide the fact. "For two years, already."

"I am very sorry," the actor responded sincerely.

He had no desire to question the priestess on that story. The news was doubly bad; how could he compete with the dead?

Lana perceived the Lorelien's trouble. She didn't want to give him any false hopes, but she couldn't stand to see him so sad.

"Rey," she said gently. "You saved my life twice in the Deep Tower. I am deeply grateful for your courage and consideration. Without them, I wouldn't be here. I will pray for you."

"Blessed be Eurydis!" the actor said cynically.

There were no more jokes for the rest of the day, and after lunch Rey chose to ride alone, leaving Corenn to take his place next to Lana.

The convoy stopped well before nightfall in Deshine, the last town before the wild and deserted Wet Valley. Grigán couldn't help but notice that their first traveling day hadn't taken them very far, and that at this pace it would take them more than a dékade just to reach Pont. But as long as the entertainers earned money only with their arts, Deshine was a nonnegotiable stopping point.

Apart from the size, the town looked exactly like Romine. Once again they were surrounded by tall, painted houses showing the Uranian eagle, and narrow streets leading from house to house. A few dangerous-looking natives with brocaded capes marched in the streets like tormented souls. Deshine looked like a simple outskirt of the Rominian capital, and Yan wondered how the artists made any money visiting sad little towns like this one.

They left the wagons outside the walls, as the laws of the city demanded. The street performers quickly installed their camp. The chore had been done thousands of times before, and the camp went up without a hitch. When dinnertime came, each of the "families" ate separately. The heirs followed suit, happily hosting Gallop and Anaël—the master of wolves—who shared the same wagon.

Yan had heard about wolves in the Matriarchy, so he kept an eye on the beast they called Merbal. That fact that the beast bore the name of the legendary brigand who drank his victims' blood didn't help ease Yan's fear of the wolf. Quickly, though, he got used to the elderly animal's presence, as did his friends, and they all waited their turn to pet his ears when he came around. Only Léti had to push him away, two or three times, the wolf being attracted to the strong smell of her fresh leather armor.

Bowbaq had made friends with the wolf without the use of his erjak powers. It was just more proof, if they needed any, that the giant had a way with animals. Though the wolf was attracted to Bowbaq, it helped that he fed the animal more than half of his meal. The heirs couldn't tell if that was to befriend the creature, or to keep its attention while the rest of the group finished their meals undisturbed.

Yan watched the giant's method, looking for tricks he could use to refine his magic. Bowbaq appeared to be without any, though, or at least none that one could call a method. What

Bowbaq would teach him would go beyond natural charm or gentility. It would be something greater: an expansion of his mind. Yan knew he needed a delicate and sensitive touch to be able to enter an animal's spirit without making it mad with fear.

With his good-natured demeanor and his poor practice in the Ithare language, Bowbaq might not be the best professor for something so complex. This thought crossed Yan's mind briefly, and as soon it did, shame surged through him.

The colossus Nakapan came around to call the troupe together, and Gallop and Anaël left to prepare for the show. The chief stopped long enough to propose that Rey join them, following Gallop's advice.

"We can never have enough amuseurs here," he explained awkwardly. "I will pay you a half-monarch for the night, if it interests you."

Politely, Rey refused the offer, and the man left without insisting. But the exchange didn't go unnoticed

"*Amuseur*?" Léti asked. "What exactly is that?"

"It's a pretty boring job," the actor responded. "Amuseurs don't do their own numbers. They simply act like idiots and make fun of a few people in the crowd in between other parts of the show. The Rominians love it."

Grigán responded, "And to think, we had one for free all this time!"

"Never would I dream of making fun of a lord such as you," Rey retorted maliciously.

The warrior walked away without responding, not at all sure he would win an exchange of words like this.

As they had arranged with the entertainers, the heirs were in charge of keeping an eye on the camp during the show. And while there was some trust between the two parties, the artists still left someone to keep an eye on the heirs.

For Yan, Léti, and Rey, their curiosity got the better of them, and they left camp to see the show. When they insisted that some of the others come as well, Corenn and Bowbaq joined them, leaving the camp guarded by only Grigán and Lana. Given the proximity of so many hostile Rominians, the two were left feeling alone and unsettled.

The warrior watched his friends walk through the gate, and felt uneasy. If he could have, he would have forced them all to stay at the camp.

Every time they separated, catastrophe followed. There was no reason to think this time would be an exception.

The troupe entered the city with their costumes on, accompanied by a raucous jig on a vigola. Their goal was obvious: to attract as much attention as possible. Yan, Léti, Corenn, Rey, and Bowbaq followed the colorful parade from a distance. The heirs were torn between a desire to participate in the party and the wisdom to not get mixed up in it.

Each artist showed off a taste of their talents. First came the three horsewomen, displaying five magnificent horses with skin as white as cream. The horsewomen were also acrobats in their own right, and they pulled off a long series of somersaults and mount changes without ever touching the ground, and then they stood on three horses riding side by side.

The horsewomen opened a pathway through the crowd for the others, and the remaining actors all surged through the gap. Behind the horsewomen was Nakapan the colossus, who took the place of honor as much for the prestige as for an excuse to keep an eye on his two daughters. Nakapan shouted to the crowd to follow if they were curious. His only performance was to occasionally flex his muscles, moving his body into awkward positions to show off his strength. By the grace of Eurydis, he didn't notice that the Rominians were more impressed by Bowbaq, whose mere presence was enough to steal the show.

Behind Nakapan, his wife, typically a fire-breather, played an echoing vigola. Right behind her was Gallop, juggling five wooden balls that were replaced one by one with objects the clowning dwarves stole from the onlookers. The Lorelien soon returned the stolen goods to their owners, then replaced the fire-breather at the vigola, allowing her to spit fire and show off her skills.

Then came old Anaël and the wolf, Merbal, outfitted for the occasion with an impressive spiked collar and held back by a short leash, which his master held with two hands like a great huntsman. The wolf played his role perfectly, growling at anyone who came too close.

Behind them came the amuseur, who was just as Rey had described. The man wore a gaudy costume covered in the cross of Jérus. Even for a Rominian, the robe was over the top. Everyone knew how the Uranians hated the Jérusnians, and the outfit had its desired effect, especially when the amuseur made his character look daft: falling, tripping over the smallest obstacle, even letting himself be "bitten" by the wolf.

Tonk, the cruel master of monkeys, was next. His favorite trick was to let his chained animals scurry up to an onlooker and dishevel their clothes until he yanked the mimastins back. Inevitably, the victims would lose buttons, brooches, sometimes hair, leading their friends to burst out in laughter. Corenn began to understand the troupe's success; the Rominians got pleasure from the misfortune of others. If she were honest with herself, they weren't that different from other people.

The next artists, two acrobats staging a battle, were less entertaining. One had a pair of sabers, the other a poleaxe with rounded edges, covered in ribbons that highlighted its arching movements. The two men wove in and out of the crowd, spectacularly attacking each other while avoiding the onlookers.

"What a shame that Grigán isn't here," Rey joked. "He might have been able to teach them a thing or two."

"Grigán is much better than they are," said Léti, who had taken Rey seriously.

Bowbaq nodded and said, "I think so too."

Rey didn't add anything. He was obviously of the same opinion, but his friends were too distracted to pick up on his joke.

The two last entertainers were shrouded in mystery. One wore a long black robe embroidered with obscure runes, walked with dignity, and carried a gold-filigreed spellbook. The other was a young woman made up to be an imp. She jumped in circles around her "Grand Master" to create space around them.

Closing the procession with these two characters was smart, as it engendered a final burst of curiosity in the crowd. A large number of the crowd joined the heirs, following the troupe to the show.

Many of them stared at Bowbaq and the beautiful, warriorlike Léti, wondering if they too were part of the spectacle. Rey noticed, and he had a few choice words with the ones who ventured too close. Each time, the Rominians walked away, their bodies and eyes indicating great respect. The actor laughed, hard, but refused to translate the exchanges for the other heirs.

The parade stopped in the town's central square, and the crowd made a circle around the artists, guided by the dwarves and the acrobatic warriors.

Like the others, Yan was ready to see a show, and he let the pleasure of anticipation overtake him without ever wondering what might come next.

The remaining acrobatic troupe member left Lana and Grigán alone so he could personally guard his pillow—a task he did so well that Grigán and the Maz could hear him snoring.

Being alone with Lana made the warrior more nervous than he was willing to admit. He thought he was so different from the priestess that they would have nothing in common to discuss. Ever loyal to his habits, Grigán didn't say a word but paced vigorously. He circled the camp twice, doing his rounds and instinctively straightening his absent mustache. With nothing more to do, he came back and sat down next to Lana awkwardly.

Up to that point, the Maz had not been loquacious either. At first, she had kept quiet to respect the warrior's own silence, but soon she was searching for the words that would help the Ramgrith share his burden. It was clear that the warrior was ill at ease, and Lana remembered an old proverb as she watched him struggle: *To find a man's heart, it's enough to be a woman.*

"Grigán, do you believe in a god?" she asked finally, with no other introduction.

The warrior fixed his gaze on her. This was exactly the kind of conversation he wanted to avoid, talking about religion with a Maz!

"What difference does it make? Do gods believe in me?" he responded sharply.

He immediately regretted his aggressive tone. Lana didn't deserve such an attitude.

"Yes, I believe in gods," he continued softly. "How could I not, after what we have seen. Usul, the Mog'lur, the portals to Jal'dara, and everything else? I would have to be an idiot not to believe!"

"That's not what I mean," Lana explained. "Do you believe in a god? Do you pray?"

"Excuse me, but I find this question to be too personal."

The Maz didn't add anything. The worst way to try to ease someone's conscience was to interrogate them. Tolerance was one of the three virtues for a reason. People always ended up understanding that if the priests kept their silence, they would equally respect their secrets. Perhaps they could help in some way or another. Was not the Maz one of Eurydis's teachers?

Grigán was no exception. Lana's silence and her attentive, caring expression did a better job of opening him up than anything else could have.

"I don't believe... I don't believe in *a* god, as you mean it," he continued haltingly. "Formerly, in Griteh, they taught us to pray to Alioss and Lusend Rama. But I was only a child, so what I thought then doesn't matter. I lost my devotion when I grew up, and I stopped praying completely when I left the Lower Kingdoms."

Lana didn't share Grigán's opinion about the value of a child's faith, but she said nothing.

"Do you believe in something like... nature?" she asked gently. "The forests, seasons, animal spirits... something like that?"

"Do you think that's stupid?" the warrior asked, slightly offended.

"No, of course not. It's normal that having passed your life on trails in forests, you might find divinity in the rising dawn or in the birth of a fawn more than in the dry leaves of a religious text. It's a commendable kind of faith, Grigán."

"Thank you," the warrior mumbled, still nervous. "But you... you aren't mad at me for..."

"For Eurydis?" the priestess finished his sentence. "That only depends on you. How would you take it if you saw all the Maz chanting the praises of nature?"

Grigán thought for a moment, trying to look for the trap he was falling into. He felt like he did when he was losing an argument with Corenn, when he never got the last word. But Lana was not Corenn; the Mother wielded diplomacy to influence political and economic decisions, while the Maz worked with religious conviction. Moreover, their methods were radically different.

"I don't know," the warrior confessed. "I suppose it would be nice to see other people respecting my beliefs," he finished, looking out at the horizon.

"Well, then you are faithful to Eurydis in your own way," she said. "Don't worry, I have no intention of interfering with your beliefs. I simply wanted to tell you this: our faiths are similar. Both of us are thinking along the same lines."

"Which is?"

"The universal quest for the Moral, of course. Knowledge, tolerance, peace. You defend these values, Grigán, even unwittingly. You help humanity progress. It matters very little whether you invoke the name Eurydis, or nature. It's said that the goddess will come for the third time to this world, to help us take the last steps. Mankind will live in harmony with nature's creatures and all living things. Over time, men and gods will mix and become a single race of intelligent beings. They will never feel suffering, desire, cruelty, or other flaws of our soul. We call this radiant future the Age of Ys. Don't you think your beliefs belong in this future as well? Don't you think that your respect for a tree or stream is something like this future?"

"If you say so," the warrior agreed, out of his element. "But the cult of Eurydis could, with this explanation, include all the world's religions. That seems too easy to me."

"Not all religions, Grigán," the Maz contradicted him. "All *moral* religions, yes. But where can you see a place for the Züu in the Age of Ys? What could we do with the followers of Phiras? And Valipondes?"

Lana stopped her sermon, realizing she had let herself go. Eurydis asked for tolerance. The universal quest for the Moral would be a long one, for it would take mankind a long time to forget the black gods. The Maz were patient, but Zuïa's messengers killed, K'lur's disciples tortured slaves, and Soltan's daughters sacrificed themselves, day after day, year after year, for how many more centuries?

Could Maz Achem have been right to ask for a crusade against the demonist cults? What had he seen in Jal'dara?

Lana was troubled. Suddenly, she doubted one of Sage Eurydis's teachings. What if it all were false, and the Age of Ys would never come?

Grigán noticed her consternation and tried, in his own cumbersome way, to be sympathetic.

"Sometimes we can't help but feel powerless, you know?"

Lana nodded silently, tears coming to her eyes. She held them back.

The warrior continued, "Rey told me something earlier... that you are a widow. Is it true?"

She nodded again, without looking up. She couldn't hold herself together much longer.

"I am sorry," Grigán said as he stood to make another round. When he was at the edge of her vision, he added, "Me too. I lost my wife. But please don't tell anyone. I only wanted to share with you that time heals everything."

Alone, Lana let the tears wash over her. But Grigán wondered if he should have lied. Even after twenty years, some of his wounds would never heal.

Rey admitted that the players' show was one of the best he had ever seen, and his friends agreed. All the artists were masters of their craft, or almost all of them.

The fire-breather went first. She didn't only vomit flames, but could walk on coals, push needles through her body, and inflict other tortures on herself with no apparent effect.

The amuseur posed in front of the flames during her show, grimacing and exaggerating her pain, and making her seem like a martyr for enduring such torture. This drew both laughter and long silences out of the crowd. The applause and ovations were boisterous, and more onlookers joined the growing mob.

Nakapan the colossus used the moment to harangue the crowd, and Corenn translated for the heirs.

"How many people of the beautiful city of Deshine are ready to pay to see the rest of the show?" he asked in a rhythmic boom.

"Our troupe has played for royal courts. Our troupe has played in front of the Great Maz of Odrel. We would be happy to play for you, noble people of Deshine. But art alone will not feed us..."

As he spoke, the rest of the players went around collecting coins. Nakapan counted on them to harass the richest-looking individuals, and to sniff out the onlookers who tried to hide or leave during this part of the show, only to return for the next number. Those who did were sure to be the amuseur's next target.

One of the clowning dwarves brought the bag of coins they had collected to Nakapan, who frowned in disappointment. It was enough to take a risk.

"We have a master of wolves and a master of monkeys," he shouted to the crowd. "We have a juggler, the best of his kind. We have acrobatic warriors whose battles are legendary. We have one of the most powerful magicians in the known world," he finished, nodding to the man in the black robe. "Noble people of Deshine, do you want us to play?"

The second collection lasted a few more moments, and it would be renewed throughout the play. For the time being, Nakapan judged the takings sufficient, and the show continued.

Anaël, the master of wolves, or rather, master of a single wolf, had the next number. Merbal gave an excellent performance, letting himself be led through a diverse set of tricks—walking on two feet, playing dead, and, most difficult, catching a particular ball out of many that Anaël threw.

Next came the horsewomen, who showed off all of their talents before leaving the stage to Nakapan. The colossus first bent a few pieces of metal, each one thicker than the one before. Sweat poured from him as he bent one and then the next. He then invited a few volunteers to confront him in a game of tug-of-war, winning each of the matches with ease.

Tonk, the unlikable master of monkeys, was next. He walked to the middle of the courtyard with an arrogant expression that irritated Corenn. His first movement was to crack his whip in the middle of the mimastins, creating a general panic among the chained animals. He had done it only to provoke Bowbaq, and he leveled his gaze at the giant as the whip landed.

Unfortunately for Tonk, his efforts hit the mark too directly, and Bowbaq's face pulled into a menacing scowl. The giant crossed his imposing arms over his massive chest and waited for the number anxiously.

No number ever really came. Tonk's exercises were accomplished through fear and whipping. With each crack of the whip, Bowbaq's arms rose higher upon his chest, as he clenched his fists and breathed heavily. Corenn knew what was going to happen next and tried to pull the giant away, but it was too late. He politely, but firmly, refused.

For the next exercise, the monkeys had to walk across the firebreather's still-smoldering bed of coals. The beasts' cries left little doubt that the fires still burned hot. Still, three mimastins accomplished the task, preferring to burn their paws than to be cut and maimed by the whip.

The last animal was less willing. After a few failed commands, Tonk started to use his weapon, hitting the animal once, twice, a third time, the look on his face exposing how little he cared for the creature. The little monkey could no longer move.

But the sadist had no opportunity to hit him again. Bowbaq stormed across the square like an enraged bull. Tonk, in his cruelty, raised his hand for another strike, but Bowbaq was upon him and blocked the Rominian's next blow, ripping the whip out of his hand. Tonk, who had been waiting for an excuse to unleash his anger on Bowbaq, punched the Arque in the face. Enraged, Bowbaq angrily threw him to the ground, where the Rominian stayed, checking to make sure that he still had all his teeth.

The heirs gathered around their friend, and the street performers, other than Gallop and Anaël, gathered around the master of monkeys. Léti kept her eyes fixed on the acrobat warriors, who were waiting only for a sign from their chief. Was this the end of their trip together?

"Noble people of Deshine, the show continues!" were the only words to come out of Nakapan's mouth.

The entertainers relieved Tonk and started a different number. The chief motioned to Tonk and Bowbaq to follow him, fury smeared across his face.

Bowbaq followed him carrying the little mimastin, who seemed to understand the gravity of the situation and clutched the giant tightly with his little hands. Behind, Tonk, mumbling curses at Bowbaq and eyeing Rey, Léti, Yan, and Corenn, dragged the other three monkeys.

"What do you think you're doing?" Nakapan shouted at Bowbaq. "Are you stupid or something?"

Corenn translated for the giant, not mentioning the insult. It was Corenn, not Bowbaq, who responded next.

"Our friend is erjak," she explained. "He can't stand to see people torture animals, it's as simple as that. Rest assured, it won't happen again."

"Wiar!" intervened Tonk, who had lost a few teeth and couldn't pronounce a few letters through the swelling.

But the excuse had been sufficient for the chief of the troupe. Erjaks were like living legends among the entertainers; the presence of one in their troupe was a promise of success. Nakapan decided to be an exceptionally gracious host with that one.

"He ftook my monfkey!" Tonk shouted, upon seeing Nakapan's decision.

"It's true that you are brutal, in any case," Nakapan responded. "And you are always complaining about that one. You had already decided to sell it!"

"He muss' pfay!"

"Well, he'll give him back to you or buy it, what a good deal! Right?"

Corenn asked, "How much do you want for him?"

"Fifthee' monarchs," Tonk responded defiantly.

"Fifteen monarchs, agreed," Corenn said, pulling out the money.

"No! Not fifthee, fifthee!"

"We agree then."

And the heirs, confident of the chief's support, walked away, leaving the sum in the Rominian's hand.

"What's the monkey's name?" Yan asked, turning back to Tonk.

The master of monkeys stared at him strangely, as if the young man had just asked him for the name of his hat.

"Ifdiot!"

And so the heirs, after losing Frog in Romine, adopted in Deshine a female mimastin named Ifio.

The show finished relatively shortly after the incident with Bowbaq. This allowed the heirs to return to Grigán and Lana early that night, with plenty of time to heal the injured Ifio. Rey had wanted to stroll through town, maybe visit a few taverns, but he changed his mind and followed his friends. Gallop had also mentioned a certain bottle of liquor in his possession . . .

They found Grigán loyally keeping an eye on the camp, and the warrior was relieved to see them return safe and sound. Corenn told him how Bowbaq had come to have the mimastin, trying to keep the story vague, but the retelling was clear enough that Grigán cursed Tonk *and* Bowbaq. The giant endured the warrior's reproach, looking abashed and genuinely sorry. Eventually, Grigán calmed down. After all, compared to what they had already faced, this was not a big problem.

To prevent any act of vengeance from Tonk, or any kind of aggression, the warrior suggested they set up a night guard around their wagons. He would take the first watch. As usual, he wanted only the men of the group to do the chore, but he made an exception for Léti, after she insisted that she do her part. Their plan set, they all got ready for bed. Some slept, another patrolled, one healed an injured monkey, and one savored a liquor made from pure petaya fruit. All settled in for a peaceful night.

Léti and Corenn found Lana in the wagon the women slept in each night. The Maz was nodding off over her prayer book, where her translated poem from the Deep Tower was inserted into the open pages. The priestess had spent a significant part of her night working on it, but she woke as they entered.

"Are you ill?" Corenn asked, seeing Lana's teary streaks and tired eyes. She had never seen the Maz look so gloomy. It couldn't have simply been a bad dream.

Lana sat up from her bunk and massaged her face before responding to the Mother, in a serious voice. "I am scared, Corenn. Horribly scared of the things that hunt us. Scared that I won't be able to handle the truths at the end of our quest. Will we have the same courage as our ancestors?"

"What do you mean?" the Mother asked as she sat next to the priestess. "What truths?"

"I know no more than you do, of course, but I feel . . . I feel they will be a *heavy* responsibility. Don't you feel it too?"

Léti nodded, as did Corenn, after a brief hesitation. Having sacrificed their homes, their wealth, and even their lives, the emissaries of the past must have borne the crushing weight of a terrible secret. A secret much more powerful than even the knowledge that Jal'dara existed.

"This poem," the Maz continued. "I call it the Poem of Romerij," she added, as if the idea had just come to her. "Have you noticed that young gods are never mentioned, in any religion, ever? Child gods? This poem is the exception. It alone could throw into doubt all of human belief."

"It doesn't seem that important to me," Corenn offered, trying to temper Lana's interpretation. "What does it matter if the gods have the appearance of children at first? Take Eurydis; did she not first appear in Ith in the form of a little girl?"

"No, the opposite. It's extremely important," the Maz objected. "The poem says, 'Man or god, same naïveté.' Naïve gods! Do you realize how important the meeting between them and our ancestors was? Do you realize that last century's drama may be irreparable? That Jal'dara, the birthplace of gods, was perhaps changed forever?"

Corenn and Léti exchanged a panicked look. Lana was giving their journey and duties a much deeper spiritual meaning, and the young Maz's words were deeply pessimistic.

Their enemy was not only powerful, he had perhaps committed the worst crime imaginable: bringing the gods' wrath down upon humanity, for eternity.

The troupe and their pilgrims got on the road early the next morning, starting the hardest part of their journey: the trek across the Wet Valley.

This territory stretched from the Brantaque Mountains to the Murky Mountains, the two main mountain chains in Romine. The Wet Valley was nothing more than a corridor between southern Arkary and the Old Country. The landscape was filled with swamps and few trees, swept by an unceasing frozen wind.

The place was inhospitable to the point of near desertion. Only a few recluses and listless farmers claimed land here. Unfortunately, the wild, lawless landscape attracted a third kind of person: mounted brigands, horsemen ready to kill for the smallest silver monarch.

Merbal of Jidée had been the most famous, and his reputation, along with his successors', helped keep Romine isolated from the other Upper Kingdoms by blocking off the easiest trading route.

Luckily, the heirs wouldn't have to travel through the entire length of the valley. They just had to reach the Murky Mountains on a fairly safe route, navigated by generations of Lorelien merchants. They need be vigilant for only two days, and then they would reach Semilia, a town that represented a relatively safe haven.

Deshine was the last frontier before this wild country, and as soon as the town was out of sight, they saw no more signs of civilization. The wagons waded through deeper and deeper puddles, the road dissolving into a path—a path that started to disappear in places. To prevent the wagon wheels from getting stuck in the heavy pond muck, the troupe took a number of detours, which slowed their progress. Each detour greatly irritated Grigán, who was mounted and had no trouble cantering through the puddles.

"We should abandon the wagons and follow our route alone," he proposed to Corenn. "We're losing too much time."

"We will need the troupe to ease our passage at the frontier," the Mother responded.

"We'll find something. It wouldn't be the first time."

"And we'll die of cold in the mountains, with no wagon to shelter us," Corenn continued. "We have no choice, Grigán."

The warrior reluctantly agreed. It was still easy for him to plan as if he were traveling alone, as he had done for so long. Having lived for two years in Arkary, he didn't worry too much about snow or cold nights, and alone, he would have made it to Semilia in barely two days. He knew that it would be too much to ask everyone to do the same.

The winds began to howl. They wouldn't stop until the troupe reached the Murky Mountains. Coming from the north, the winds were strong, cold, and dry, and they brought with them the occasional hailstorm.

"The wind," commented Léti, who rode next to the smaller wagon, the one reserved for the women of the group. "It sounds like the ghosts' singing, in the library."

Neither Lana nor Corenn responded, but they silently agreed, and found no comfort in the sound. The Maz added another layer to her travel clothes, and her friends quickly followed suit.

Later in the day, they directly crossed a three-hundred-foot-long lake, never more than two feet deep. Grigán had found the ford on his own, which saved them at least a dékade. If Nakapan was skeptical at first, he was full of compliments once they had reached the other side.

"I hate rainy places," Rey said, looking out over the half-frozen muddy ponds. "To think that last dékade, we were in the Land of Beauty!"

"It never rains here," Grigán corrected him. "The water comes from snowmelt in the Brantaques and the Murky Mountains. In five moons, this lake will be three times larger than today and at least five feet deep."

The actor contemplated the landscape, which endured such intense seasonality. How could anyone live here? Even flora and fauna were hard to find.

Old Anaël, who had befriended the heirs, told of how he had found the wolf cub, Merbal, in this valley. The animal had gotten caught in the rapidly rising waters, which had transformed a long stretch of land into a shrinking island. The Rominian saved him from his mistake, and thus a juggler became "the master of wolves."

He shared his knowledge of the land with the pilgrims, pointing out the valley's leathery plant life, gray algae, Burak's willow, preacher's herb, selsasses, swamp bushes, and other plants unique to this harsh place. The animal life was no less diverse: vorvans, capped gulls, margolins, domalianders, gerbils, and even a viper's nest that they cautiously avoided. No one wanted to see hundreds of snakes biting at their horses' ankles.

The person who would have most appreciated this knowledge was conspicuously absent. Bowbaq was occupied with something else that was just as captivating. He was teaching Yan to be an erjak.

"Animals... they don't think like us," the giant told his captivated student. "They don't think at all, actually. They don't need to—everything they do, they do naturally. If they're hungry, they eat. If they're tired, they sleep. If they sense danger, they flee. Simply put, if an animal hesitates... it wouldn't be one. It would be like you, me, the others: an intelligent being. And it would be dead in a few days."

Bowbaq was almost talking to himself, tirelessly working with poor Ifio. The giant had not yet removed the poor creature's chain, but he hoped to try it soon, as soon as they were able to coax the creature to calm down. The mimastin would be a perfect example for their lessons. The little monkey would be more than just a test subject. The giant wanted to give something to the animal, something that would heal her wounds.

Yan guided their wagon, distracted by the conversation. Everything Bowbaq had said seemed like obvious fact, but what the rest of the world simply intuited and guessed at, Bowbaq's experience made clear and true.

"You don't have to wait to form words," Bowbaq continued. "Feelings alone will work, or, even better, images. Your mind translates these into words, but animals do no such thing."

"I understand."

"That's what I can teach you, my friend. I don't know a recipe for how to enter a mind. I can't explain how the power functions. If you can't do it yourself... I can't help you. I can only help you get used to... uh... to what you see in the animal's spirit."

"We agree then." The young man nodded. "When can we start?"

The giant didn't know how to respond. He would have preferred to save this for much later. His timidity resurgent, he worried that his lessons would be pointless, and that he wouldn't be able to teach his student, who was so much smarter than he.

Yan could sense his concerns and took charge. "The best way to do it would be for you to explain the main ideas before I try anything. You must have a stack of warnings to give me? With Corenn, my lessons always start with those."

"Yes," the giant confirmed, calmed by his friend's confidence. "For example, there are three cases where it is useless to try to contact an animal: when they think their lives are in danger, when they think their babies are in danger, or when they think of you as prey."

"That I can understand easily," Yan said.

"It's equally difficult if the animal is injured—impossible if you injured it—or if it thinks you are threatening its territory."

"I didn't know there were so many conditions for this to work."

"Yes, of course. You can always establish a contact, but sometimes a dialogue is impossible."

"A little bit like Grigán, actually," Yan joked playfully.

They smiled together. Making fun of Grigán's seriousness was typical of the group's jokes, ever since Rey established the precedent. Jokes aside, they both held the warrior in the highest esteem, just as all the others did.

"In a general way," the giant continued, "it's easier to contact females. With males, there is always a fight for dominance. It is something difficult to handle. It's easier with predators as well, because their motivations are fairly similar to our own, actually. Selfish.

"On the other hand, grazers have a kind of herd mentality that we struggle to understand. Apart from their own survival, their behavior follows that of the chief, the dominant male. In fact, it's easier to communicate with a bear than a horse."

Yan nodded often, engraving all of Bowbaq's wisdom into his memory. The giant talked, and talked, and talked. And Yan learned more and more, driven by simple curiosity and intellectual interest, without knowing that someday soon, it would save his life.

Zamerine shivered with excitement. Never, in his many years serving Zuïa, had he enjoyed his work so much. A true frenzy of activity buzzed around him, the sound of it so engrossing that he had used all of his intelligence and leadership to accomplish his task.

The High Diarch, his master, had finally revealed part of his plans, and the Judge felt his admiration for Saat double. What genius! What ambition!

The plan Saat had etched was the largest undertaking in human history. But was Saat even human? This idea and the possibilities it would bring matched the audacity of its creator. Unbelievable. Eternal. Perhaps demented? The gravity of the plan was too much, and the Judge pushed those thoughts aside. There was work to be done.

Not only did his master have the vision and the courage for such a plan, he also had the means. Over eighty thousand souls had been enslaved in only a few moons by Gor the Gentle's army. Now, the killer understood, they were finally going to put these laggards, who had only slowed the army, to work. Saat had always known their purpose, but he had announced it only when they reached the army's current encampment, where they would remain until they launched their massive attack.

Until that day, Zamerine had been put in charge of the work, and Dyree assisted, along with eighty-five of Zuïa's messengers. Through pain and suffering, the slaves had learned to fear the red killers, and to obey their orders. The Züu were the best guards for hopeless men.

Prior to learning their fate, Zamerine had suggested that the workers not be allowed to sleep or eat, as they were so easily replaced. This would have saved time and resources, but Emaz Chebree had improved the idea. To only the most fervent worshippers of their god, Somber, would be given a little water, a little bread, and some time to pray . . . or sleep.

Immediately after this command was relayed to the troops, the cult had a resurgence in faith, and the High Diarch was quite satisfied—a rare occurrence. Even his son seemed to stir a little and occasionally acknowledged Saat's apostles, Zamerine, Chebree, Gor, and Dyree. No one else mattered to the young master.

Their army held a strong position, controlling the entire territory between Col'w'yr—more simply referred to as the Gray River—and the Liponde's warm waters. Raids continued in the Thalite Kingdom, but the most important work was done here, at the foot of the mountains.

Zamerine raised his eyes and contemplated his next adversary. The size of the task was considerable, and they would certainly encounter many obstacles, but with his resources, nothing seemed insurmountable. And the stakes were worth it, absolutely worth it.

Before the end of the year, his master would conquer the Upper Kingdoms: Goran, Lorelia, Romine, Ith, Kaul, and Arkary.

What Saat wanted to do with these kingdoms held little interest for Zamerine, as long as he found himself governing Lorelia, as promised. From his seat of power, Zuïa's laws would reign supreme.

The heirs, like the street performers, were happy to see an end to their first day in the Wet Valley. After numerous detours, stuck wagons, and the constant threat of attacking brigands, they were all exhausted, and Nakapan had them all stop to rest as the first tendrils of fog rose from the swamps. It was the evening of only their second day of travel.

Grigán protested halfheartedly, but even the warrior, anxious to reach Pont, had to submit to nature's forces. The decision made by the colossus proved to be a good one. In less than a centiday, the entire party was surrounded by a thick fog. Corenn's suggestion that no one go far from camp was unnecessary. No one wanted to stray too far in such a fog.

With nightfall still far away, the heirs searched for small tasks to busy themselves and pass the time. Corenn and Lana sat on their wagon and discussed their theories on the Poem of Romerij, while Grigán and Léti proposed to train with the acrobatic warriors. The other heirs gathered to watch what promised to be a memorable battle.

The two acrobats, one with his two sabers and the other with his poleaxe, were confident enough in themselves that they took the idea lightly. They were quickly disappointed. Starting out reserved, almost timid, Léti's and Grigán's attacks quickly became more rapid and violent. The heirs had taken the first few passes to study their opponents' movements.

The way the warrior and the young woman fought side by side impressed even the most skeptical in the troupe. The two heirs dressed in the same black leather outfits, sported the same concentrated face, and sometimes even simultaneously attacked with mirrored techniques, as if part of a rehearsed dance. The acrobats' condescending smiles soon faded, and were replaced by angry grimacing. Who were these foreigners, showing up the professionals?

The touches were done softly, but were no less humiliating. Léti was "injured" twice, as was the man with the poleaxe. The acrobat holding sabers was less fortunate, having been "wounded" four times. Naturally, Grigán left the game unscathed. Seeing the faces of his opponents morph from frustrated to angry, he stopped the fighting before it devolved into a more serious affair.

Yan joined Bowbaq and Rey, noisily congratulating the victors, while their adversaries saluted them courteously. Léti planted her rapier in the ground and ran to her friends, throwing her arms around a surprised Yan's neck.

Yan put his arm around her, trying to figure out how he had earned the pleasure. He quickly abandoned the thought, deciding it better to enjoy the feel of her against his chest, if only for a few moments. The embrace stretched for a beat, and then the young woman untangled herself with a smile and rejoined Grigán for the rest of her training.

"With your white hair and red face, you could be our very own amuseur," Rey said in a mocking tone.

Yan took his eyes off Léti and looked at his friends, blushing more intensely. The actor winked complicity, while Bowbaq smiled so all his teeth showed.

"She's happy she won," Yan said, naïvely pointing toward Léti.

"We saw that," Rey said with a knowing smile.

Yan regretted having talked to the actor at all. It would only make him the target of more salacious mockery. The same thing he had feared in Eza, six dékades earlier, in a distant past. He decided he had nothing more to say.

Rey turned toward Corenn and Lana, sitting twenty feet away next to a campfire. The diplomatic Mother and the moralist priestess talked as they studied a sheet of paper. Apparently, they disagreed on a few points, but they each tried to calmly acknowledge the other's understanding of the text. The comedian couldn't hear a word they said. He only had eyes for Lana.

He approached Yan, who had refocused on the combatants. Then he whispered, in a serious tone, "What are you waiting for? Why not ask for her Promise?"

Yan swallowed and looked at the actor, bewildered. It was the first time anyone had spoken to him so frankly.

"The day is past," he whispered back. "Next year..."

"Or the year after? Why not right now?"

"Why..." The young man couldn't finish his thought.

Rey was right. Why not, after all? Here, in the middle of the Wet Valley, while surrounded by friends? They were lost in the mist with a troupe of Rominian entertainers. He had no better reason to do it than the very best of reasons: the desire he felt for her.

Why always wait for another day? The future could bring better times, or there would be no more chances. What better time than now?

Yan took a step toward his friend, then a second, before freezing. He remembered why not. Usul.

He Who Knows had foretold their Union, the one thing Yan desired most in the world. But the god had also foretold Grigán's death and the crumbling of the Upper Kingdoms. Yan would do his best to stop that future, but what he didn't know was if Grigán's death could be prevented by sacrificing Léti's Promise.

Once again, the young man was paralyzed by his knowledge, and incapable of acting for fear of causing the coming evils, or preventing his greatest wishes.

With a lowered head, he returned to Rey's side. The actor made no comment, but if Lana weren't a Maz, he knew exactly how he would act.

The next day in the valley was similar to their first. Spared from attacking brigands, the column arrived at the feet of the Murky Mountains with no trouble. They started their climb at dawn on the Day of the Weaver, six days before the Day of the Earth and Pont's festivals.

Passing from muddy, swampy terrain to a wide mountain trail with gentle slopes was a relief to humans and animals alike. But their gratitude was short-lived and soon forgotten when the slopes steepened later in the day. To relieve the animals, the troupe and the pilgrims stepped off the wagons and walked on foot. The cold grew increasingly more bitter as one deciday slipped into the next. The frigid air troubled all but Bowbaq, whose thick furs attracted considerable envy.

Lunch was a good excuse for a short halt, and they took it with relief. The hike only got more difficult. Not used to such physical effort, Lana struggled, and Rey tried to help her as best he could by quipping on any subject.

The only memorable break in the monotony was seeing a pair of crowned eagles soaring in majestic flight.

Snow appeared on the ground, first in patches and then in large swaths. Eventually it stretched wide in all directions, and the group found themselves in an immaculate blanket of white. Without the wind, the cold was less biting and cruel, but the less well-equipped voyagers soon had wet and frozen feet.

Night fell on the exhausted travelers, but the column didn't stop. Nakapan lit a few lanterns and asked for a volunteer to lead the way, so they wouldn't lose the trail. Grigán offered his services, as the chief had hoped.

They continued like this for more than a deciday, practically without speaking, everyone saving their breath for another step in the snow. Three men, who were regularly relieved, helped clear a path for the first wagon, which needed to be pushed occasionally, and the rest of the group followed in their tracks.

By the time Yan, Bowbaq, and Anaël stepped forward to lead the convoy, the horses were exhausted, and regularly needed to be pulled along. Once again, Yan wondered what had brought him here. With snow up to his knees and a lantern in hand, he was now guiding a Rominian wagon on a barely visible mountainous pass with not a single Kaulien companion at his side. A cold gust of wind blew the nostalgic thought from his head, and Yan concentrated on the task at hand: reaching Semilia.

His patience was rewarded when Grigán returned from his scouting trip to announce that the town was near. The warrior was greeted with sincere cheering, and the news gave the group enough energy and courage to slightly speed up their progress. Seeing the town's lights at the top of the pass gave them even more comfort and energy, and they finished the last mile amid the sound of relieved laughter.

Semilia was much smaller than Yan had imagined. From the top of the pass, they could see almost the entire town hidden at the bottom of a cirque. Protected by a natural shield of mountains and an outer wall much larger than the town itself, the city looked like a fortified square compared to its Lorelien brethren. Semilia had once been a simple military outpost in the era of the Two Empires. Under the protection of the merchant kingdom, it had become a principality that anchored northwest Lorelia. The task of keeping marauders at bay fell to the snowy hamlet.

As they descended toward the gates, Yan thought that the place must be beautiful in the warm seasons. All of the hills covered in snow would exchange the white for green, making a paradise for trappers and shepherds. The mountain runoff would provide chilly water for endless creeks and waterfalls, before pooling into the twin lakes at the base of the cliffs. Even in the Matriarchy, the largest one was reputed to be rich fishing grounds.

The young man had never thought he would see it with his own eyes. But wasn't he jumping from discovery to discovery? Where would his companions be in a dékade?

He suddenly noticed the similarity between Semilia's landscape and that of Jal'dara, and he scrutinized all around, his heart beating furiously. He was looking for proof that Jal'dara was near, but even in the obscurity, he had to admit: this valley was less beautiful than the one seen through Ji's portal. Less beautiful than a brief vision seen through a magic portal whose function they still didn't understand.

Entering a Lorelien city always required taxes, and Semilia was no different, even though the principality was economically independent from the rest of the merchant kingdom. Luckily, the tax collectors respected the right to free passage traditionally given to entertainers, and only checked the contents of each wagon. As the collectors waved the group through, Nakapan dropped a few coins into their hands for form.

Semilia also had an open-farm, a generous name given to a few dilapidated buildings left to travelers passing through, since the town had few inns. The troupe, used to these kinds of arrangements, quickly set up camp inside the buildings, pulling the wagons and horses into the open barns and lighting two peat fires, which produced ample smoke and a good deal of heat.

The grimy rooms had been used as sleeping quarters, kitchens, living quarters, and, if the smell was any indication, cesspools. Two homeless men, sitting next to a fire, grumbled when their new company arrived, then stopped when they realized how large the group was. One of them wore a necklace made of teeth.

"This is a long way from the Broken Castle," Rey said, sniffing the air. "What if we looked for an inn?"

"Diplomatically, that would be a bad choice," Corenn said. "This shelter is free to us, thanks to the troupe; to refuse it could be perceived as offensive."

"Maybe," the actor insisted. "Maybe Lana might want someplace more comfortable, though?"

"The wolf smiles but we can see his teeth," the priestess recited with evident pleasure, which her friends soon shared.

Rey didn't respond and went to look for Gallop, hoping that the juggler might at least know a place where they could have a few pints.

The two men left soon thereafter with Nakapan, his son, the clowning dwarves, Tonk, and the amuseur, along with a few others.

The heirs decided to clean part of the room before setting their blankets and bags in a corner. Once they had changed and eaten a hot meal, the open-farm seemed less disgusting. Almost welcoming.

Grigán was the first to succumb to sleep, surprising them all. They had gotten so used to the warrior keeping watch over them as they nodded off. Yet the journey to Semilia had been much more tiring for him than for anyone else, as he had covered nearly twice the distance as their scout. The heirs conversed in whispered voices, to not trouble his sleep.

Time flowed by slowly, and the exhausting day would have finished nicely for the heirs if a horrible incident hadn't sown trouble in the group.

With a loud bang, the barn door swung open, and Tonk crashed into the room, stumbling and mumbling incomprehensibly. Dead drunk, he swept his gaze over the heirs, laughing heavily. He walked toward Bowbaq, dragging something behind him.

Léti stood and grabbed her rapier. Yan followed and tried to remember where he had put his broadsword. Lana, Corenn, and Bowbaq sat, immobile.

"You stole my monkey!" he yelled. "You can have the others!" And he threw three mimastins at the giant's feet, their throats still bleeding from where Tonk had slit them.

Bowbaq looked silently at their little, bloody bodies, still chained. Léti and Yan took a step back, not for Tonk, but to get closer to their friend.

"That's horrible," Lana whispered, crying.

"Bowbaq, he doesn't know what he's doing," Corenn said, trying to temper the giant's reaction. "He's drunk."

"Me, I'm not," the giant responded as he slowly stood, placing the bodies gently to his side.

The floor planks groaned when Bowbaq took a step forward, staring at the Rominian. Through the haze of his drunken stupor, Tonk began to understand the gravity of his mistake.

Léti ran over to Grigán to wake him, but Bowbaq had already put his immense hands on Tonk before she could reach the sleeping warrior. She watched as Bowbaq lifted Tonk off the floor as if he were an empty bag.

"If I ever see you again," he said slowly, "I will do the same thing to you."

He held the Rominian up in the air until Tonk started to panic and gesticulate, then he set the man down with a strained look on his face. Tonk looked left and right, wondering if he should gather his things, then decided it would be best if he left as soon as possible.

"Grigán!" Léti called out, panic in her voice. "Grigán won't wake up!"

As she reviewed her elite troops by torchlight, Chebree realized how much she loved to watch the ordered ranks they formed. There, before her very own eyes, stood the powerful warriors of the largest army in the world. Their army. Her army, soon, if she continued to maneuver without any mistakes.

A lieutenant followed her, naming each of the four hundred companies, represented by the four hundred men present. Their companies had, depending on their origins, anywhere from ten to two hundred warriors. Chebree enviously admired the pike men, the cavalry, the foot soldiers, the archers, the proud gladores, the thistles, the bearded ones, the dragons of Oo, the legendary Wa'r'kal, the Farikii and their horde of rats, the Yalamines, the Headless, the horsemen of Egosie, and more. They were Wallatte for the most part, but also Solenes, a few Thalittes, Sadraques, Grelittes, and a few Tuzéens.

The lieutenant didn't have to repeat what she already knew, and she barely listened to his droning. The only thing that mattered was to see these people from different corners of the world filing up for her, and for her only.

Before Saat came, she had been Queen Che'b'ree Lu Wallos of a small Wallatte clan with small holdings. As Queen Che'b'ree, vassal to Gors'a'min Lu Wallos, her only ambition was to guard her small territory from attack by the Thalittes, or the Solenes, or even her own lord.

She had rallied to Saat's army from the first day he arrived, though at the time it was only a disparate group of mercenaries and vagabonds banned from their own clans. Yet the Goranese man had so successfully commanded the group that it struck fear into the hearts of those in even the most well-defended villages. Chebree recognized his power and chose to become his ally before she could be declared an enemy and be thrown into a conflict she had no chance of winning.

Her secret hope had been to use the army against Gors'a'min, now Gor the Gentle, and to firmly grasp the rest of Wallatte territory. But the colossal barbarian king, celebrated for his drunkenness, his frequent raging, his sadism, and most of all his two-handed axe, thwarted her nascent plan by joining Saat himself.

As a vassal, Chebree was forced down a rung in the hierarchy of captains who served the High Diarch. To stay at the top, she became their master's lover, his only concubine who wasn't a slave, and the only one to have survived five moons at his side.

Five moons, already, she thought to herself with a clenched jaw. *And still nothing.*

Saat had seen in her uncommon ambition and intelligence, and had named her Grand Emaz of a new cult, one no one had ever heard of: Somber, He Who Vanquishes, the black god of conquerors.

Chebree invested all of her energy into building this new cult: the priesthood, the ceremonies, the praises to Somber at every captains' meeting. She became an apostle. After only a moon, half of the army had converted to this religion that promised riches and powers to the worthy. By the time the next moon fell, all the warriors would start their days by swearing fealty to Somber, the diarchs, and the apostles.

Emaz Chebree converted their slaves with the same success. Her discourse to the enslaved was, of course, different: Somber was still their conqueror, but the vanquished who submitted to his will would be freed when they entered the coming era of peace: the New Order.

Saat told her he was satisfied. Saat, her master. Saat, who would soon rule all of the eastern realms, the Upper and Lower Kingdoms, the entire known world. Saat, to whom she could offer only one thing. To rule at his side. To control life and death over all humanity.

Unconsciously, she slid her hand over the golden breastplate that covered her stomach. She thought of the man whose face she had never seen. The High Diarch, their master, who undressed only in the most profound darkness, and whose skin was as dry and wrinkled as a withered apple. He who had the body of an ancient man and the strength of a Tuzéen warrior.

He who was waiting for a son that no concubine, free or slave, consenting or forced, could give him.

The open-farm, so calm just a few moments earlier, was now the scene of an all-encompassing chaos. The heirs, soon joined by the rest of the troupe and the two homeless men, gathered around Grigán's unconscious body. All held their breath watching Corenn and Lana's coordinated effort to reanimate him.

"He's so pale!" Bowbaq said quietly, going pale himself.

"He's so cold, Corenn," Lana warned. "We need to bring him closer to the fire and cover him in blankets as best we can."

Ten pairs of arms moved to lift the lifeless body, but the giant had already picked up his friend before any other could reach him.

He laid Grigán down next to the hearth and backed away, leaving room for his friends to examine the lifeless body.

"Deremin is our healer," said one of the horsewomen. "He's in town with the others. I'll go find him."

The young woman only took the time to find her coat before heading out into the night. Léti accompanied her; she could speed things up if needed. Besides, she couldn't stand being in that room any longer, watching the man who had saved her life, the man who had saved all their lives, fight an invisible enemy.

In the most difficult situations, one finds true friends. Even though most of the Rominians were haughty, arrogant people, the troupe showed their loyalty by offering to help in any way they could. Some even offered up suggestions on how to treat him. What ailed Grigán was no typical illness, though. In all the world, there was no known remedy to the Farik sickness, and the healer in Three-Banks had confirmed the fact. The warrior's only chance lay with his own ability to resist it.

They had thought he was healed, but by appearance, they had been wrong. Grigán showed the same signs as in his previous fits, on the island and with Sapone. The sickness seemed to come in cycles: the heirs counted five days between each attack. Or perhaps it wasn't cyclical at all, merely striking when the warrior was at his weakest, after a long day of hard work. It was irrelevant now, because either way, the warrior wasn't moving.

"Lana, look at his eyes," Corenn said suddenly.

The Maz leaned over to look at his eye while Corenn held back his eyelid. The priestess changed positions to avoid blocking the light, and then suddenly jumped back. The onlookers, including Yan and Bowbaq, pressed her with questions.

"His eyes . . . ," Lana responded, trying to control herself. "His eyes are completely red!"

"It must be the fever," Yan suggested, approaching the warrior to see for himself.

Lana was right. Grigán's irises had changed from the familiar dark blue to a red as fiery as cinder. Yan waved a finger in front of Grigán's face, but the warrior didn't respond. The young man stood back, saddened and scared, and Corenn gingerly closed his eyelid.

Yan watched as everyone piled blankets, furs, and coats on top of Grigán, but he knew the warrior was finished. Usul had said before the year's end. Why now? Already, after only a dékade? Why could he not survive the night?

"Hold him," Yan said as an idea struck him. "I am going to try something."

Bowbaq and Corenn each grabbed one of Grigán's wrists, as gently as possible, without taking their inquisitive eyes off of Yan. He got on his knees, inhaled noisily, and grabbed his friend's ankle, before brutally yanking at a toe.

The warrior seized violently and kicked Yan in the face as he struggled like a drenched standing-sleeper. Corenn's grip slipped, but Bowbaq held Grigán down. They needed four more men to keep the warrior down until he calmed and fell back asleep. The whole time, Grigán hadn't recognized any of his friends.

"He will live," Yan said confidently, rubbing his cheek and jaw. "He'll never stop fighting."

Corenn, Lana, and Bowbaq watched in silence as the young Kaulien walked away. Discovering such strength in the frozen warrior's body was hardly reassuring. Twenty years as a fugitive had changed the warrior, down to his unconscious mind, providing him with a deep instinct for survival.

Of course, they didn't know that he was fighting something as powerful as a divine prophecy.

Léti and the helpful horsewoman returned shortly after Grigán's episode, accompanied by Rey and the other entertainers who had gone out for the night. The actor and Léti were only partially relieved to hear that the warrior had shown a burst of energy. All they could see was a feverish, unconscious Grigán.

The healer Deremin was none other than the entertainer who wore the embroidered robe and carried a golden spellbook. Though he wasn't really a magician, spell-caster, or thaumaturge, the man still had a genuine knowledge of healing. The results of his exam brought the heirs little hope, however, as his conclusion was "Let the fever pass, let him rest, and avoid angering him."

If he had known Grigán and their situation better, Corenn thought, the Rominian would have laughed at his own nonsense. Since they couldn't do anything else for the warrior, everyone did their best to get ready for bed after a difficult day and night. Bowbaq hesitated at length before approaching Nakapan to relay his message for Tonk. The colossus was not surprised by the episode, and he apologized to Bowbaq himself for it. He had sent Tonk off earlier in the night after the man had quarreled with others in the troupe, who had had enough of his belligerence.

"If he had thrown those monkeys' corpses at me, I would have punched him in the face," the Rominian concluded.

"He wasn't armed," Bowbaq mumbled as an excuse, before returning to his friends. The chief watched enviously the man who was so sure of his strength that he preferred his enemies have a blade, to alleviate his conscience.

The night felt long, especially for Yan, Rey, Lana, and Bowbaq, who traded watches over Grigán. It was worse for Léti and Corenn, who never left his side. If one let the other sleep, she would be reproached for having left her friend to sleep too long. After only a deciday, though, the warrior had regained regular breathing, and a peaceful expression settled on his face. Carefully, Corenn pulled his eyes open and found that the dark blue had quenched the red that had burned before. Even so, the two Kauliennes wouldn't leave his side until dawn.

Early sunlight slowly roused the town of Semilia, and as residents awoke, they found their city blanketed in fresh snowfall. A guard came to the open-farm as the second deciday bells rang to take a head count of the guests and see if their accommodations were acceptable. Nakapan lied about Grigán's health when the guard pushed him, and he later explained that strangers with grave maladies were immediately kicked out of town.

The chief of the troupe had planned to do a show at noon and then start on the path for Pont. Wanting to keep the group together, and after hearing Corenn's arguments, he agreed to delay their departure until the next day. The Day of the Earth's festivals wouldn't start for four more days anyhow, and they could find hundreds of ways to make the delay useful, with buying provisions, performing maintenance on the wagons, accounting, and other work.

Grigán continued to sleep, though he reacted by moaning or turning over when Corenn shook him. It was reassuring to see that the warrior had enough energy to protest, so the Mother allowed herself to rest. Léti decided to join her.

Rey brought Lana with him to watch the entertainers' show. Bowbaq and Yan burned the dead mimastins, as the ground was so frozen they couldn't possibly dig a grave. Out of decency, the giant forced Ifio to stay away while he finished the difficult task. It was the first time in four days that they had separated. The little monkey celebrated the giant's return like a puppy.

Bowbaq liked seeing the monkey run along his expansive shoulders and arms. In the open-farm, they were the only two without a chore to do, along with Yan, who enviously watched Bowbaq play with the monkey.

"Do you still want to be an erjak, my friend?" Bowbaq asked, smiling. "I think Ifio is ready now."

An animal's first reaction to an erjak's powers was always one of intense fear, followed by a fierce anger. If the erjak wanted a lasting contact, he had to attenuate these harmful effects by preparing the animal for human presence before the first contact. Yan and Bowbaq had already accomplished this part.

The giant had been a model of thoughtfulness and gentility toward Ifio, so much so that the female mimastin, far from fearing the bearded Arque, always strove to be near Bowbaq—standing on his head and shoulders, hiding in his fur coats. Yan did not escape these marks of affection, and the mimastin would often perch on the magician's neck or shoulders.

"Still, it's better that I leash her first," Bowbaq said. "There's little chance she will hurt us, but she could run away and die from the cold."

Putting action to words, he attached the old leash to Ifio's collar. The animal saw this as the first signs of a coming torture, and fled as far as the leash allowed. It took the two men more than a deciday to regain her confidence, with the help of many sweets, soft words, and a few games.

"Now you can try, if you want," the giant announced. "The most important thing is to start slowly."

Yan swallowed before concentrating. He had hoped that Bowbaq might offer some more advice before his first effort, but the giant offered no further guidance. At least Bowbaq was true to his word; he had told Yan at the beginning of this undertaking that he didn't know how an erjak's power worked. The only thing he could teach was how to help Yan interpret what he would see in an animal's mind, and how to give animals simple directions with something similar to a dialogue.

If Yan could reach the animal's mind, he would be an erjak. If not, Bowbaq could do nothing for him.

The young man recalled Corenn's many warnings and advice. Everything, whether an object or living being, could be defined by the five elements. water, fire, earth, and wind were the primary elements, with recept a fifth element that dictated how strongly an object would resist magic. Yan had the rare power, when he was concentrating, of seeing this spiritual composition, which was something the Mother called the Sublime Essence.

Magicians used their Will to allow them to use the energy in their bodies to alter one or more of the five elements. The most easily manipulated was earth, true matter, which magicians could mold like clay in their hands—deforming or destroying with ease—as long as they could handle the spell's languor, its power growing in proportion to the spell.

Reading someone's mind required little concentration. The only thing that a magician needed was a keen sense of observation and a feel for the target's wind. A rock held practically none of this element; the same rock used to build a statue would have a little more. Plants had more than stones, and the largest wind element in plants could be found in the oldest trees of magical species: maoals, sterile apple trees, blue pines, and others.

Wind was primarily an element in animals, where there was another hierarchy. Insects were the least endowed, sometimes having less than large-limbed plants. Then came fish, mollusks, and crustaceans, slightly more bright than any fly. Higher up were reptiles, then birds. Finally mammals, humans, those that nursed their young, as Bowbaq described it.

The giant had never penetrated the mind of anything other than a mammal. Certain Arque legends mentioned connections between erjaks and birds of prey, but he had never seen it. They said that an animal's spirit grew with its shell, and that if an erjak were to find a three-foot-long mosquito, it could be asked about the taste of human blood. Bowbaq wouldn't want to try it.

Yan had already touched another living being's wind element: Grigán's. Because he could see the Sublime Essence, he was capable not only of reading minds, but of modifying them. With this power, Yan could change memories, personality, intellect, convictions, even the deepest of feelings. Corenn had warned him against this power, so much so that Yan was reluctant even to try it anymore. Whenever he used the power, he avoided pushing his concentration to that level. The thought that he could have done damage to his friend's mind frightened him and made him respect the power he wielded.

Considering all these possibilities, he proceeded with caution with the mimastin. The ease with which he could see Ifio's essence scared him a little. Even when he tried to hold himself back, it appeared almost instantly. Contrary to an earth spell, the wind spell left Yan aware of the outside world. He could see the little monkey twitch subtly and pull away from him with terror.

"Wise one," he said sluggishly, "it's nothing. It's me."

"You're there?" Bowbaq asked

"I'm there, yes. The poor beast is scared to death."

Ifio hid under the giant's arms, and he walked away slowly. "She needs to understand that we are not torturing her. The surprise will go away soon. What do you see, Yan?"

"A sphere," Yan responded, his eyes hazy. "Sand on the bottom, split by a fissure where it disappears. On top, a small piece of ice surrounded by fire. The emerging mist is Ifio's spirit."

"I've never seen anything like that," Bowbaq commented, shaking his head. "Normally, I imagine a kind of fog."

"That's it," Yan confirmed, seeing the vapors rise in the sphere. "That's exactly it."

He extended his hand to Ifio, who didn't calm down. Feeling cornered, the mimastin jumped and bit Yan's hand, before running back to Bowbaq and howling stridently.

"Don't let go!" Bowbaq warned, while his friend shuddered in pain. "If you stop now, it will be harder next time."

Yan tried to concentrate, following his new teacher's advice. At this stage, if Ifio could have controlled her thoughts, she would have closed off her mind to any intrusion, as a human would have done. But the little mimastin could only think to flee, to escape what felt to her like the most dangerous possible attack.

Yan focused on the mystical sphere and the rare spectacle of seeing a living being's essence. Minuscule currents of vapor turned, changing direction and twisting together in beautiful lengths, thicknesses, and shapes. By narrowing his perception to just these wisps of wind, Yan could discern particular traces, following them with his eyes and watching them slow, deform, and suddenly rebound with a slightly different trajectory. The color patterns turned out to be full of beautiful nuance. If he didn't focus, the ensemble could be described as a simple fog, but Yan could see so much finesse and beauty in the evolving swirls that he felt it was something divine.

What would a human spirit look like!

He vaguely heard Bowbaq announce that Ifio had calmed down. He already knew that, though; he could see the relaxation as the currents slowed down.

Soon he was close enough to touch them. He imagined his own body next to the sphere and extended an ethereal hand through the glassy recept; it was soft, like breaking the surface of water, with none of the thickness like Ji's portal.

His hand grazed a vaporous current, and Yan *knew* the painful scars on Ifio's back, as if the monkey were a part of him now. He touched other vapors, and felt affection and fear toward Bowbaq.

Yan felt emboldened, and he brought his other hand into the sphere, then his entire body. He was little Yan in the monkey's spirit. The currents passed through him, revealing their information. Most of these were physical impulses, but a few emotions burst through: fear, fear, hunger, fear, gratitude, fear, cold, hunger...

Yan flew through the storm with the joy of a new experience. Of course, he was careful not to fully live it: only his perception of the Sublime Essence allowed him such a voyage, which was no more than a waking dream. His body was still in the open-farm, next to Bowbaq's, but his spirit had plunged into the monkey's.

He continued his progression with the sense of pending discoveries. At the heart of the sphere, the winds were more violent, numerous and charged with information. Yan suddenly felt the fleeting sensation of Ifio's feet on the wood; an instant later, he perceived Bowbaq, his own body, and the wall behind them, as if from the monkey's eyes. This sensation kept repeating, more and more often, and Yan grew aware of the monkey's limbs, one by one, and then all of her senses. His own body seemed far away, and in his concentration, he lost a sense of his own form.

He saw Bowbaq—even more gigantic from this height—grab his immobile body and speak to him softly. It would be funny to surprise him now!

He did three somersaults, surprised he could handle this new foreign body so well. Then he stepped back and leaned on the wall like a human.

"Yan," Bowbaq stuttered, horrified. "You are *in* Ifio! You have reached her *deep mind!*"

Seeing his friend's panicked expression, Yan pulled himself out of the euphoria that had overcome him and brutally lost his concentration. It was then that the languor floored him.

The first thing the young man saw when he woke was Corenn's angry face, and Bowbaq's anxious one behind her. Thinking about the coming lecture, Yan had a painful migraine that sent him back into the shadows.

When he awoke again, he was more successful at maintaining consciousness. Though his mind had returned, his body was drained. Yan felt weak, cold, sore, and sleepy, and he had a splitting migraine so strong that it blurred his vision. If he weren't already laid out on his back, he would have collapsed again.

He knew exactly where all the pain was coming from: the languor. But he had never felt it last for more than a few instants, even when he had lost consciousness. What he was feeling now was something different. Corenn had described the sensation to him before as a persistent languor, the *apathy*. This was the punishment for a magician who pulled too much force from his body.

"Yan? Can you hear me?" the Mother asked, her voice resonating as if in a dream.

The young man wanted to speak but his throat was dry. He slowly nodded his head.

"Can you see my finger?"

Corenn waved her index finger in front of his face. He followed its trajectory with some difficulty, blinking his eyelids often.

"He takes a while to respond," she said to Bowbaq with a reproachful sigh. "He still needs to rest. And now we have two sick! I suppose you're proud of yourselves?"

Yan couldn't respond, unlike the giant, who said timidly, "He touched the *deep mind*!"

"And so what?" the Mother asked, calmer now. "Is such a feat worth dying for?"

"No, no, friend Corenn," mumbled Bowbaq, who had intervened more to apologize than to excuse Yan. "He shouldn't have, it's true . . . And I should have warned him. But all the same, *he touched her deep mind*!"

The Mother began to understand what this meant for the giant, given his insistence on the point. But she couldn't help but be distracted by Yan's comatose state, which Bowbaq had brought to her attention only a few moments before. His frozen hands and empty eyes; it would make Léti suffer, and that would be her responsibility.

Even if her student seemed to be out of danger, she had to tame her own curiosity and leave the discussion on the famous deep mind for later. Yan and Bowbaq, despite their discoveries, needed to understand the gravity of their errors.

"I don't give a margolin's ass about that, Bowbaq," she declared. "Don't you see that Yan could have gone mad, because he went too far? And you pushed him there."

The young man succumbed to his weakness on hearing this last reply. Weren't the heirs all mad already? The threshold of going too far had already been crossed by several leagues and several times over, ever since they saw the wonder of Ji's portal.

Seeing Yan unwell, Léti took the opportunity to ridicule her aunt about the supposed dangers she herself faced when training with Grigán. If the young woman regularly had small bruises and wounds, those healed quickly and had never forced her to stay in bed all day, unlike the effects of magic on the apprentice magician.

Lana came back enchanted by the troupe's show. Léti noticed that Rey was still holding the Maz by her waist as they entered the room, and felt somewhat jealous. Not out of affection for the actor, but because she and Yan rarely had such moments together.

Before the Züu massacred all the other heirs, perhaps they had shared such moments, yes. But not after. What was she to him, exactly? Now that they had traveled a good portion of the known world together, what could Yan want with a little Kaulienne?

As was typical, she shook off these agonizing thoughts to concentrate on the reality in front of her: after more than five perilous dékades of travel, the remaining heirs were still alive, and even if the future were uncertain, at least they were going to confront it together.

Thinking about Yan and their journey, Léti listened, feigning interest, to Maz Lana's account of the troupe's abilities. The priestess had little interest in the amuseur's ridiculous games, but the rest had amazed her. The acrobats, the horsewomen, Gallop the juggler, Anaël and his wolf, and the last number with Deremin and his assistant, which the others hadn't been able to see.

His number was surely a fraud, and the Rominian didn't pretend it was anything else except to please the crowd. Beyond simple sleight of hand, his favorite trick was to surprise the spectators with purses that "magically" appeared in their pockets. The clowning dwarves placed them there throughout the show, ahead of the finale, but the crowd loved this last trick. Deremin confessed shamelessly that the purses came from spectators who had left the show early.

Nakapan always gathered a meager offering in Semilia, but giving the town a show was a custom, an unwritten law. It was a way to thank the prince for granting them the open-farm and free passage, which were things the ruler could take away at any time.

The day of rest in front of a warm fire served the heirs well and passed too quickly. Yan and Grigán woke at nearly the same time, just before dusk. They both listened attentively while the others explained their mishaps, but this didn't take away from their recovery. They felt so good, in fact, that when it was time for the others to sleep, the young man and the warrior felt more than a little disappointed to have missed the day.

They spent part of their night talking, mostly focusing on Grigán's plethora of travels and experiences. That night around the fire, the two men were peaceful and spoke freely, as if they weren't pursued by the Grand Guild, on Zuïa's blacklist, hunted by an invincible demon, and menaced by a man turned immortal. The conversation was pleasantly strange, as if they were two men who still had time for domestic pursuits.

Time passed, and Yan felt close to telling Grigán the truth: the one concerning the warrior's pending doom. He couldn't find the courage or an excuse to share such a burden, though, so he left that conversation on the tip of his tongue.

"Do you still feel sick?" was all the young man could awkwardly ask.

"I don't know . . . No, I don't think so," the warrior added, after reflecting on it. "Why, do I seem like it?"

"No, I was just wondering how we might ensure your good health . . ."

He didn't need to say anything more. They all knew that Grigán could suffer another episode, one day or another. The episodes kept getting worse, and the next one could kill him, but they were powerless to stop them.

The troupe and the heirs left Semilia shortly after dawn, traveling together for another day, the end of which would be their last as a group. Grigán and the others would head for the Holy City, while Nakapan and his troupe would set up in Pont and stay there for the festivals of the Earth.

It was with a certain sadness that they set out for their final day together; they had become friends, in spite of the Rominians' apparent indifference just a few days before. The heirs were going to miss Anaël and his wolf in particular, Gallop the juggler, Nakapan the giant, and even the false mage Deremin, who had shown himself to be an agreeable and jolly man. No one had seen Tonk, and even the other entertainers were relieved by his absence.

The mountainous route between Semilia and Pont was easier than the last one they had taken: larger, cleared of snow, and at a slight downhill angle. They crossed the last band of snow well before noon, and soon walked on hills covered in short grass and scattered rocks. If the cold were still present, at least they could stay in the wagons and enjoy the countryside, instead of struggling through thick snow.

Despite Lana's advice, Grigán refused to quit his saddle for the entire day. Locking himself up in a wagon felt like a sign of weakness to him, and the warrior was forever wary of seeming weak. What's more, he felt perfectly healthy, and he continued to remind his friends of this. Corenn, who knew his personality so well, did nothing to change his mind. Even her persuasive words wouldn't accomplish anything in the face of his exaggerated sense of pride.

Taking the previous day off had served the horses well, and they kept a brisk pace. It seemed like the travelers would see Pont within the fifth dékade, well before Nakapan had planned.

The convoy's monotonous progression was troubled on one occasion, when they came across two wagons similar to their own. Nakapan waved to the eight people inside, two Rominian families, minor nobles by the look of them. Unfortunately, the strangers were bearers of bad news.

"Turn around," one said in a disheartened tone. "They blocked the King Bridge!"

"They refused you passage?" Nakapan said, surprised.

"It's swarming with military! Like a war or something."

The crossing wagons passed out of earshot. Grigán, who had heard every word, spoke with the troupe's chief. After a fruitless discussion, they asked Corenn for her advice.

The King Bridge, which gave the town its name—*pont* being Rominian for "bridge"—had been build by the Rominians in the time of the Two Empires. It was one of the three greatest achievements of mankind, along with the Palace of Freedom in Goran and the Sleeping Statue of Hamsa in Cyr Heights. The bridge spanned a cliff more than two leagues long, was wider than six feet, and rose above the ground below by four hundred feet. By the mountain passes, getting around the cliff would take three days. Three days for only six hundred feet, as the crow flies.

The marvel, entirely made of wood, didn't rest on any foundation, as building columns four hundred feet high to support it was an unthinkable undertaking. The cliff's width equally prevented a rope bridge, which wouldn't have supported its own weight. The Rominians had had the idea to build a suspension bridge placed twenty feet *below* the chasm's edge, held there by solid ropes attached to the walls. Unique in its kind, the King Bridge was tactically vital, and the Loreliens who had inherited it guarded it jealously.

Access was reserved to soldiers and members of the nobility. Following the long-standing tradition of free passage, they also let entertainers and messengers from any country use it. This privilege was not permanent, and the crown could remove it at any time, which is precisely what seemed to have happened to the heirs.

"We can't afford to lose three days," Grigán contested, without being able to explain himself to Nakapan.

Every detour slowed the heirs down in their quest and gave Saat time to achieve his plans, whatever they were.

"Have they ever refused you passage, Master Nakapan?" Corenn asked, after thinking for a while.

"Not yet. The militia sometimes need to be asked twice, but only to swell their purses. By Odrel, I've crossed this bridge more than twenty times."

"As have I, twice," Grigán said. "It was easy enough to pretend to be a messenger. Normally, they aren't too vigilant. If they've closed access, it's because something serious happened."

The Mother looked at the sun's position to guess how long they had before nightfall.

"Are we still far from this famous bridge?"

"Two leagues, or around there," Nakapan responded. "Perhaps a bit less."

"Good! To be so close, we won't lose much by at least trying, and if nothing else, we will learn what has put them on such high alert," she said. At the last part, she looked at Grigán knowingly.

The warrior understood what she meant. The Mother had a feeling, the same one that had tormented him as soon as they had heard the news.

If Lorelia, the freest of the Upper Kingdoms, closed her frontiers, it could have something to do with Saat and his plot.

Trying to maximize their chances, Corenn suggested that they present Gallop and Rey, two typical Loreliens, as the troupe's leaders. The idea didn't exactly enchant Nakapan, but he agreed to it under his wife's insistence. She didn't relish the idea of staying two more nights in the Murky Mountains.

The Mother also proposed that the troupe put on their costumes, so as to emphasize their role as entertainers. She borrowed a few brightly colored garments from the Rominians and dressed herself up, along with Yan, Lana, and, most importantly, Rey. The key thing was to convince the militia that they were a troupe of entertainers; if even one of the guards respected the free passage tradition, he might be more open to a troupe so full of the brightly dressed amuseurs.

Because of his size, Bowbaq needed no disguise; anyone could guess what kind of numbers the giant did. The same idea applied to Léti and Grigán, whose leather Ramgrith outfits could mark them as acrobats.

To avoid the curious eyes of a brother in the Grand Guild who might by chance be at the bridge, Corenn scattered the heirs among the eight wagons in their convoy. She took her place next to Rey and Gallop at the front, and signaled to continue.

The troupe had lost all of its joy as they traveled the last few miles before King Bridge. However, once they could see the small fort guarding their side of the bridge, the travelers became animated, and music rose from their wagons, mixing with the sounds of animated conversation.

All the noise and false cheer was part of Corenn's plan. If the guards' orders weren't strict, they would act according to their own judgment, and it would be better to present them with a friendly mood.

A sentinel rang the bell in his tower as they approached. The small fort's gates were still open, a good sign. Seven hundred yards ahead—practically the other side of the world—a few weak lights shone through the fading light: lanterns from the fort on the other side. A bit beyond that was the town of Pont, and Lorelia.

Eleven guards appeared and haphazardly arranged themselves on the fort's walls, looking at the new arrivals. Only two were armed with pikes, while the others kept their blades sheathed. There was a tenseness in their movements even as the guards paced and chattered animatedly.

Corenn noticed with horror that there was a *jeleni* among their ranks. The dog masters were the heart of the royal elite troops and were never stationed at frontier posts. Whatever had happened in Lorelia, it must be serious. Worse, the heirs had already confronted the jelenis. Some of the treasure the heirs had stolen from the Small Palace still rattled in their wagons!

She anxiously watched the man approach. If he had been present that day, if he recognized Rey, or her...

"Good day to you, sir," the actor said, without dismounting. "Quite a few people out to greet us, I see."

The jeleni stepped right past him without answering, and walked along the entire convoy before turning back to them. The only word he said was to call for his mastiff, who was pulling at his chain trying to get at Merbal.

"Who is the chief of this troupe?" he said authoritatively.

"I am, and my younger brother here, soldier," said Rey. "We took over from our father, an artist you have surely heard of: Grigán the Rambler? People called him that because he had the strange habit of—"

"That doesn't matter to me. Where are you from, and where are you going?"

"We come from Romine, and we arrive here for the festivals of the Earth, of course!" Rey said joyfully, miming the action for beating a drum. "But why so many questions? Typically we cross this bridge without any difficulty."

"Lorelia has prepared herself for war, my friend," the jeleni said condescendingly. "The Goranese are already up in arms. If we don't react quickly, they could be in Riders' Square by next dékade."

"War with Goran?" Rey and Corenn exclaimed together.

"Maybe. Maybe not. The Grand Empire is proclaiming that they need men in the Warrior's Vale, but we have never seen them raise such an army to hold back a few marauding Thalittes. Instead of just waiting to find out, the king is preparing for the worst. If the Goranese truly have problems in the east, we may go to help them. But if they're covering up something else . . . we will be ready to greet them," he finished with a vicious grin.

Corenn drank in his words, her heart pounding furiously. They were lucky that neither the troupe nor the heirs had a Goranese in their ranks, but the rest of the soldier's speech was bad news for the heirs.

Was Saat responsible for all this? the Mother wondered. Was he in Goran, planning to invade Lorelia? Or with the Thalittes, preparing to attack the Upper Kingdoms? How? Why?

"If war is coming, better for us to be inside our kingdom's borders," Rey said, his tone turning very serious.

"That is impossible," the jeleni responded. "To prevent any spies from infiltrating, no one is allowed to cross the King Bridge until we hear otherwise."

"But a detour will cost us at least three days," the actor insisted. "By then, we will be too late for the festivals."

"I'm sorry," the guard responded, happy to see his command so readily respected.

"And if I promise that we have no spies in our group?" the actor responded, winking at the jeleni.

"There are too many of you. I can't take the risk."

"Come on! We are *Loreliens*!" Rey protested, using his best argument.

Corenn intervened before they lost their chance. Rey was a great actor, to be sure, but he hadn't mastered diplomacy like the Mother.

"Sir," she started, "I suppose at the end of our detour, we will face another frontier post?"

"More than likely," the jeleni responded, sounding suspicious.

"I also can guess that, for the same reasons you have just explained, they will hesitate to let us in?"

"They will simply verify that you are who you say you are. The frontiers aren't closed, they are merely surveyed." The man spoke as if he were speaking to a child.

"Well then! Why not verify right here!" Corenn exclaimed. "You will save us a costly detour, and gain our . . . gratitude. Everyone will be better off."

The man stared at the Mother attentively. Corenn looked back with a knowing smile, hoping he wouldn't misunderstand it. She was trying to grease his palm, not seduce him.

"It's a great responsibility," he responded, lowering his voice. "Giving free passage to such a large troupe . . . I would be risking my head."

"We are only entertainers, sir," Corenn said. "We need to cross the bridge in time for the festivals of the Earth. What misfortune could find you, when the two of us will forget this conversation?"

The man looked behind him, to see if anyone else could hear her. The other guards were spread out along the convoy, as much to look for possible spies as to satisfy their own curiosity regarding such a bizarre troupe.

"It's a *great* responsibility," he repeated finally.

Corenn searched through her bags and gave the jeleni a purse heavy with coins, which she had prepared ahead of time in case the need for a bribe ever arose. The man quickly hid the purse in his jacket. Rey and Gallop were smart enough to not interfere with the exchange.

"That purse only contains beautiful Lorelien terces," Corenn whispered, trying to seal the deal before he could change his mind. "Don't worry, we aren't traitors."

The last remark seemed to relieve the jeleni enough to eliminate his final misgivings. The soldier hadn't practiced acting as the entertainers had, and he smiled from ear to ear with obvious pleasure for his profit.

What immoral acts would he allow himself to commit, if the conflict really exploded? Corenn thought to herself sadly. What would they all do, the sadists, the ambitious, the perverted, the greedy, the intolerant, the jealous, frustrated by the tapestry of unfair laws, when things began to crumble.

Her mind was drawn to Kaul. The Matriarchy had been spared from famine and conflicts for so many years. Goranese and Loreliens ravaged by marauders and war; wouldn't the Kauliens be next? Was this the future for all of the Upper Kingdoms?

"You may pass," the jeleni announced once he woke from his daydream. "If they interrogate you on the other side, say that you are family to one of the guards on this side. Don't come back here until the war is over," he ordered.

He turned heels, gave a few orders to his subordinates, and disappeared inside the fort.

Rey said mockingly, "I bet you he is already counting all his coins."

"I won't take that bet. Too easy for you," responded Corenn.

"How much was there in that purse, Corenn?"

"Just enough. Too much and he would be suspicious. True entertainers don't buy their free passage in gold."

"Rey was right," Gallop said enthusiastically. "You really are a woman of the mind."

Corenn smiled at the young Lorelien's compliment as they guided their wagon inside the fort, followed by the others. They stopped only when the guards opened the interior gate, which led to the sloping path toward the King Bridge, twenty feet below the cliff's edge.

The slope was fairly steep, and they all had to walk to lighten the wagons. This gave them a chance to learn how Corenn, Rey, and Gallop had gotten them through and the reason for all the militia. The news was welcomed by the troupe, who rejoiced to avoid a three-day detour, while the heirs were saddened by the possibility of a coming war.

Yan's spirits sank more than anyone's, the weight of the truth weighing heavily upon him. Usul had told him this would happen and, worse, what its outcome would be.

"The Upper Kingdoms will lose," he said out loud. "In less than a year... only a year..."

"What did you say?" Grigán asked.

Seeing six pairs of eyes turn toward him, the young man realized his mistake. He had said too much to retreat. And since the prophecy seemed to be coming true, he didn't have much left to hide.

"Usul let me see...," he explained vaguely. "I couldn't understand what it meant then, but now I see."

"Saat is behind all this?" Corenn asked

"Probably, yes. Usul wasn't clear on that."

"Where is he, in Goran or Thallos?" Rey intervened.

"I have no idea! I wouldn't hide something like that!"

They agreed, but all of them were concerned that the young man hadn't told them about the coming war until now. No one knew what Yan had experienced with Usul; they only saw his white hair marking the painful experience.

The convoy advanced toward the bridge, and two guards walked alongside. They were there only to help the travelers avoid falling off, and they stopped at the bridge's edge. Alone, the travelers advanced out over the abyss. The way was lit only by lantern light, and wood cracked under their weight. The wind howled past their ears.

A few entertainers marveled at the beauty of their own lights illuminating the void between stars and earth. Others preferred to grab hold of the railings, worried that one of the horses might knock them over the edge. The heirs were as unconcerned with the bridge as one could be, their minds elsewhere and full of worry.

"If Saat really has an army, we can't do much against him," Bowbaq remarked gravely. No one corrected the giant. His pessimism was full of good reason.

"All the frontiers will be closed soon," Grigán said. "We will have to gallop straight for Ith, with no more stops."

They reluctantly agreed. Maz Achem's journal—a century-old notebook whose contents might be useless—still represented their last, best hope.

Somber dreamed, and dreamed. More and more he didn't need to sleep to dream. All he had to do was open his mind a sliver, and thousands of thoughts filled him, bringing images of war, conquest, domination, and adoration.

He was starting to control his powers.

At the beginning, mortal minds imposed on his dreams, taking root, deeply embedding themselves in his still-virgin conscience like corrupting parasites. Somber fought in vain against these intrusions, and yearned for the time when only Saat shared his dreams. When they hid, the two of them, under the mountain of Jal'karu.

Little by little, Somber learned to draw strength from humanity's prayers, fears, cruelties, and ambitions. He feasted on them. He found his identity in them, and from the dreams came his name: He Who Vanquishes. He had been this forever, in the depth of his soul he knew that, but the revelation came from mortals. He was born from man.

Stronger. Smarter. Brighter.

He could easily penetrate any mind, but it was only recently that he had learned to recognize a few key faces and remember the important names. Emaz Chebree, his priestess. Gors'a'min, Saat's war chief. Zamerine, his strategist. Dyree, his executioner. And their ally in the Lower Kingdoms, whose face remained unknown, but whose name was often spoken.

All these people spoke to him, calling him the Young Diarch. For a long time, their plans seemed strange to him: obscure, confused, unimportant. But as Somber's mind grew, he discovered ambition and deciphered the plans. From human prayers he realized his superiority, and the strange circumstances that made him a god among men. The immortal being saw only dreams of battles, murders, and conquests, all the values man had forced on him.

He understood Saat's projects perfectly. They would, together, conquer the mortal world and impose their reign. The New Order, for eternity.

Somber rejoiced to think of the power that would come with all of humanity's worship, how he would be strong enough to stamp out any resistance. He was He Who Vanquishes.

As his consciousness awoke, Somber's memories came into sharper focus as well. He could also remember the past. Jal'dara. His brothers and sisters. Nol. Jal'karu. Seeing them were bad omens. He often remembered his painful contact with Usul. The immortal hated his younger brother. Usul knew. What did he know?

The Undines. The whispering lake. Somber remembered a Truth from the dark creatures in the depths of Karu. An Adversary would be born, and he alone would be able to defeat He Who Vanquishes.

Somber didn't know who or when, or even how he could fall. Humans were laughably weak, and his brethren were powerless to stop him.

But a Truth wasn't conditional, and Somber needed to prepare for his coming Adversary . . . the only one, for all eternity, who would have even a chance of defeating him.

He worked on the task with a savage joy. Saat no longer needed to advise him. Somber was nearly full grown, and understood the stakes perfectly. Of his own initiative, he searched for their enemies' spirits.

His shadow flew over the mountains, towns, rivers, and plains, faster than thought. Touching and exploring thousands of minds. Crossing kingdoms, listening, spying, rummaging through it all for seven spirits out of millions.

He knew them well, having seen them several times already. One of them could be the Adversary. Somber doubted it, but it was beyond his power to verify.

It took a while to find them, a few diversions. Almost a milliday passed.

Their enemies had traveled a great distance since their last contact. Somber briefly flew over them, immobile and invisible in the skies. Seven riders, mortal, and with no power to speak of. These seven were the greatest threat to the diarchs' reign.

The god searched their minds, scowling. One of them was particularly repulsive, completely devoted to his sister, the insipid goddess Eurydis. Somber rejoiced to think that her cult would soon be annihilated. He would burn all her temples, exterminate her followers, torture her Maz. It would be a shining proof of his superiority.

The mortals were too weak to even detect his presence, and he found what he wanted easily. Then he felt a moment's hesitation. The situation required him to ask his friend's advice.

The hundreds of leagues separating them were no problem. After a century together, Somber reached out to Saat's mind easily, and his friend shared his most intimate thoughts. He was ready to talk, he had always been ready.

They have almost reached their destination, Somber said, without introduction.

The god was taciturn, for good reason. Saat and he always understood each other.

Do they know where we are?

No.

Good. I will warn our men in Ith.

For the High Diarch, the moment was over, but Somber didn't break contact.

Is something bothering you, my friend? Saat asked

Why don't I just kill them now? the god responded, brooding like a child.

Can you do it without materializing? Saat asked hopefully.

Somber thought, checking his power and the distance from his body.

No. I would have to sleep for a long time after.

So, we will wait. If one of them is the Adversary, he could defeat you and conquer us. Remember the Broken Castle.

The Adversary could already be dead, the god countered. *Without ever having seen me.*

In a few days, that will be a fact. Unlike them, we have all the time in the world, my friend. Endless time.

Somber took a last look at the riders and returned to his body, thousands of miles distant. The camp resonated with slaves working against the mountain, and prayers sung in his honor.

I am He Who Vanquishes, he repeated to himself. *He Who Vanquishes. He Who Vanquishes. He Who Vanquishes.*

It took the heirs only three days of travel from Pont to reach the royal city of Lermian. At dusk on the Day of the Earth, they camped outside of the city of artists. The festival drumbeats echoed throughout the night, cruelly reminding them of their friends in the troupe. They had left with the promise of a future meeting, and no confidence they could keep it.

Riding without rest, they were about to cross into the Grand Empire, sneaking past the border under the shadow of night. The two southernmost provinces in Goran and Lorelia were mostly, as of yet, unaffected by the pending war between their kingdoms. The heirs avoided passing through the larger cities and spent their nights sleeping under the stars. They had to be cautious. In times like these, tempers flared easily and any stranger could be seen as an invader.

Day after day, Corenn learned as much as she could from travelers venturing south. Trying to separate the truth from the endless set of preposterous rumors, it turned out that the Grand Empire was indeed having problems along its border in the Warrior's Vale, and that they had no plans for Lorelia. The merchant kingdom was waiting only for an official request from the Goranese emperor to send reinforcements and rise to the Upper Kingdoms' collective defense. But each kingdom suspected treachery from the other, so they continued to amass troops at their borders, waiting for something to happen.

All eyes were on the north, so the heirs easily entered Ithare territory on the third day of the dékade of the Earth, seven days after leaving Pont. Nearly two dékades had passed since their foray into the Deep Tower.

The nights between days of exhausting riding always seemed to be too short. The heirs were tired and sore, but, finally, they were close to their destination.

When Grigán gave the signal to halt that night, he did so with relief on his face. As they had done on all the other nights, they ate dinner quickly and went to bed early, saving their energy to reach Ith as soon as possible.

None slept well that night. The next day, they would discover if their efforts would lead to any reward. Would Maz Achem's journal hold any vital information, or would it reduce their hope to nothing?

Ith was an open city, which meant that anyone could enter without paying taxes or being inspected at the gates. This worked out well for the heirs, who were always worried about being noticed. Their aim was to reach the Holy City, though, and gaining access to the religious neighborhoods would be quite the task indeed.

As Lana couldn't help Grigán form a plan, the warrior had no other choice than to wait and see for himself before improvising an approach, something he hated to do. With pounding hearts and tense bodies, they covered the short distance remaining to Ithare's capital, two moons after Yan had first heard mention of the heirs.

Lana seemed to come alive as they approached her childhood home in the bright sun. Each ruin, landmark, and neighborhood reminded her of a personal memory or historic anecdote: there King Li'ut gave a speech, here she would come to walk, over there had been the last battle of the Ithare Empire.

The heirs listened attentively to the Maz, invigorated by her expressiveness, which was such a contrast to her typical reticence. Rey was the most tenacious with his questions, punctuating Lana's tales with gently mocking commentary and making his friends laugh every time.

Corenn lost herself contemplating the Alt's vibrant waters, the high Curtain Mountains—dressed in white, gray, and ocher—cutting through the blue sky, the Holy City's domes, an undulating plain like a rug set out in front of Mount Fleuri. And hundreds of pilgrims who had walked calmly to the capital searching for miracles, spirituality, and peace. If the situation were different,

Corenn would have found the day to be marvelous. The heirs had not come to Ith to find serenity, though. Indeed, they could only be disappointed, or shocked like their ancestors had been, 118 years earlier, when they returned from Ji.

Soon they were at the city's gates, simple travelers among hundreds of others who came to pay homage to their cult. There were a large number of Eurydians wearing masks and robes adorned with the goddess's protective symbols. The other cults had their followers as well: Ivie-the-Night, Mishra with the head of a bear, Wug, Eeti, Dona, Sad-Odrel, the Serpale twins, Brassisse, Aliandra of the Sun, and dozens more that the heirs didn't recognize, not counting the pilgrims who showed no sign of their cult, and whose beliefs were hidden.

"There," Grigán pointed scornfully. "Valipondes."

They all turned toward the group of four riders who kept their distance. They wore leather lace–trimmed green shirts with long golden necklaces tied in complex knots. One of them carried a cage holding three copper-toned margolins. The crowd avoided these characters, making a wide detour around them.

"How can you tolerate the Valipondes," Grigán said, turning to Lana. "Demonist child murderers, banished from all other kingdoms!"

"The Holy City is open to everyone," the Maz responded, with a hint of regret. "The king makes sure that they stay harmless. But, outside of human sacrifices, everyone is free to make their offerings as they wish . . . the law doesn't prevent animal sacrifice."

"What!" Bowbaq said angrily, jumping off his horse and giving the men in green a dark look.

Yan put his hand on Bowbaq's shoulder, hoping to calm him down. The giant looked back and forth between the demonists and the young man, not understanding why Yan held him back. Suddenly, the cage's door broke off, allowing the rodents to flee and causing a ripple of turmoil in the crowd.

Their owner swore in an unknown language, and swore even louder when his companions started to yell at him. Bowbaq thanked Yan with a big smile, and Yan responded with a wink. Opening the cage with magic had been easy, and Yan hardly felt the languor from his spell.

Yan's spell hadn't been enough to satisfy Bowbaq, though. He used his erjak powers on one of their horses, whose rider's hands were busy insulting his peers. The scared beast reared back, throwing the Valipondes pilgrim to the ground under a rain of laughter from the crowd. Bowbaq walked away with a satisfied expression, ignoring Corenn's wrathful glare.

Carried away by a surge of pilgrims, they soon came to the city's gates, which, while open, were still narrow. Lana guided them to a nearby enclosure.

"It's forbidden to ride into the Holy City," she explained. "Even in the lower city, riders are somewhat looked down upon. Ith's streets are older than Romine's, and have never been repaved. The king does his best to conserve the vestiges of the old empire. I always thought these enclosures were a good idea."

"I thought the city was led by the Emaz?" Léti said, surprised.

"The Emaz validate the king's decisions. Sometimes they propose laws, but power always resides in the bearer of Li'ut's crown. The great priests hardly concern themselves with commercial treaties or other dull tasks, and the king doesn't interfere with Temple business. It works quite well this way," Lana explained with conviction.

Corenn sighed doubtfully, thinking of the supposed integrity of the Emaz and the actual extent of power given to the king of such a small kingdom. But it wasn't her job to relieve Lana of her illusions. The priestess had plenty of time to learn the twisted ways of mankind, or at least she would have plenty of time, should they ever reestablish a normal life.

They left their horses at a stable, along with a few coins, and headed up the busy street. Lana confidently guided them, having spent her whole life in the city.

"You're taking us to the Holy City, right?" Grigán verified, suddenly struck by a sense of foreboding.

"I think it's best we buy some masks first," the Maz explained. "Without those, we have no chance of entering."

"And where do you plan on buying a mask where no one recognizes you?"

Lana stopped, lowered her eyes, and blushed before confessing, "I hadn't thought of that. I was going to take you to my parents' supplier."

The warrior turned around, walked a few steps, and took a deep breath. He always had to think of everything. For everyone. They were but seven fugitives, but by traveling together the risk multiplied by twenty.

"We could still go there," he said as he approached Lana, forcing himself to sound calm. "You just can't enter, that's all."

Lana felt completely foolish. As they started walking, she realized that being in Ith had made her lose all sense of caution. The Holy City, her clean, winding streets at the base of Mount Fleuri, the shaded squares, the colorful gardens, the bridges spanning the Alt... And yet, it was also the place where the Züu had tried to kill her. She had to remember why the heirs had made this voyage, and that danger followed them.

She looked at the crowd, searching the eyes behind the polite masks. Was there a killer among them? Several, maybe? Had the heirs already been seen? Were they being followed?

"This crowd is far too calm for my taste," Rey said, gazing thoughtfully at the passersby. "In Lorelia, half as many people make twice as much noise."

"*Faith is unmoving*," Lana recited, trying to forget her dread. "But don't trust appearances, Reyan... as the prayers end, Ith will seem much livelier."

They arrived at the shop of the mask maker, a profession exclusive to Ithare, and Corenn and Rey took care of buying classic masks for each member of the group. The faces on the masks were expressionless and sexless, with a rough finish. Grigán complained that his obstructed his vision, and Bowbaq said his was too small.

"Either way, Bowbaq and I are easily recognized," the warrior said as he removed the mask. "And I refuse to change my clothes."

"Me too," said Léti, who had grown attached to her outfit.

Nonetheless, the warrior agreed to wear the novice's robe that Rey had filched from the Züu, and Léti did the same with Lana's own robe. Seeing a group of strangers changing in the middle of the street shocked none of the passersby, who must have seen an endless stream of eccentricities in the strange city.

The heirs themselves saw a few bizarre sights as they approached the Eurydian corner of the city, one anonymous procession among many. Lana successively pointed out the famous Lurian singers, a family of Thébian Donors, an inn run by a "priestess" of Dona, and the bridge where, long before, a lookout spotted the coming army of undead Goranese.

She cried out and averted her eyes when they found a man hanging on a side street. The man had apparently killed himself, but this hardly lessened their shock.

"It's been more than two days," Grigán commented. "What kind of city lets someone hang and rot from their balcony for two days?"

"Detach him, Grigán, please," Corenn asked.

The warrior checked to make sure they were alone, then cut the rope with one blow from his curved blade. The body fell to the ground, and Grigán led the group away.

"He was a Brassisse," Lana explained. "They think that you keep your physical appearance for all eternity when you die. Many commit suicide as they age."

"But the guards don't do anything?" Yan said, surprised. "Why do they just leave them there?"

"They probably hadn't found him yet," the Maz explained. "The officers already have a lot to deal with, with the Valipondes, the K'luriens, and the Yooses. And there are so few of them; the Temple has less than two hundred men to guard the Holy City. The king has a few more, maybe three hundred and fifty, but they watch over the entire kingdom."

"Five hundred men for the entire kingdom," Grigán commented, shaking his head. "With my horsemen, I could have taken the city in . . ."

His face darkened and he left his sentence unfinished. The memory of his Ramgrith cavalry brought back other, more bitter memories best left alone.

"Goran protects us," Lana asserted. "Whoever attacks the Holy City must first defeat the Grand Empire. And that day has never come," she said, hoping she was right.

Emaz Drékin felt old and weak. His faith in Eurydis was intact, but serving the goddess had lost some of its joy from his first years as an initiate. Reaching the Temple's highest levels, he had discovered the Grand Temple's influence in the world, political, economic, or simply human.

At first, this too had inspired him. Now it only left him with the bitter taste of power's tortuous path. Rather than a great priest, he saw himself as an able manager. Certainly, he had contributed to the Temple's blossoming growth, but not to the goddess's.

With these thoughts, he set out to finish his chores, dékade after dékade, cloistering himself with the most boring and monotonous tasks to atone for his sins. Until today.

"Your Excellence?" one of the novices on his service asked. "A few visitors are asking to be seen. One of them says she knows you; she wouldn't give me her name."

"Let them enter, my child," the Emaz responded, happy to have an unexpected diversion.

His joy turned into surprise when a disparate group of seven entered his study without a word. One was a giant with a monkey on his shoulder—hardly the type of people he typically spoke to. Then his surprise turned to joy when one of the strangers took off her mask.

"Lana! You're alive," he said, his voice full of emotion. "Oh, you're alive!"

Despite his obvious joy, the two priests maintained a respectful distance. He saw tears in her eyes, saying more than words ever could.

"I can't believe it," the old man continued. "Why did you leave Mestèbe? Why leave us in the dark for so long?"

"It's a long story, Your Excellence, and time is not on our side. I can't tell you much, anyhow, to protect you. You shouldn't even have seen me."

The Emaz's face darkened, and he took a step back, looking at his old student's companions. Who were they, and what did they want? It couldn't be . . .

"We need your help to get into the heart of the Holy City," Lana said, imploring Drékin. "It's the only reason I came here. And the only request I have of you."

Drékin shuddered. He was convinced now. They were looking for the book. These strangers wanted the book.

"You're a Maz," he said, buying time to think. "You don't need me to get in."

"I can't reveal myself," Lana explained. "It would be too dangerous."

"And what are your intentions?" he dared to ask. "What will you do once you get in?"

"It's better that you never know," Lana responded. "Rest assured, it is nothing that goes against the Moral."

Drékin paced, thinking. He couldn't show his suspicion. Thirty years in power made it easy.

"You are my friend before anything else," he declared seriously. "You need my help, and I will give it, hoping that you won't betray my confidence."

He hugged the priestess.

"I will find a robe for each of you. I am so happy to see you again, Lana," he said, before leaving the room.

Waiting behind the door until the strangers started talking again, he locked it noiselessly. Then he sent his servants away for one thing or another, before leaving the house himself, heading straight for the Holy City.

He had waited too long for this moment. Always putting it off for another day. For it was, according to Eurydis's teachings, a monstrous crime he was about to commit.

The book had to be destroyed. The book, Maz Achem's journal, returned to the priests a century before, could upend all of the world's religions.

"I don't know if this was a good idea," Rey said as they waited in the priest's study. "We should have stuck to the original plan and gone straight to the Temple's archives."

"Access to the Holy City is guarded," Grigán reminded him. "You saw it yourself."

"The outer wall is covered with cracks, chips, and ivy! Even a child could sneak into the gardens and walk around unnoticed."

"I disagree," Lana said. "Ith is pacifist, but that doesn't mean her guards are incompetent."

The conversation died, as no new arguments could be made. The heirs waited patiently, roaming the large room and admiring the numerous paintings, rugs, and sculptures that represented a diverse set of stories from the goddess's mythology. Corenn paused in front of a large collection of religious texts.

That's when doubt crept into her mind. A horrible doubt. She should have known.

"Lana, what authority manages the archives of the Grand Temple?" she asked.

"The Emaz of Treasure, traditionally," Lana responded. "Emaz Drékin, actually."

Corenn exchanged a look with Grigán, and the warrior ran to the door, to see if their fears had come to fruition.

"It's locked," he said gravely. "We're locked in."

His gaze swept across the room, looking for an escape, but the rare windows were too small for all but Léti. He turned to the door and tested its sturdiness by kicking it twice. The wood was young and had a metal frame. Even with Bowbaq's help, breaking it would take time.

"Reyan, do you have an idea how to open it?" Lana asked, an idea forming in her head.

"And why would I have one, me more than any other, I ask you?" the actor said, feigning surprise. "Do I have such a bad reputation? Do you think, maybe, that all Loreliens spend their youth picking locks?"

The Maz didn't respond, ashamed to have vexed her friend. She had been clumsy and desperate, and had turned to him for help with the hope that he could pull her out of this mess as he had done before.

Bowbaq and Grigán looked for something to ram the door, while Yan discussed with Corenn using magic to get out. Rey simply pouted.

Finally, he announced, "It happens to be true that I have a skeleton key that might be of some use now, but I don't want you to think it's my custom to break locks. I took the object from my cousin's murdered corpse."

Putting action to his words, the actor pulled out a small, complicated key that he jiggled in the lock. The mechanism resisted briefly, and then they all heard a liberating click.

To apologize, Lana gave Rey a deeply grateful smile, which the actor couldn't resist. He gave up pouting and returned to normal—confident, cynical, seductive.

Grigán pushed the door open and jumped into the hallway, blade at the ready to confront any guard. Seeing an empty passage, he signaled to the others to follow him.

"We have to leave this place as quickly as possible," he ordered, as they started walking. "If it's not too late. We might be surrounded already."

"Emaz Drékin wouldn't hand us over," Lana objected, trying to keep up with the warrior.

"Emaz Drékin wasn't supposed to lock us in a room either," Grigán countered. "Where do you think he is right now, if he isn't rounding up the guards? Maybe even the Züu?"

"He went to find the book," Corenn said in a flat voice. "He's the only one who has had access to it for the past nearly thirty years. He knows its contents. He figured out that we were looking for it."

Grigán slowed down as the Mother spoke, then stopped, perplexed. If Corenn was right, they needed to change their plans.

"That's impossible!" Lana persisted. "Why would he hide it from me for all those years? Why keep it secret?"

"Your answers are in your ancestor's journal, friend Lana," Bowbaq declared wisely.

The Maz looked at the ground for a few moments. Grigán looked impatient, but Corenn signaled for him to stop pacing.

When Lana woke from her reverie, her eyes were full of tears. Though she knew a Maz shouldn't pity herself, she found herself doing so again.

"Eurydis has watched over us from the beginning of this quest," Lana said, in a voice she wished sounded more confident.

"The goddess wants us to see it through, and that's what we will do, despite this betrayal. The seven of us, against the world . . ."

The heirs listened to the Maz, disturbed by such frankness, and by the new wave of tears they could see rising to her eyes. The priestess was fearful by nature. From now on, she would know to trust only her traveling companions, those whom, just a few dékades earlier, she had thought of as a lively bunch of madmen.

"We have to find the journal before Drékin does," she said, clearing away her tears. "Grigán, clear our path please. My feet follow yours from now on."

The warrior obeyed without a word. He wasn't insensitive to the fact that the Maz had been betrayed by her mentor, but they had lost a lot of time. Too much.

Drékin wore only a frayed robe and heavy clogs, and when the northern wind blew, it chilled him to his bones. The Emaz wasn't worried about his frail, tired body, though. His greater concern was the persistent feeling that he was being followed, and he cast his eyes over his shoulder frequently. Several times, he thought he saw shadows disappear behind him.

He couldn't say if it had started when he left his home, or when he had entered the Holy City, but the feeling hung on him. The two Temple officers guarding the Tolerance Gate should have stopped anyone shadowing him. Tonight was strange, though. Normally the guards liked to accompany him on his trips to the Holy City, only too happy to assist an Emaz, but tonight there were none. Why had the guards not caught up to him after finding replacements for their gate? Why had their conversation stopped so abruptly once he was out of sight?

Drékin wasn't so bold as to turn around and ask after the guards. No one was following him. The shadows slipping behind him didn't exist. The guards were at their stations and alive; his imagination was getting the better of him.

The only thing that mattered was the book. The cursed journal that destiny had placed in his hands. The book he had dreamed of destroying thousands of times, without ever finishing the task.

Today he would do it. What did knowledge and tolerance matter if these virtues disturbed peace? How could Eurydis's teachings protect something that would challenge their very foundation?

Drékin started to run, something he hadn't done since he was a child. Running, to escape the shadows, death, his responsibilities as Emaz. Lana shouldn't have to bear such a heavy burden. No one could bear it. And the journal's secrets could never, never fall into the wrong hands.

Still running, the Emaz crossed through the Theology Academy's orchard. He passed Aliandra's temple, skirted the rainbow headstones, before reaching the Treasury buildings and, finally, the House of Ancient Archives.

Only then did he stop to catch his breath. He no longer saw the shadows, but he was certain they were there. His own echoing steps couldn't have made so much noise alone . . . a group must have followed him the whole way.

But now, he saw no trace.

Panicked, Drékin rushed over the small bridge to the archives, covering the twenty yards as fast as he could. He threw himself at the door and frantically unlocked it, often glancing back at the bridge. Finally, he scampered into the building and closed the door behind him.

Still, he didn't rest. Breathless, blood pounding in his temples, he lit a candle and held it high to light a wide stairwell covered in dust and debris. At the bottom, he walked across a large, deserted room to reach a hallway.

The shadows still seemed to be hunting him, though the old priest imagined that they might have done so every time he came down here. Every time he had tried to destroy the journal. Every time he had abandoned the task in his cowardice.

"This time, I will do it!" he shouted to the darkness.

Even the sound of his own weak voice scared him as it echoed in the empty rooms. He trembled as he opened the last door, the one leading to the hidden archives, to the dangerous writings, born in the hands of priests whose convictions had grown apart from the Moral of Eurydis.

Drékin scrambled behind a column, squatted, and opened a trapdoor. Climbing down into the cave brought his fear to its peak, but he had no choice. He let himself slide down the ladder, sweating from the effort and a feeling of dread. There was no need for him to search through the piles of journals and papers piled haphazardly in the room—the journal was in the same place as always, where he put it back every time.

He grabbed the book and its blasphemous pages in one hand and held out his candle in the other, bringing the two objects closer. As paper edged toward flame he hesitated, and reconsidered. The shadows danced around him, closing in. The demons in the dark tormenting his conscience.

Drékin slipped the book into his robe and left the cave. The shadows followed, encircling him. He told himself he was going mad, that they were only illusions that would disappear when he took the time to calm down, but time was something he no longer had.

He walked back through the halls, across the large room, and climbed up the stairs, though not as fast as before. He was moving slower than a youth would walk, but he felt the need to run, to flee and leave this cursed place from which he had just stolen a powerful treasure.

He unlocked the door and stepped outside. The light of day blinded him, and he stumbled toward the bridge as if in a dream. There, more shadows emerged from the sun's light. It was Lana and her friends, running toward him with their weapons drawn. They seemed to be yelling something to him.

Watch out?

Drékin stopped in the middle of the bridge and turned around slowly. A dozen novices, dressed like so many others in Ith, approached him—with the slow saunter of predators.

They carried daggers as thin as needles, and their eyes reflected the shadows that still danced around him, impatient to take his soul.

Grigán realized that they wouldn't reach Drékin before the Züu did. He slowed, dropped his sword, and notched an arrow.

"Move!" he yelled at his companions.

Without stopping, the heirs separated enough to give the warrior a shot. They heard a whistling by their ears, and the first Zü fell to the ground. Then, almost instantly, two more whistles and two more felled assassins. Now Drékin himself was in Grigán's way, blocking the Züu.

"What an idiot!" the warrior said as he abandoned his bow and started running again.

Out in front of his companions, Bowbaq saw the Emaz stand on the ledge of the bridge spanning the Alt. Not in haste, not trying to escape his attackers. Like he was waiting.

The high priest pulled an object from his robe and stared at it, fascinated, right up to the moment when ten hati stabbed through his body, sowing their poison in his veins.

Drékin briefly shuddered, then fell into the river's lively currents, bringing Maz Achem's journal, and the heirs' hopes, down with him.

Lana stumbled, shocked as she watched a pack of Züu attack her mentor. Corenn ran to her side and helped her stand. The best thing for them now was to flee; the heirs had nothing else to hold them in the Holy City.

Grigán ordered the retreat, and Yan, Bowbaq, and Rey immediately obeyed, aware of how uneven their odds were against a dozen assassins—but Léti stayed her course.

The older warrior swore and ran back to his bow, realizing he wouldn't have enough arrows. He nocked one and struck down the killer closest to the young woman. How many more were there? Ten? Twelve? More?

Yan and Rey turned around to help Léti, and Bowbaq followed. Grigán kept firing with the energy of the hopeless and trapped. The Züu seemed unconcerned by their losses, and even the injured ones continued to advance, pushed by their fanatical devotion to Zuïa and an endless rage.

This is how I shall die, the warrior thought. *In Ith, two against one, without ever knowing what happened on Ji.*

Out of arrows, he abandoned his useless bow and rushed headlong to meet the Züu. The odds were not with them—five more or less inexperienced heirs running heedlessly toward a band of fanatic assassins—but they were resolute in their charge. Léti, out in front, looked impressive with her rapier and black leather. Yan, behind her, brandished his broadsword, which he had never used. After them came Bowbaq, the nonviolent, and Rey, who was better with his words than with a sword.

Léti took a sharp turn and ran along the river's banks, ignoring the two killers who detached from the other six survivors to follow her. Bowbaq threw his mace at a Zü as soon as he was close enough, to crack the assassin's skull with a dry thwack. Yan stopped abruptly and stayed motionless, waiting for the killers to come toward him.

Grigán turned to help Léti, and two more killers followed him. The warrior saw that the others wouldn't reach Léti, so he turned to face his own pursuers.

Rey and the giant stopped next to Yan, and watched the last three fanatics close the gap between them.

One of them convulsed and let out a painful scream. An instant later, he stabbed both of his accomplices with his hati. The two men collapsed, confusion flashing across their eyes. The stronger one found the energy to reach out and stab his attacker. As he did so, Yan lost consciousness, crying out in pain.

Léti finally found what she was looking for, and jumped into the river. The current was strong, and the water came up to her chest, so she struggled to reach her goal: Emaz Drékin's body, held in place by a submerged tree root.

The two assassins following dove in after her and did their best to gain on her, but their ample robes slowed their progress. Breathless, trying to control her disgust, Léti pulled the journal from Drékin's dead, clasping fingers. She hurried to the other side of the river and climbed out.

Grigán had seen the entire thing, but couldn't intervene. His attackers were trying to surround him, and only his remarkable speed saved him. *Firm footing*, he told himself, repeating his own lessons for Léti. Against two men armed with daggers, he would normally have the upper hand, but a single scratch from a hati would be enough to defeat him.

Rey rushed to his aid, skewering one of the killers in the back, cold-bloodedly. Grigán didn't let the opportunity slip away, and he attacked the second Zü, who was surprised to lose his companion. The surprise was sufficient, and the warrior's final struggle was to pull his curved blade out of the man's body.

Léti ran along her side of the river, stabbing at the Züu who pursued her and preventing them from getting over the bank. But the men quickly realized that they needed to separate. Indecisive, the young woman chose one and stabbed him with her rapier, crying out.

The other Zü removed his wet robe and walked toward her, with a cat's quick, careful movements. Léti faced him, gripping her sword's wet handle, her eyes full of tears.

A crossbow bolt suddenly appeared through the killer's forehead, and he tumbled forward. Léti let him fall to her feet, looking for the person who had saved her.

Corenn was on the other side of the river, still holding the weapon and unable to believe what she had just done. She wasn't even sure she knew how it worked; she had never killed anyone before.

Léti grabbed the journal. A small, wet volume, with thick parchment brimming out of a leather cover hardened with age.

To the Memory of Men. Maz A. d'Algonde.

The young woman delicately opened it and read the first few lines, thanking Yan for having taught her to read. With a fluttering heart, she noticed that the ink had been partially erased by the water. She hoped that the most important parts were intact.

> *What we survived on the island of Ji, and elsewhere, will forever be the greatest disruption to ever threaten humanity . . . and it still threatens us, because this story is not finished. Others will carry our curse. To those, I say: Caution! Your responsibility is the heaviest anyone has ever borne, because your choices and your actions will affect generations of lives.*
>
> *I have no ambition to write a new* Book of the Wise One. *However, this text represents much more than my own memories. It is a tale of eternal warning.*

BOOK VII:
TO THE MEMORY OF MEN

What we survived on the island of Ji, and elsewhere, will forever be the greatest disruption to ever threaten humanity... and it still threatens us, because this story is not finished. Others will carry our curse. To those, I say: Caution! Your responsibility is the heaviest anyone has ever borne, because your choices and your actions will affect generations of lives.

I have no ambition to write a new Book of the Wise One. *However, this text represents much more than my own memories. It is a tale of eternal warning.*

Against all logic, I will start my tale with its conclusion, the one that justifiably terrifies all of the Grand Temple's Emaz. A number of them have reproached me for sowing trouble; even more accuse me of madness and profanity. I am only an apostate, having lost my title and responsibilities. A pariah of the Holy City. Even as my faith and love for Eurydis have never been stronger.

To the Emaz, the Maz, and all the preachers in the world, to all my mortal brothers and sisters, I deliver this message: It is not the gods who inspire evil thoughts. It is man's evil thoughts that breed demons.

Each voice that invokes Phiras gives him more power. Every prayer to Yoos makes mankind more evil. Every sacrifice from the Valipondes creates nightmarish monsters—more and more, stronger and stronger. And it will continue until a time when men no longer dream of the Age of Ys with hope, but rather with nostalgia, like the memory of a beautiful dream, never experienced.

The teaching of Sage Eurydis advocates tolerance and peace. I have defended these values my entire life, and I deny them now. Do we heal wolves that butcher children? No, of course not. So in Ith, why do we host the dark souls who have decided to openly worship our goddess's enemies? Why should we, in our universal quest, pander to the very enemy we are fighting against?

Because that's exactly what this is: a battle with no possible truce, and one that will end by annihilating one of the two sides. The moralists or the demonists. Virtue or black magic. Good or Evil.

I can remember letting myself get carried away during my speeches. Letting it slip that I think we must resort to force, to war even. We must begin a crusade, one that cannot end until all mankind has forgotten the names of the black gods.

More often, the idea filled me with shame, and I rejected this contradictory violence with the same reasons I used to incite it. But sometimes . . . sometimes I think that infringing on the Moral would be a lesser evil, difficult to accomplish and painful to our conscience, but perhaps a necessary preparation for mankind to defend the threatened Age of Ys.

You, the Emaz, have declared me a heretic for defending these ideas. Very well, forget the crusade, and let the souls of evil men proliferate in the Holy City. But prevent them from converting weak minds, the lost, the unsuspecting, those who live and let live, and all the naïve idle minds that fill their ranks.

I deny Tolerance. Every mortal who dedicates himself to the black gods does more than just delay the arrival of the Age of Ys. He becomes its enemy.

I deny Peace. We have always thought it was enough to wait. An error. We have to fight.

Victory is not assured, simply because we represent Good. There is no universal law that gives us an advantage. All is in equilibrium; the other side has as much a chance as we do.

Lana stopped reading. Her companions thought she needed to pause to gather her thoughts, as she was obviously suffering from an array of powerful emotions. That wasn't the case, though.

"The rest is illegible," she said. "I can't read it."

"It's erased?" Corenn asked, worried.

"No . . . but his words don't make any sense. It looks almost like a foreign language. Maybe a code?"

The Maz passed the journal to her friends, who glanced at it before returning it to her. Together, Lana, Rey, and Corenn knew six languages, but none of them recognized the particular use of the Ithare alphabet used for the rest of the text.

"Look at later sections," Grigán proposed. "Maybe there are some easier passages?"

The Maz did just that, despairing that she couldn't satisfy her curiosity immediately. Léti had given her the journal a deciday earlier, on the riverbank, but Lana hadn't had time to examine it as they fled the Holy City. After only a few pages, such disappointment! By the grace of Eurydis, what a cruel destiny.

"Achem must have written everything related to Ji in code," Yan suggested. "A way of respecting his oath."

"But he already betrayed that oath," Rey argued, "by revealing some of Jal'dara's secrets to the other Emaz."

"He never mentioned Jal'dara," Lana corrected. "Neither in his speeches, nor in this text. He did not betray them."

"He still used the information to influence the Temple," the actor responded. "Either way, it's not important. Who other than a Maz could care about these barren discourses on good and evil?"

Lana interrupted her research to stare at the actor. *She* had understood all of the implications of the text, and had imagined that her friends understood as well.

"It goes much further than theological debates, Reyan," she said in a serious voice. "Did you not understand? The secret of our ancestors is here, laid bare, *black and white*. All this is why they suffered!"

"I don't think I understood either, friend Lana," Bowbaq intervened timidly.

The Maz looked to Corenn for support, hoping that she at least had understood the revelations. Luckily, that was the case, and the Mother summarized the situation much better than the Maz could have.

"If Achem is telling the truth, a god's power is linked to the amount of attention humans give. To be more clear: the more a cult spreads, the stronger their god becomes."

"At least, while they are still children," Lana clarified. "The Poem of Romerij only mentions children."

"If that is true," Corenn continued, "then men and women could gather and together *form* a new god, endowing it with a name, a character, and particular powers to suit their own purposes."

"Excuse me," Rey interrupted. "How can one *use* a god? I don't mean to be offensive, but do you know what you're saying?"

"Try to have an open mind," Corenn advised. "Having seen the portal on Ji, the ghosts, the Mog'lur, surely by now you must believe in gods?"

"Their existence, yes. Now, yes. But from belief to thinking we can invoke them by snapping our fingers, and have them do our chores..."

"It's certainly possible," Lana responded, "if a god is *formed* with this in mind. By Eurydis! All of this is so disturbing. Sacrilegious!"

"Impolite?" offered Bowbaq, who looked more and more disturbed himself.

"In a way, yes. Mankind can create gods and make them slaves . . . What a horror! What chaos! We aren't ready for that power."

Finally, they all understood their ancestors' curse, and their responsibility. An informed humanity would either undergo a great spiritual evolution or tumble into madness. Should they share the secret, or not?

From then on, the heirs would also bear this burden. From then on, they would fear the Züu for another reason, much more serious than their own survival. And if Zuïa were one day powerful enough to walk among men? If Phiras, strengthened by prayer, materialized and became the oppressive demon his followers worshipped? And if Soltan, Yoos, and K'lur manifested?

Perhaps they already had. Perhaps man's dark thoughts had brought demons into the world already, in the kingdoms where they were strongest. Perhaps, even, man's fear was enough to give the gods strength . . . as much as the adoration of their reckless worshippers.

From then on, the heirs would be unable to hear a demon's name without trembling, without thinking that, somewhere in the world, or in another close by, the entity existed and was listening.

"Revealing this secret would unleash mayhem," Grigán said.

"But it can't be that easy," Léti said. "There must have to be thousands, hundreds of thousands of believers to *create* a god. It must take many centuries."

"Maybe. Maybe not. How can we know?"

No one responded. The implications of this discovery were endless, and they understood so little. They could spend days discussing it without making any progress—as their ancestors probably had. But whereas their ancestors discussed only theories of gods, their heirs faced the real thing. An immediate threat, of which Bowbaq reminded them.

"Could something in here help us defeat Saat?" he asked, without much hope for a positive answer.

Corenn shook her head regretfully. Nothing that they had found in the Deep Tower of Romine or in Maz Achem's journal hinted at how Saat could have reappeared a century after his death, filled with power and a desire to exterminate the heirs.

"The solution might be in the rest of the text; we just have to figure out the code," Lana said.

"And what should we do until then?" Rey asked. "That could take days."

They turned toward Grigán and Corenn, waiting for their leaders to make a decision. For the first time in dékades, the pair were indecisive.

"We can't stay in Ith," Grigán confirmed. "Not after what happened. The Züu will find us."

They all agreed on this point. They didn't know how the killers could have been waiting for them in the Holy City. It was as if their enemy knew their every move.

"Saat is somewhere behind the Curtain . . . ," Corenn suggested softly, waiting to see Grigán's reaction.

His eyes opened in surprise, then his expression turned pensive. He stood, paced, and looked at the tall mountains looming over the forest where they hid.

"I don't think so," he started to say, turning back toward the group.

Six people were waiting for him to decide. Six people counted on him, to show them their path forward. But Grigán saw no better way than Corenn's. If he had been alone, he wouldn't have hesitated.

"All right," he said grudgingly. "We will find Saat on the other side of the mountains."

For the first time in years, the warrior would travel to unknown territory, hoping to find the man who haunted their lives, and who shared Jal'dara's secret.

That night, the heirs camped on the banks of the Beremen, one of the two rivers that crossed the capital of the Grand Empire to join the Alt. After several decidays, they had already crossed a third of the empire's eastern expanse.

Although the Curtain Mountains had the reputation of being impassable, particularly at the start of the cold season, some Goranese patrols roamed the mountains to prevent enemy infiltration. Thanks to Grigán's experience, the heirs had already avoided two of them, and had been inspected by a third with no trouble. The Goranese gave them no grief, and Corenn deduced that they were truly at war with the Thalittes, and not against Lorelia. This helped confirm Saat's presence behind the Curtain.

They hadn't stopped moving since Lana had read the introduction to her ancestor's journal, and they hadn't discussed their immediate problem: the next direction to take. As they rode, they all had time to meditate on recent events. They didn't speak about the luck that had kept them all alive during their confrontation with the Züu in the Holy City.

Grigán and Corenn reproached Léti, more for form than anything, for ignoring the command to retreat and putting the entire group in danger. But since her initiative had paid off, the lecture was useless. Léti accepted each critique, but saw gratitude from the rest of the group, especially Lana.

The Maz confessed she was shocked by Rey's actions.

"Attacking from behind, that's not a fair fight, Rey."

"They just stabbed Drékin," Rey reminded her, a little annoyed. "Do you think they deserve a fair fight?"

"*The stupid get drunk, the wise only want to,*" the Maz recited pedantically. "We don't have to act like them, Reyan."

"And what should I have done, according to you? Asked him to turn around? Give him the chance to stab me?" Rey asked incredulously.

Lana didn't know how to respond. Eurydis defended Peace, but was silent when it came to situations where that was impossible.

"Excuse me, Reyan," she asked soon after. "I spoke with the ease of ignorance. I didn't fight. And I have no desire to lose you," she finished softly.

The actor accepted her apology with a smile, and changed the subject by complimenting Corenn's unknown talent with a crossbow.

"To be honest, you are better with it than I," he said. "If you want, I will offer it to you as a gift!"

The Mother shook her head, looking embarrassed. She did not regret what she had done; she regretted having the need to do it. Killing a man in cold blood.

Yet it wasn't really cold blood. When she saw Léti fall for the assassins' trap, the Mother lost control of herself. If she had been thinking, she would have used magic against her enemies, breaking a rule she had repeated hundreds of times to Yan: *Never call upon your Will under the influence of rage, suffering, or liquor.*

She looked at the timid young man, who hardly spoke during their discussions. Everyone knew, without him saying as much, that he had used magic to kill three of the assassins. Yan had entered another person's mind and taken control of his body. It had only taken a moment, and it appeared to be easy. Too easy.

When the moment came for him to tell his story, the conversation died. For the nonmagicians, the astounding growth in Yan's powers was too frightening to be casually mentioned, so they tacitly avoided the subject. For Bowbaq, the event was more evidence of Yan's aptitude. Yan had touched another's deep mind, and Bowbaq could only feel respect for his young friend.

For Corenn, watching Yan's growth was an immense joy... and brought an even stronger feeling of dread. It exceeded her abilities to help, as more and more things did.

If Yan, a magician for only two moons, was capable of such wonders, what powers might a two-hundred-year-old sorcerer have? And what could they do against such a man?

An execution ceremony. The largest Zamerine and Emaz Chebree had ever organized, to serve both as an example, and as a way to reinforce the respectful fear the slaves felt for Somber.

Five Thalitte prisoners had tried to escape, and three had been caught the next day by the Züu who had been sent after them. The two other prisoners had had no better luck; their heads had simply been added to the others decorating Somber's altar.

Rumors circulated that the god's temple, once it was finished, would hold the skulls of the more than eighty thousand slaves who built it. It would be a gigantic building. However, that wasn't the reason for all of the work. Even after building Somber's altar, a palace for Saat and his captains, and other houses and fortification walls, Zamerine hadn't known what to do with the hundreds of quintals of rock extracted from the mountain.

Giving in to a fantasy, he ordered the construction of arenas similar to those in Lus'an. The idea greatly pleased the High Diarch, and building the arenas became a priority equal to the temple. The High Diarch's encouragement also served as the impetus for this ceremony.

To highlight the event's importance—the first of its kind for the New Order—Zamerine had selected eleven additional agitators, including two Wallattes from their own army. Along with the three fugitives, he had fourteen victims who would suffer a memorable ceremony.

When the day finally arrived, once again, after many years, Zamerine sat as a Judge. Thousands of miles away from Lus'an, Zuïa's law spread over the world.

Behind him sat the diarchs, one wearing his ever-present helm, and the other with an unreadable expression. Two chiefs, inflexible, confident, respected. Feared.

To Saat's right was Emaz Chebree. The barbarian queen, grand priestess, attached to her master's side with a predatory smile. Like the others—maybe more than the others—she waited with morbid fascination to see the torture.

Zamerine had been placed to the Young Diarch's left, but didn't have the courage to stay there. A few dékades earlier, the Judge had complained about the laconic young man's silence and absolute indifference, which scared him more than he could explain. His feeling of dread was worse now that the Young Diarch had woken. His laughter was scornful and cruel, his gaze pierced Zamerine's soul, and his voice, on the rare occasions he used it, was heavy and oppressive, carrying a hidden menace. The Zü did his best to avoid him.

Half of the troops from their army filled most of the arena's bleachers. The men present in the audience had earned the honor by luck or as a prize for a job well done.

On the other side of the arena was a much quieter crowd: several hundred slaves, chosen to carry tales of Somber's power, and the cruelty of the diarchs and their captains, to their brothers and sisters.

The first convict was brought to the arena's center by a group of Egosie horsemen, chosen by Zamerine for the way the other warriors, even the proud gladores, respected them. The prisoner was naked and weaponless in the sand.

Three Farikii walked out into the arena to great applause. The vampire rats' handlers each had five beasts that they released simultaneously, to the crowd's delight.

The condemned man screamed and ran, but there would be no escape. Soon the fifteen famished monsters caught up to him, and he tried to fight them off, screaming and struggling, before succumbing to a second round of attacks. While he shrieked in pain, the warriors laughed deeply and the slaves looked on in horror.

It was only an introduction, a first course. Soon the laughter faded, and the Farikii gathered their rats, letting the convict wither on the ground, his body almost bloodless and riddled with wounds.

Saat spoke briefly to the crowd once it was done. Zamerine knew his master's words well, even when reformulated and embellished. They always served the same purpose: to push and galvanize men by evoking images of conquest, wealth, and power. As always, the thickheaded brutes who composed their army let Saat's powerful oration overwhelm them, and his final words were greeted by the clamor of hundreds of blades hammering against armor. Versed as he was in diplomacy and manipulation, Zamerine was almost bored by the whole demonstration. What followed, however, surprised him greatly.

Saat invited Chebree forward with a gesture, and she stepped up hastily. This wasn't part of the program. She wasn't supposed to talk until the end of the ceremony. Had they changed the plan without warning him?

Building Somber's cult had never been a priority for Zamerine, who remained loyal to Zuïa. Still, he helped Chebree whenever he could, whether that meant supplying soldiers and slaves or building the temple. He didn't follow their new god, but was that a sufficient reason to remove him from important decisions?

"Today is a great day," Chebree shouted. "Today, the reign of He Who Vanquishes begins!"

A thundering applause greeted this introduction, though it hardly revealed anything. The next part elicited even more applause:

"Today, Somber condescends to join us! In front of you, in this arena. Punishing the faithless who oppose his will."

Zamerine heard the warriors cry out in ignorant joy. A *god*? A god would appear, invoked by a bunch of barbarians who hadn't known his name the year before?

The strange couple, Saat and Chebree, sat, and the Zü signaled for the ceremony to continue, vacillating between impatience for the promised event and disbelief.

Rambunctious cheering greeted the two men who entered the arena next. Most of this applause was directed at Gor the Gentle, the warrior's warlord, rather than for Dyree, Saat's official executioner. While Gor strutted and waved to the crowd like a street performer, Dyree, who had no taste for fame, waited for the condemned.

Eight were pushed into the arena, hungry, harassed, and desperate. Gor insulted them in all the languages he knew, followed loudly by the violent crowd.

One of the victims decided to get it over with quickly and approached the apostles. The Wallatte giant charged him after a few steps. Gor threw him to the ground, kicked him while he was down, then picked him up and crushed his skull with a loud crack.

Gor thanked the cheering crowd with a bow. The remaining condemned huddled together, whispering. Five separated from the group and walked slowly toward the apostles. These ones wanted to at least try to survive.

The giant grabbed his two-handed axe and smiled. In sharp contrast, Dyree looked bored, holding only a simple dagger and leaving his hati sheathed. Against all expectations, he threw the dagger at the feet of the two slaves who hadn't yet moved. To Dyree, they were either the smartest or the most cowardly. The Zü liked a worthy adversary.

The larger of the two condemned men grabbed the blade and approached, staying as far away as possible from Gor and his whirring axe. The other followed at his heels.

The two men tried in vain to surround Dyree, who effortlessly slipped out of their circle on one side or the other. Eventually the Zü stopped, crossed his arms, and let the unarmed slave circle around him. Finally the man jumped, trying to distract Dyree and hoping his friend would have enough time to stab him.

But Dyree was too fast. He turned and hit the man's exposed throat with his open palm. The man collapsed, unable to breathe. With three rapid steps, the Zü escaped the armed man, whose attack wasn't fast enough to take advantage of his partner's death.

Gor handled his battle with as much skill. He could have disposed of his adversaries in a few leisurely movements with his immense axe, but the giant enjoyed playing with his prey, injuring, mutilating, and cutting off limbs before splitting heads with a precise swing.

The man with the dagger glared at Dyree nervously. The killer stood only three feet away, hands behind his back, smiling. They were both waiting for the other to make the first move.

Dyree showed his empty hands and signaled the warrior to approach. The terrified man didn't want to move an inch, so the killer closed the remaining distance between them. Then the slave committed himself fully and jumped at his adversary. He didn't even see the hati as it pierced his throat. With extraordinary speed, the killer had unsheathed and struck.

Gor had also finished his "battle," and the crowd hailed their captains as they left the arena, satisfied with a job well done.

Emaz Chebree returned to the stand for another speech. It was incredible how quickly silence spread over the raucous crowd. The eastern tribes were quite superstitious. Was it possible that a god would really appear?

The last five men were pushed into the arena, joining the nine corpses left in place, along with a few limbs and a great deal of blood. Seeing what waited for them, the slaves fell to their knees and begged for mercy, in the name of He Who Vanquishes. They had no idea that they were being sacrificed to him.

The Emaz asked for a long silence, and a hush descended over the crowd. Then Chebree invoked the god's name in a whisper, which grew louder and louder as she signaled for everyone to follow her lead. The entire arena, then the encampment, resonated with the sound—"Somber! Somber! SOMBER! SOMBER!" shouted by thousands of voices, the name of the god echoing off the mountains.

Even the victims prayed, hopeless and mad. They stopped when a form materialized in the middle of the arena, obscuring the murdered bodies and blood. Everyone stopped, even the shouting warriors, to better observe the horrible monster appearing out of the ether.

The last slaves died as quickly as the others, but it was Somber who killed them, with sophisticated, implacable cruelty.

He was He Who Vanquishes. Not He Who Takes Pity.

While the crowd watched, fascinated, as their god demonstrated his power, Zamerine glanced at the Young Diarch. And he knew. Seeing the face, usually so impassive, deformed by hate, he knew.

No one knew the name of Saat's presumed son. It was simply the Young Diarch. Now, now he had one. His reign was beginning. Somber. Somber. SOMBER.

On the fifth day of the dékade of the Earth, the heirs stopped for the night at an inn near the Warrior's Vale. The narrow band of earth between the Curtain Mountains and the Ocean of Mirrors was the best route to reach the Eastian Kingdoms, and, in truth, the only practical one. The other involved traveling close to Yérim's coast, then through the Sea of Fire before crossing the desert called the Sea of Sand on foot.

Apart from the innkeeper and his wife, the establishment was empty; times of war weren't favorable for commerce. The heirs were treated like kings for a time, until the Goranese learned their destination. After that, they were asked to pay for all the services they had been offered.

"You don't seem too confident we'll return," Rey commented. "Yet your inn is perfect for expeditions east; you must have built it with that in mind."

"Mister, I gave credit to one such traveler, who had gained my trust after being a client for many years. He visited Thallos, Sola, Greloes, and other mysterious places. He bartered for goods, learned their languages and customs, and brought back souvenirs. Then he headed back to the east, his mind full of foolish dreams of easy money and discovery. Mister, for six moons, no one has come back. It's really a war over there, you know. In the past dékade, more soldiers have come to my door than I've seen my whole life."

After his tirade, the innkeeper turned and walked away, showing no desire to discuss his demands for immediate payment. Since Rey had asked the question only out of curiosity, he didn't bother to pursue the subject further.

Corenn worried that Grigán would change his mind after such a warning, and watched the warrior's face for a reaction. But he stuck to their decision, for he had known the dangers well before they had gone down this path.

The heirs rested and ate in the inn's small common room, decorated with diverse objects from the east. Hanging from the wall or leaning on the stairs were numerous weapons and pieces of armor, a few tapestries, diverse tools, hunting trophies, and other curiosities. Léti noticed a thistle and a spitter, both weapons she had seen in Junine, but that was only a small sample of the eastern warriors' genius. Every blade, arrow tip, and pike tip was barbed and equipped with hooks that ripped flesh. The innkeeper showed them a Yalamine shield, which had sharp, lengthened edges, allowing its wielder to use it like a scythe.

Bowbaq demonstrated his progress with Ifio by having the monkey do a set of tricks, including bringing them bread and soup and even refilling their empty glasses. They all enjoyed the distraction, especially the monkey, who seemed to prefer Bowbaq's training methods to Tonk's.

Yan hadn't used his erjak powers since the episode in the Holy City. Penetrating into a monkey's mind was one thing, but in the heat of action, Yan had invaded and controlled a human spirit. Worse yet, an assassin's, and the memory left a bitter taste in his mouth. He wanted to speak to Bowbaq, but the giant feared Corenn's rebuke. Hadn't she told him to stop discussing the deep mind?

After they finished their meal, Lana took her leave and returned to her room. They all understood the Maz's solitary focus. She had but one goal: to decrypt her ancestor's journal, something she had failed to do thus far.

Grigán followed her lead, to everyone's surprise. Rey and Yan exchanged a glance, fearful that his sickness was coming back. Annoyed by their worrying, the warrior assured them that he felt well, but the coming days would be difficult. He counseled that they all needed to get some sleep.

Bowbaq obeyed Grigán's advice like an order and quickly went to bed, Ifio following at his heels. Corenn and Rey followed soon after, leaving Yan and Léti alone for the first time in what felt like years.

The young Kauliens smiled timidly, disturbed by their rediscovered intimacy. Neither of them wanted to ruin the moment. Neither of them knew how to say so.

Léti played absentmindedly with the medallion Yan had given her, and the young man distractedly grasped his three-queen charm, idly turning it over his fingers.

"Will you show me someday?" the young woman asked, looking at the coin.

Happy to please her, Yan placed the coin on the table and applied his Will. An instant later, the metallic disk rose slowly from the table and began to gradually turn. Léti was enthralled, and her face lit up. Seeing this, Yan made a goblet float as well, then a pair of knives, then a plate, then a half-full pitcher, and eventually all of the dishes were floating a foot above the table. Their reflections glistened in front of an awestruck Léti.

"It's magnificent," she whispered, sparks in her eyes.

As are you, Yan thought. *Do it, tell her, now! Tell her. Ask for her Promise. Now.*

"Horrors!" a voice cried behind him.

Yan's concentration broke and all the dishes clashed on the wood, before smashing on the floor. The innkeeper was standing at the kitchen's entrance, his eyes like saucers. Only Usul knew what he was thinking.

"I'm sorry, I woke too quickly," Yan mumbled, blushing to his ears. "I will pay you."

The man nodded, lips sealed, contemplating the destruction, and the young warrioress, who laughed so hard she couldn't breathe.

Yan helped the man clean up, and Léti joined them. She didn't lose her smile, the same knowing smile from when they were kids, but Yan felt like crying. It felt like only Usul's darkest prophecies were coming true.

Someone knocked softly at Lana's door, and she peeked out to find a smiling Rey with a bottle of green Junian wine.

"The teachings of Eurydis encourage hospitality," he reminded her boldly. "May I enter?"

Lana moved out of the way, letting him into her room, half-amused and half-worried. She wasn't as naïve as Rey thought. It was clear he was doing his best to charm her.

Then, looking at his noble bearing, his gracious movements, and his look that seemed to drink her in—and remembering his courage, his thoughtfulness, and his inalterable optimism—she realized it was already done. Rey made her happy. Consequently, she had to be much more careful.

"The Maz never drink, Reyan," she warned him, looking at the bottle.

"No matter, it was only for me," the actor retorted, laughing. "I'm kidding, I'm kidding," he said, seeing her blush. "How goes the decryption?"

"Not well, I'm afraid," the Maz responded, delighted the subject had taken a turn. "Do you want to see my progress?"

"I would love that."

Lana gathered her notes, conscious that Rey cared more about her presence than her work.

"You see," she said, showing him the journal, "the place where the introduction ends. The rest is written with words that are all shorter than four letters, for the most part. One out of five has only one letter. And they make no sense, in any language from the Upper Kingdoms."

"You summarized that very well," the actor said, staring at Lana's face.

"I had hoped there would be other legible sections," she continued, "in the pages stuck together from the water. I did my best to save them . . . but that wasn't enough; it was too late. Look for yourself."

Regretfully, Rey turned his eyes to the old notebook. On the open page, the text was almost entirely erased and illegible. The remaining, faded ink had been turned into a series of smeared lines, melancholy and meaningless on the warped parchment.

Rey softly picked it up and cautiously leafed through a few pages. The same damage repeated itself throughout the central part of the journal. More than three-quarters of Maz Achem's confession was lost for good. Only the first and the last pages, partially protected by the thick leather cover, had survived the disaster.

"We have to tell Corenn," the actor asserted, suddenly very serious. "And Grigán."

"Not yet, Rey," Lana tempered. "Will it change our plans? No, not at all. I finally have a role in our drama, and it's not so urgent that we need to tell the others immediately."

"But . . . why not right now? If Grigán catches wind of this secret, you can be sure he'll knock me on my ass for it!"

"We should protect their hope, Reyan. If only for Léti, who took such a great risk to bring this book back to us. I won't tell them until I have decoded the rest," she said.

The actor nodded, pensive. He wasn't sure he agreed with the Maz. The idea of protecting hope seemed absurd to him.

"Hidden truths are polite lies," he said, instead of contradicting her. "But why did you tell me?"

Lana blushed again and avoided his covetous gaze. She looked for an innocent response, but couldn't find one, and left the question unanswered. For once, Rey had the tact not to insist, and he focused instead on the encrypted text.

"If Achem wrote an original version that he recopied and encoded in this journal, we may never find the key," he said after considering the text. "But if he wrote *directly* on these pages . . ."

Lana listened to Rey and admired his thinking. Although she was the one who had been working with the text for three days, she had never thought to put herself in her ancestor's shoes. She thought of herself as intelligent, and at least aware, but the Lorelien was clever.

"If he wrote directly," he continued, "it's useless to look for some complicated code of numbers and letters replaced or moved. He would have to have written *almost* naturally. How would I have done it . . ."

The Maz had never seen Rey look so serious. His sudden interest in Achem's journal was enough for him to forget Lana. If he was speaking out loud, it was more to help him think than to explain his thinking. Lana saw a part of the actor she hadn't known: although he was sometimes rebellious, thoughtless, rude, and cynical, he was also capable of respect and clearly enjoyed problems of the mind. She was convinced now that she could teach him to appreciate the virtues of Eurydis. And this idea, for very personal reasons, filled her with joy and hope.

Rey looked at one of the pages in silence. He was already certain that the letters didn't correspond to syllables, at least if the text were composed in Ithare, as the introduction had been. It was useless to try mixing and matching the clusters of letters.

Examining more closely, he realized that the letters had been written one by one; the fine lines linking each proved that Achem had picked up his hand after each letter. *The Maz was spelling out words.* Since he had already rejected the idea that Achem had written in a code where letters replaced other letters, Rey hoped that each letter corresponded to exactly the words Achem wanted to write. Spelling the words across lines? Maybe across an entire page, or several?

Impassioned by this discovery, Rey tried to associate the first letter of the first line with the second, then the second with the first, but with no results. He tried again, alternating between the first and third lines, and his heart pounded as he read: *n-e-v-e-r.*

"I think I found it," he said feverishly. "A stroke of luck," he added, considering Lana, who had struggled for two days with the mystery.

But the Maz had no unhealthy pride, which prevents one who fails from admiring others who succeed. She asked him for the solution and transcribed, on a new parchment, the first part of Achem's story: *Never had I expected . . .*

"Thank you, Reyan," she said, her words brimming with emotion. "Thank you for giving me hope."

The actor found the moment ripe for a kiss, and Lana briefly enjoyed the embrace, before gently pushing her friend away.

"Forgive me, Rey," she said, with a ravishing smile. "But, I have to know," she said, pointing to the journal. "I need to know."

Rey placed a finger to his lips and left the room with a wink.

Alone, and despite the torrent of emotions rushing through her, Lana grabbed the journal and began her transcription. She woke Corenn before the night was over.

Never had I expected to be absent from the Grand Temple for six dékades, when I accepted the mission to Lorelia. Never had I imagined that we would leave Ji, our meeting place, for a distant destination where our assembly would decide something no less important than the relationship between gods and men.

At first, I took Nol the Strange to be a hoax, a man cherishing his hoarded secrets and the mysterious play he was directing. On the Day of the Owl in the year 771, he had us wait until nightfall to hear any explanation. If I hadn't been concerned about a lost opportunity for the Ithare people, I would have immediately taken the ship for Maz Nen, leaving Nol to his fantasies. Later, I learned that many of the emissaries had felt the same way.

Many nations were present that day. I met Prince Vanamel Uborre and his counselor, Saat the Treasurer, whom I knew already from when I was an ambassador to the Grand Empire. There were many other royal characters, most of whom would become my dearest friends. King Arkane of Junine, Reyan Kercyan, the honored Mother Tiramis and her guard, Yon, son of Kaul's Ancestress. There was also chief Ssa-Vez from far-away Jezeba, the general Rafa Derkel of Griteh, and finally the wise Arque, Moboq.

From we ten, only seven would return from our strange voyage. King Arkane would lose an arm. All of us would end up losing money, titles, land, and the respect of our peers. Our vows of silence made us pariahs, even, as we thought, we protected humanity.

But I'm getting ahead of the story. That day, as dusk approached, we could think only of Nol and his mysteries. Of the coming revelations that he had hinted would be overwhelming. So, as night fell, we followed him through the labyrinth of rocks without hesitation. Without hesitation, but with plenty of surprise. Hadn't he promised to bring us somewhere else?

Nol led us deep into the island. I think he intentionally followed a few false trails to discourage any shadowing from any of our nations. We emissaries, impassioned by such mystery, joked in quiet voices. I spoke with the wise Moboq, only too happy to demonstrate my knowledge of the Arque language.

After a time, though, only our destination filled our minds, and, following Nol's mute lead, we walked in complete silence, drinking in every aspect of the landscape.

The strange man soon brought us into a grotto, and we followed him down into the dark, with a rising fear. What if this were all just an elaborate kidnapping, as many had predicted? Were we headed straight for a trap?

I noticed with relief that there was no one and nothing in the grotto, and my mind turned to wondering why Nol would have brought us here. Was he expecting us to negotiate something, by lantern light, seated on the sand?

But Nol didn't stop, and he walked deeper into the cavern before turning down a narrow, natural hall hidden in a recess. We walked down this new, gently sloping passage to arrive at the edge of an underground lake more than one hundred yards wide.

It was dead quiet. We already knew that our escorts would have trouble finding us if anything went wrong, and Nol wanted to take us even deeper underground. The adventure was taking a fantastic turn, so extraordinary and bizarre that we all felt a heaviness in the air. And we hadn't even seen anything unnatural or supernatural. Not yet.

Nol guided us along a ledge that circled the lake on the left and ended at a fissured wall. He checked that we were all still there, and then he confidently walked through the narrow fissure.

I followed, between Moboq and Rafa de Griteh, wondering if there really was an exit to this cave. A gallery opening in front of me was my answer, and I filed into the new room with the others. It was a large space, though smaller than the one with the lake, and its ceiling reached high above us.

With a sign, Nol signaled to us to wait while he crossed the cavern alone, wetting his feet in a small freshwater pond. By the distant sound of waves and salty odors, I realized that the ocean wasn't far: probably at the bottom of the chasm over which our guide was leaning.

I decided to see for myself and joined Nol cautiously, accompanied by Moboq and Vanamel. Nol seemed somewhat vexed by our presence; not angry, but worried. Enough so that he broke his habitual silence and spoke:

"What happens next, do not fear, do not cry out, and do not flee. Do not intervene; you are in no danger."

Rather than reassure me, his warning did the opposite. I leaned out over the edge to try to see the bottom, in vain. I was tempted to drop my lantern to get a better look, but I needed its reassuring light.

All the emissaries soon joined us, and Nol motioned for us to step back and to wait along the rocky walls. Then he spoke, though his words weren't meant for us. From his mouth came an unknown language, and he spoke it directly to the void. Again and again he repeated the same sounds as he looked into the darkness. It seemed as if he were calling someone, or something.

And something responded.

Something alive climbed up to the ledge. We heard it well before we saw it. The noises were so dreadful and powerful that I thought I wouldn't have the courage to wait for its arrival. It sounded like an immense body pulling itself out of the water, followed by the din of crashing waves and a swirling sound, like the pulling up of a large anchor. Then came a loud breathing, ten times louder than a wild bull. Then the scratching, scurrying sounds of giant claws climbing the cliff walls, intermingling with the sounds of panting, growling, and the crashing waves.

Despite the warning, Ssa-Vez of Jezeba pulled out his bow and nocked an arrow. Nol saw and signaled for him to put down the weapon, advice the Jez, nearly in a full state of panic, didn't follow. Nol's gaze turned to the bow, which suddenly snapped in half. Ssa-Vez fell back onto the wall and didn't move, his terror rendering him mute and immobile.

My nerves were shaken too, and as I scanned the faces of my companions, I could see that none of them had much courage for what we were about to face. We stood stock-still, afraid to breathe, ready to run. We stared into the obscurity and waited for the monster to arrive.

First we saw an enormous hand, or something more like a paw, grab the edge of the floor. It had scaly, leathery, dark-blue skin that shimmered in our lantern light. It had four fingers that ended in claws like ice axes. Then came the rest of the arm, as tall as a man and as thick as an oak trunk. Finally, the creature's head appeared.

No one breathed. No one moved. The monster stared at each of us, its eyes as big as fists, and growled. Hostilely, I thought.

Nol spoke, and the creature quieted, though it didn't stop staring at us with its contorted face, even as the Strange calmed it with his soft voice.

What we could see of its body resembled a human's, in a general way, except for the head, which was as wide as a barrel and as deformed as ozün fruit. It had no eyelids and no nose. Its neck was swollen with strange gills that regularly flared out. Its mouth was enormous, and had several rows of pointy teeth, like so many bear traps. The creature from the abyss stared at us hatefully.

It started to move again, and Nol stopped talking. I hoped that it was a sign of victory, and not of failure. I wanted to look for Nol's reaction, but my eyes couldn't stop watching the monster finish its climb.

The rest of its body looked nothing like a human. Apart from its hips, the creature had all the parts of a gigantic crustacean. Eight legs with many joints protected by a thick carapace, of which four legs had impressive claws folded underneath. The monster was three times taller than any of us, and at its full height it loomed above our heads like something born out of our worst nightmares.

It walked past us slowly, with an unreadable expression. The sharp clicking of its claws and the hissing of its gills echoed off the walls, strangling us with dread.

"But . . . what is this thing?" Moboq found the courage to ask.

"One of the Eternal Guardians," Nol responded. "One of your oldest gods. He is called Reexyyl, one of the last Leviathans."

"One of our gods? What do you mean?"

Nol ignored the question. Later, we would have all the answers we desired and more, but right then we couldn't keep our eyes off of the monster as it approached the cavern's center.

A light buzzing began to fill the room, growing louder and louder. Soon it became a jarring whistle, and my eyes searched for its origin in vain. The terrible sound seemed to come from everywhere, though it soon quieted, with a kind of hiccup.

In the center of the room, where the Leviathan had stopped, the shadows were strangely agitated. They faded as a light appeared. The light was small at first, just a pinprick among the shadows, or a distant and dying star, but soon it began to grow, reaching high into the air, bathing the cavern in a pale glow.

It was then that I finally saw the symbols carved into the walls and ceiling of the cavern, even as something else pulled my attention away. The light diminished slowly, leaving behind a blurry view, as if something was hidden behind a slowly lifting fog. As it lifted, I saw a landscape. Not the cavern in front of us, but a beautiful valley with a promising dawn rising.

The creature seemed to completely ignore the phenomenon; it simply turned toward us, or more toward Nol, seemingly waiting for something.

"What is . . . What is this place that we can see, against all logic?" Vanamel asked.

"It's the gardens of Dara," Nol responded gently. "Our destination."

Everyone, me included, was eager to get closer and look into the beautiful valley, but the creature's proximity froze our heated desires.

"Just how well can you control this Leviathan?" I asked nervously. "By Eurydis, he doesn't seem to appreciate our presence! Is there any risk he will attack in a sudden rage?"

"Not Reexyyl," Nol assured us, after reflecting. "Not as long as I am with you."

Later we learned that Nol had sometimes lost control of certain Eternal Guardians, the last having been the Wyvern of Oo. If he had told us then, I don't think we would have walked through the portal.

However, at the time, that's exactly what we did, guided by the Strange right up to the extraordinary portal to the gardens of Dara. Nol walked through first, then came back to show us that it wasn't dangerous. He touched each one of us, mysteriously, then encouraged us to try it for ourselves. The spirited Vanamel was our scout.

"It's very strange!" he said, thrilled. "I can see you in the cavern, and I am here on the other side! Can't you see how beautiful it is here? It almost feels like we are in some sort of spell."

Forgetting all caution, Vanamel ran down into the valley, amazed by every flower, rock, tree, or bird he came across. His counselor, Saat the Treasurer, hurried to join him, and everyone else followed, one by one, crossing the narrow window between the two worlds with palpable excitement.

I was the last. Eurydis's teachings can prepare a man for many things, but not that. Although the experience was exciting, I felt something grave in it. What happened next proved my point.

"How is this possible?" I asked our guide. "What is the magic in this portal?"

Nol smiled and looked up, into the eyes of the Leviathan, anxious to return to its marine abyss.

"For the most part, the magic comes from the Guardian," he explained gently. *"His presence alone opens the portal, and to enter, you must dare to approach, and have been touched by a divine being."*

What Nol was saying then already shook my convictions, and I was speechless. The Strange had to take my hand to bring me into Dara. In his . . .

"Why did you stop there?" Léti shouted, after a few moments of heavy silence. "Maz, continue, I beg you!"

"That's all there is," Lana revealed sadly. "From there on, the text is illegible, except for the last ten pages. I haven't yet transcribed those. First I wanted to share this."

The heirs couldn't hide their disappointment. They had learned so many things in so few pages that losing three-quarters of the journal was truly a disaster.

What if their last chance had just disappeared for good?

Though Lana had woken them up in the middle of the night, the heirs couldn't fall back to sleep. Lana's reading had been lively, and Achem's tale astonishing.

"The description is exactly what we saw in Ji's cavern," Corenn commented. "The portal, the pond, Jal'dara, there's no way it's a hoax."

"It's the first time we have heard of this Leviathan," Grigán noted, not trying to contradict Corenn. "After all those years our ancestors spent searching for clues about Ji?"

"The poem names the Eternal Guardians," Lana reminded him. *"Promised day when gods will hear the voices, open the portals, bind the guardians,* they are the same thing."

"But how can you explain that *we* have never seen this monster, nor our parents or their parents?" asked the warrior.

"I don't know," the Maz conceded.

"Perhaps you have to call it forth," Rey proposed, "as Nol did from the top of the chasm. Or maybe the Leviathan only comes forth in certain conditions?"

"Like?" Léti asked.

"A certain date, the color of the sky, the moon's period, what do I know! Or maybe it's just dead."

"That would surprise me," the warrior mumbled.

No one disagreed. Even if the Leviathan weren't a god, it was difficult to imagine something capable of killing it.

"That's why we couldn't walk through the portal," Yan said. "Its Guardian was never there."

"Yet we saw Jal'dara," Léti responded. "Aunt Corenn, Grigán, you saw it every time! At every reunion!"

"Perhaps the Leviathan wasn't far," Corenn suggested seriously. "Waiting for our call."

They all could see a terrifying image of the monster climbing the cavern's walls, watching their movements. What if they had done something the Leviathan found . . . punishable? Something like destroying the symbols on the portal? Or trying to walk through it without the Guardian's approval? They had no idea if that was even possible.

"I think the creature is dead," Bowbaq announced, more to convince himself than really argue. "Surely they can die. The Sohonne Arch is also a portal to Jal'dara, but we have never seen it function, because there is no monster in the area."

"No? And the Undulating Drake?" Grigán retorted, as the idea crossed his mind. "He would suit the role perfectly!"

Bowbaq looked at the warrior and grew pale, distraught.

"Have you seen this Drake?" Léti asked. "You yourself?"

"No, and neither has Bowbaq, actually. It's an Arque legend that they bring out anytime there is an unexplained death. Even a lion like Mir couldn't cut up a body like the Drake does, and the legend stems from the Sohonne tribes!" Grigán concluded triumphantly.

The normally tacit warrior's excitement spread to the rest of the group. How could they not revel when they finally had some evidence that stacked up, where the facts seemed coherent, and even logical? The secret of Ji, the core mystery in their lives and those of their ancestors, was revealing itself little by little.

"It's a shame that the journal is damaged," Léti complained. "We could have learned so much more. Achem must have written the emissaries' entire story."

Yan consoled her by saying, "There's still the last pages. They may be informative."

Everyone turned to Lana, but Corenn saw her tired eyes and cut them off.

"It can wait until tomorrow," the Mother said. "Don't you think we've covered enough for tonight?"

"Corenn, I could—" Lana started to say.

"I forbid you," Corenn declared, falsely scolding. "Lana, it's your ancestor's journal. Take the time to learn from him."

The Maz agreed, relieved at the turn of events. They had all already slept a few decidays, while she had worked all night. She didn't have the energy to transcribe any more pages of Achem's manuscript.

Thankfully, no one was rude enough to offer their services. While it represented their best hope, the journal was Lana's, and they all knew the oath the Maz had made to her father at his deathbed. She had to destroy it. Reading it *before* she destroyed it was already a small betrayal; they did not want to add to her burden. She would be the first to read it.

"I suggest you return to your rooms," Corenn announced. "Try to get some sleep. Tomorrow, we will be in the Eastian Kingdoms, and we will need all our strength."

They separated with promises of sweet dreams, but few dreamed at all. A collection of dark thoughts prevented them: the portals, the Guardians, Jal'dara, the Züu, Saat and the demons of Jal'karu, the journal's secrets, and the voyage to the other side of the Curtain.

They left early the next morning, after buying replacement provisions and equipment from the innkeeper, who also managed a supply store. They didn't know when they would next come across advanced civilization, and as they left the Goranese inn, the heirs felt like they were leaving the Upper Kingdoms for good.

They headed for the trail through the Warrior's Vale at a brisk pace. Grigán hoped to make it through as quickly as possible; if there was going to be a battle, it was more likely to happen after breakfast. At dawn, providing they had not kept guard all night, men still loved life. Wars were won in the fading light of dusk, almost never at dawn.

The trail was in a piteous state, trampled by the footmen, horses, cattle, and chariots of the recent Goranese campaigns. Yan knew that Grigán had chosen this path thinking it might be less trampled than others, and the trail through the Vale itself must be even worse than this one.

A fine rain started to fall, angering everyone except the warrior, who saw it as a possibility that they might pass through the Vale without a battle. The misty rain intensified quickly, soaking them after only a few miles, only to fade and completely disappear once they had descended from the Curtain Mountains' heights.

"Thallos is over there," Rey announced, pointing to the east. "Why are we still heading north?"

"We can't take any chances, crossing blind into a region I don't know," Grigán said. "I think if we follow this trail, we will stumble over one of the Goranese camps; they can point out the enemy's position."

The warrior's uncertainty bothered his companions. They knew he didn't know the eastern territories well, but to see it so obviously... They were used to him being an all-knowing guide, and without his assurance they felt lost. What would it be like in the middle of the Thalite Kingdom, where they didn't even know the language?

They continued north, paying more attention to the landscape since, for once, they couldn't depend solely on Grigán.

The region was mostly deserted; over the centuries, the barbarians' proximity and their frequent raids had forced most of the inhabitants to flee. They could see only a few poor cottages built from mud and grass, and the fields outside these homes were ravaged by the passing troops. No smoke rose from their hearths, and the heirs concluded that their owners must have fled after the more recent combat. The ambiance added to the feeling of desolation that had inspired ancient poets to name the valley Warrior's Vale.

Continuing on their path, they passed a few vestiges of this name: rusted, half-buried weapons, ruins of old fortifications from another era, and even a few yellowed bones sticking out of the brown soil, a silent testament to battles that had been raging since the beginning of time.

How many battles had this land seen? How many men had died here? Even as far away as the Matriarchy there was a legend that no matter where one dug in the Warrior's Vale, one would find a skull. How many times had the Thalites attacked Goran? How far had they advanced before being pushed back?

As the miles passed, these morbid signs became more and more frequent. Lana said a few prayers for the warriors whose bones the horses walked over. Is this what Saat wanted? The Upper Kingdoms hadn't known a war since the last generation. Did he want to start another, as Usul had predicted?

The rain had stopped, and though the sky was still dark, the heirs could see a long way across the barren landscape, far enough to see the frontier post long before reaching it.

Goranese soldiers were ready for their arrival. Their post was a small one, with wooden ramparts reaching fifteen feet into the air and a shallow trench encircling them. Despite the fort's small size, the men seemed ready to defend it to the death.

Ten archers threatened Grigán, Corenn, and the others when they approached slowly, hands raised in peace. Still, the Goranese kept their bowstrings tense.

"We won't host anyone!" a captain warned them, from the top of a small wooden tower. "So if you weren't sent by the emperor himself, get going!"

"That we will do, sir," Corenn shouted so that he could hear. "But our affairs take us to Sola, and we would like to avoid the enemy's camps. We would be grateful if you could share this information?"

"You are crazy," the man said immediately. "Or something much worse. What affairs exactly bring you to the Wallatte border" He looked at them suspiciously.

"You are wrong to mistrust us, soldier," Corenn said. "Our reasons for crossing the frontier at such a perilous time are quite sad, actually. My brother goes to Sola once a year to sell jewels. However, he left for Sola more than four moons ago, and we never heard from him again. With my companions, his associates, we are out to find him."

"You're lying," the Goranese decided. "You are going to join the Wallattes!"

Grigán and Corenn looked at each other, surprised and confused.

"Why the devil do you think we are going to join the Wallattes, when we are headed to Sola?" Grigán asked, letting his frustration show.

"Because you are spies! Vermin from Wallos!" the man responded, pointing at them.

"You are at war with Wallos?" Corenn said, genuinely surprised.

The Mother's obvious surprise finally made the captain doubt himself, and he responded with no less hostility, but less yelling.

"Who do you think we are facing? Who do you think is on the other side of the Vale? The Kauliens, maybe?"

"We thought it was the Thalittes..."

"Thallos was razed. Almost all the northern barbarians have disappeared or joined the Wallatte army. Like you didn't already know it!"

"Of course we didn't know. Why would we ask you for our enemies' position if we were spies?"

Letting the man think through her response's logic, Corenn turned to her friends.

"There you have it, Saat's location," she whispered. "With the Wallattes. My knowledge of eastern history is fairly weak, but I think that their civilization is the most evolved after the Tuzéens'."

"Which makes him a serious threat to the Upper Kingdoms," Rey noted, regretfully.

"We still have to pass through the Vale," Lana reminded them. "The Goranese will stop their invasion, and the Loreliens won't delay to come to their aid."

"Where is your army?" Grigán asked the captain.

He smiled cynically and waved to the north.

"Don't you see it?"

Squinting, Yan and the others tried to make out something on the horizon.

"I don't see anything," Léti declared.

She turned to Grigán, who had the best vision. The warrior scanned the horizon from northwest to northeast, his expression darkening.

"It's there," he said. "The entire horizon."

Incredulous, Léti looked again, and stepped back, speechless. What she had taken for an absence of relief was the relief itself. On the horizon stretched a compact mass of camps, fortifications, wagons, horses, and footmen, invisible individually, but so numerous as to change the color of the horizon.

"Are you satisfied?" the man asked, feigning concern. "Return to your homes; it would be better for you. For in a couple dékades, when the Wallatte vermin have gathered their troops, this land will be the site for this century's largest battle."

"Sir," Lana intervened, "by the grace of Eurydis, help us. We are going to try to get through, but we will never make it unless you share your knowledge."

Lana's charm and her Maz robe, which was much respected by the Goranese, was finally enough to get the man to respond.

"For now, the Wallattes amass near the coast," he revealed. "They have built catapults to keep our ships from approaching the coast and surrounding them, something the Thalittes never thought to do. If you stay close to the mountains, you should be able to pass through just fine. But once on the other side, I suggest you head directly for Sola: stay far away from the ocean until you cross the Col'w'yr. After crossing the river, the region should be less dangerous."

They thanked him and headed east, leaving the protective Goranese army, and the civilizations they had always known, behind them. From this point forward, they would march without knowing where they were going.

Grigán pushed them hard, very hard, on their first day east of the Curtain. Using his Rominian compass, he guided them southeast, toward Sola, as the Goranese captain had suggested.

Saat was somewhere to the south, at the heart of the Wallatte Kingdom, and if they wanted to face him, they would have to penetrate deeper and deeper into enemy territory. But Grigán left this confrontation for later. This close to the Vale it was too dangerous to head straight south; better to enter the kingdom from the east than from the north. The warrior didn't dare share his pessimism about the entire endeavor.

The Warrior's Vale was equally deserted on both sides, so much so that they didn't see a living soul for many miles. But the place more than earned its name. The barbarian people cultivated the art of intimidation, and macabre trophies lined their path. The bodies of Goranese soldiers, hanged, impaled, or decapitated, had been left as close to the trail as possible, acting as so many warnings to anyone trying to enter the barbarians' territory.

They crossed fifteen bodies before Grigán suddenly changed course and headed east at a gallop. They followed, anxiously scanning the horizon and looking for something that might have put the warrior on alert. He didn't let them slow down until they reached the first few protective trees, a sign the cursed Vale was at its end.

"Did you see something?" Léti asked, as the horses caught their breath.

"A group of riders, to the south," Grigán responded, as he scanned the hills. "A dozen or so, perhaps more."

"Wallattes?" Yan asked.

"I don't know; they were too far."

"Do you think they saw us?"

"If I could see them, they could see us. Even more so because we were silhouetted on the horizon."

Then, "There," the warrior said angrily, pointing at a black spot. "Open your eyes, if you don't want to be impaled on a stake!"

"Wise Eurydis, what a horror!" Lana responded, shocked at such an image.

"Don't worry, Lana," Rey responded, with ease. "Grigán would never let them do that. Right?"

"Don't tempt me," the warrior curtly responded.

They looked out over the landscape for a while longer before continuing. They tried to stay hidden among branches, rushing between patches of trees as quickly as possible. Soon the forest expanded, and the risk of being seen lessened. Yet the heirs didn't relax, freezing at any sign from Grigán and ready to flee or fight if they needed to.

They had been riding since dawn, but their anxiety was stronger than their fatigue, and none complained. They all understood that, before anything else, they had to get as far away from the Warrior's Vale as possible, even if that meant not stopping until nightfall.

Once again, as they had done often over the last two moons, Yan, Léti, and the others slept beneath the stars. As he set up his blankets on the wet, spongy ground covered in moss, the young man thought nostalgically of their princely chambers in the Broken Castle, Zarbone's accommodations in the Land of Beauty, their rooms in Sapone's palace in Romine, and all the other places they had stayed, all the way back to Raji the Ferryman, the *Othenor*'s cabin, and the performing troupe's wagons. So many different places, already, and how many more to come? Few, probably.

Since they had crossed into the Eastian Kingdoms, Yan felt their adventure was reaching its end. It was an ominous, oppressive feeling, and images of Usul often bubbled up to the forefront of his consciousness. Grigán would die before the year's end. The Upper Kingdoms would lose in a murderous war.

Certainly the future could be changed. In fact, weren't he and the other heirs reacting directly to Usul's prophecies? If Yan hadn't revealed the coming war, would Corenn have decided to cross the Curtain? Weren't they rushing to their end, believing their actions were for the best?

He dropped his blankets and looked at his friends, hands on his hips. Bowbaq, caring for the horses and their baggage. Grigán explaining to Léti how to install "traps" that would signal any enemy's approach, like the ones he had used to catch Yan in Kaul.

Rey worked to start a fire, sharing secret smiles with Lana while the Maz prepared a meal and selected a few items from their provisions. Corenn, right by his side, helping him put out their bedding for the night.

Despite the numerous dangers they had encountered together, they had always come out alive. But what if, this time, they had made the wrong choice? What if they had taken the wrong direction?

"We shouldn't go to Wallos," he announced suddenly, struck by a decision.

The heirs stopped their activities to stare at him in surprise. But Yan was at a loss. He felt their eyes on him, but didn't know how to continue.

"Why?" Corenn asked, attentive to her student's thoughts. "Are we missing something? What did Usul tell you that we don't know?"

"Nothing else," Yan lied, thinking of Grigán's sad fate. "I only have . . . a feeling. I am not scared," he added, to justify his words. "I mean, no more than we all are. But I don't think we should approach Saat, if he is really at the head of this army. We'll never reach him."

"He's right," Grigán intervened, grabbing at the chance to share his own doubts. "With only the Thalittes, we would have had a chance; they were just beyond the Vale and small in number, compared to the Goranese. But now . . ."

"What does that change?" Rey objected. "We aren't going to fight them all anyhow. So, Wallatte or Thalitte, what difference does it make?"

"It means we have to cross more enemy lines. With seven of us, and no one here speaks their language. How will we get past even a patrol when we don't know the territory?" Grigán responded.

"But," Lana said. "I thought we could get around the enemy? Approach Wallos from the east?"

"It won't work," Grigán asserted, shaking his head. "Their generals don't seem to be idiots to me. If they thought to put catapults along the ocean shore, it's probably a sign that they are watching their backs."

"I don't understand, Grigán. Why did you bring us here if you didn't believe we had a chance? What did you have in mind?"

The warrior went to stroke his mustache, a sign of embarrassment, before once again discovering that it was hardly there at all, and hadn't been since Three-Banks. The heirs anxiously waited for his response.

None of them know what war is like, he thought to himself. Two young Kauliens, a Mother, a Maz, a pacifist Arque, a loud-mouthed Lorelien. That was his group of warriors, who naïvely thought they could slip past an entire army, an army of people who lived for battle.

"This morning, we didn't know," he finally said. "We couldn't turn around once we had talked to the Goranese captain, and I wanted to see for myself. That's done. With seven of us, we will never reach him."

"Grigán!" Corenn shouted. Then she stopped and continued more calmly. "You're not thinking of—"

"It's our best chance," the warrior interrupted her. "Alone, I could get close enough to Saat. Together, it is impossible."

"You will not go alone!" Yan affirmed, joining Corenn's protest. "You will not!"

"What other choice do we have?" Grigán said. "Fleeing is impossible. Saat can find us anywhere and send the Züu, or worse, the Mog'lur, after us. And going to Wallos together is a sure way to get ourselves killed."

"Maybe we could send a message to Saat?" Lana suggested. "Propose a compromise."

"Do you really think this man would change his mind for a letter? Only cold steel at his throat will get his attention," the warrior said with a serious expression.

"We don't know the extent of his powers," Corenn reminded them. "Grigán, you can't go alone. It would be madness."

"Well, what should we do then? If someone has a better idea, I am happy to follow it. If not, I am sticking to mine," he warned them.

The silence that followed was heavy, almost tangible. Everyone tried to think of an alternative, something less catastrophic, but no obvious solutions were found.

"I won't let you leave alone," Rey said quietly. "Whether it pleases you or not. I have a few words for Saat."

"Me either," Léti swore, her face hardened but her eyes shimmering with tears. "I would never let you leave alone."

"I will go with you, friend Grigán," Bowbaq hurried to add.

"That would be stupid," the warrior responded angrily. "Your sacrifices won't help me."

"I have something to propose," Corenn said, cutting off their angry exchanges. "It might be just as dangerous, but at least we will do it together."

They all quieted to listen. What could the Mother be thinking? It must be a desperate plan, they all thought, and they were right.

"Go to Sola," Yan guessed. "Find the portal in Oo."

"Exactly. And meet Nol in Jal'dara," the Mother concluded confidently.

Rey whistled in admiration, then said, "That seems even more difficult than attacking Saat. What will you do with the Eternal Guardian, described as uncontrollable, even by Nol? And what of the part about a divine touch?"

"You have to be touched by the Guardian to cross through the portal," Lana explained. "At least that's what I understood."

"If this Wyvern resembles the Leviathan, his touch would be a mortal wound! How do you expect us to defeat such a creature, Corenn?"

"I don't know, Rey," the Mother confessed. "We can't understand these things. The Leviathan never bothered us on Ji; we'll have to hope that this Guardian does the same."

"But, friend Corenn, the portal may not open. Ji's never actually opened," said Bowbaq with a worried look on his face.

"I know, but it's our best alternative. The only one, in fact. At worst, we will lose a dékade," she added offhandedly.

"In the worst case," Rey corrected her, "we will be added to the Guardian's eternal graveyard. I wonder if I'd rather be killed by the Wallattes."

They turned to Grigán, waiting to see his reaction. He knew that whatever he decided, the group would follow, so he took his time before responding.

"All right, we will head for Oo. Under the provision that Achem's journal doesn't warn us of another catastrophe. Lana, can you finish the transcription tonight?"

"I'll start immediately," Lana assured him. "It shouldn't take more than a deciday."

"Good, then we'll know tonight," Grigán concluded. "The Wyvern and Jal'dara or Saat and the Wallatte army."

The High Diarch turned the door handle to check that it was locked, then pulled the key out of the lock and set it on the table.

His palace was far from finished, but its construction advanced quickly. It had taken only five days for the slaves, "motivated" by their Züu guardians, to build this wing. It wasn't beautiful, but he wouldn't be here long.

In a few moons, Saat would reign over the entire world from Ith's Grand Temple. Or the Imperial Palace in Goran. Or, maybe, the Broken Castle of Junine. He hadn't decided yet. Either way, it would all be his. If he so desired, he could build a gigantic palace with stones from all three historic monuments. He had promised

Somber that he would burn the Holy City, a commitment he would take care to honor.

He blew out the only lantern in the room, and total darkness descended—though the blackness did not blind him. Saat could see in the deepest shadows almost as well as in the middle of the day. After a century underground, he had developed a few unique skills. His magical powers did the rest.

He pulled off one of his mail gloves and with his withered fingers caressed the rock wall ripped out from under the mountain. It was the same mountain, but not the same rock. The stuff in Karu's pits was much darker, hotter, and full of *gwele*, even there. Even so deep.

Saat tried to model a piece of the wall, to make a *Gwelom*, if the rock would take it. But there was little chance of it working, and he had other, more pressing projects.

He pulled off his other glove, then his breastplate, the shoulder protection, and the ridiculous dagger sheath he wore to support the gladores, his elite warriors. He pulled off his own sword and dagger, then took off the rest of his clothes.

As was his custom, he finished with his helm, pulling off the Gwelom slowly, carefully, tasting with an immense pleasure the fresh air on his face, his mouth, his cheeks.

He wanted to throw the mask away and present himself openly to everyone, but he had to wait for that. A relic of civility that he hoped would disappear, with time. He breathed deeply, and the noise of it disgusted him. He sounded like a choking dog. Though he hated the feel of it, at least the helm helped hide his struggle to survive.

He closed his eyes, concentrated, and was reinvigorated; he felt powerful, awake in his heart, body, and limbs. His muscles and ligaments unknotted, and he breathed easily. He had felt this thousands of times, but the joy of such power coursing through his body always made him feel him more than himself. He felt like power incarnate, without blemish or flaw.

He walked over to his bed and lay on the rich tanned skins that covered it. Chebree was already there, naked, immobile, silent. Impatient, and hoping to finish as quickly as possible.

Saat put a hand on her forehead and caressed her face. Chebree shivered and stopped breathing. Not from pleasure, but from feeling the High Diarch's hand. His horribly wrinkled skin, so thin she could feel his bones. He smelled of graveyard soil.

Our enemies have their doubts, my friend, Somber warned him with a thought.

Saat immediately closed off a large part of his mind. He had done it for so long, with such consistency, that the god didn't even notice.

What are they doing? he asked, still embracing the high priestess.

They talk a lot. They plan. They want to see Nol.

The old man won't help them, Saat assured him, moving his body. *And how do they plan to accomplish such a miracle?*

The Sola portal. They will open it.

You have no idea if they will. You can't see into the future.

They will open it. We have to kill them.

Patience, my friend. Say they go to Sola, and they get past the Guardian. Maybe they even see the old man. So what?

Nol will tell them of the Adversary.

Saat hesitated.

They won't get that far. I will send a company of gladores after them. They will never reach Nol, but they will still be sent to another world!

This time Somber paused.

You should let me kill them, he repeated angrily.

There are too many risks for you, my friend. If one of these men is the Adversary, he could—

I've had enough of waiting. Somber cut off the connection.

The High Diarch was alone with his thoughts, busy with a tense, inactive Chebree.

As he awoke, Somber had acquired a personality slightly different from the one Saat had prepared for. He was like an adolescent revolting against his parents, but stronger and more intelligent. He was still loyal to their common plans and friendship, though, and that was the most important thing.

Looking at the priestess's face, Saat thought of how ignorant were even his closest companions. Ignorant of his real project. Ignorant of their own power. Their heritage.

Chebree would probably never understand why he wanted to have a child with *her*, more than with anyone else.

It was understood that none of the heirs would sleep as they waited for Lana to finish decoding the journal. Given the uncertainty of the near future, the nearby presence of an enemy army, and their curiosity to see what was in Achem's journal, there was far too much tension for even the briefest of slumbers.

To pass the time, Grigán and Bowbaq decided to curry the horses. It was a substantial task, and they figured it would take up enough time for Lana to decipher the text. Yan launched into a discussion with Corenn on the subtleties of magic. Léti joined the warrior and the Arque, and Rey stood nearby without offering to help. In their circle, they debated the art of combat.

"Someone with an obvious weak point will often aim their attacks as if their adversary has the same problem," Grigán said to his student. "If he attacks your legs, attack his. If he threatens your left side, concentrate your efforts there."

"Now I understand why you always go for the head," Rey joked. "It's your weakness!"

"Should we try it out now?"

"Now he threatens me!" the actor continued. "I preferred you in the Land of Beauty. We were friends then, you remember, Grigán?"

"A moment of weakness, Mr. Kercyan. It won't happen again."

Bowbaq was too preoccupied to pay attention to his friends' verbal jousting, and he left his brush with Léti, to instead join Yan and Corenn. At least he could participate in their conversation and try to forget, momentarily, that he had no idea what had happened to his wife and children. They were still in the heart of Arkary, thousands of leagues from where he stood.

"Drawing force from outside of yourself can help you avoid the languor," Corenn explained to Yan. "But I need to remind you that the technique is dangerous. So much power can make you lose your head, make you drunk on it, make you believe there is no end to it—but there is. The power is not endless. Any object can reach a point where it shatters, which creates a vacuum of force. In this case, you can die or have a long episode of apathy."

"I understand," Yan nodded, mentally summarizing the lesson the Mother had given him.

The technique wasn't that complicated. He just had to concentrate on the object from which he would draw power, accumulate the power, then concentrate on the spell's target and apply his Will, unleashing the gathered force to act on one of the four elements. The difficulty wasn't the operations themselves but their succession. To fail at any stage could kill him.

"As an anecdote," Corenn continued, "some famous mages always used the same objects, which they kept with them at all times. Crystals are preferred—sapphires, emeralds, rubies, diamonds—but of course a grain of salt has the same properties, or almost the same."

Yan agreed. Effectively, precious gems could hold an immense power; he had felt it himself when working on Léti's opal. Working with the same object made it familiar, which helped transfer power, and Yan was drawn to the benefit of avoiding the languor. He promised himself he would try it when he came across a bit of flint, if he could find any.

"I have a question," he said. "If, after you have drawn the power, you don't cast a spell, what happens?"

"I have no idea," Corenn admitted. "I've never thought of that."

"Can I try?"

"Absolutely not! Don't you think you should master the skill first, before trying something new? Remember the apathy after your experience with Ifio!"

Yan looked at the little monkey perched on Bowbaq's shoulder. They were so used to her presence that they often forgot she was there. He remembered penetrating the monkey's mind and taking possession of her body. He had done the same with the Zü, in the Holy City of Ith.

He still had no idea what these actions had done to him.

"The deep mind is the place where the soul attaches to the body," Bowbaq said before Corenn could interrupt him. "If you can reach it, you can insert your own mind and steal a body. It's what the ghost did to me in the library."

"But what happens to the invaded spirit?" Yan asked, hoping to soothe his conscience for what he had done to the Zü. "Do they suffer?"

"From frustration, yes, a lot. They revolt, they cry out. But they can't do anything while the intruder still dominates."

"Can the power structure change?" Corenn asked.

"Yes, that happens, sometimes. There are two cases. The erjak can lose himself and become a prisoner to the foreign body, but with no power over it. He will stay there until the body's death, or until he takes control again."

"That's horrible!" Yan commented.

"Yes, and it's also possible for the invaded person to flee into the erjak's body. There are tales of men acting like wolves, bears, or other animals, until the spirits find their proper homes."

Yan shivered, imagining the Zü invading his own body and murdering Rey and Bowbaq at his side, as he had forced the Zü to do to his brothers.

Whenever he thought of that moment, he felt shame and sadness, though he knew that he had only done what the situation required of him. None among his friends had the desire or the audacity to reproach him for it. They could see his respectful fear of his own powers, and this was enough to keep them quiet on the subject.

"I finished," Lana announced suddenly, tears in her voice. "Sage Eurydis, but how they suffered!"

"'Would Saat have gone mad,'" Lana read, "'if he hadn't discovered the powers of the gwele? Even if Vanamel and Pal'b'ree hadn't followed Lloïol, the cursed little imp, into the third pit, we would have been put in danger sooner or later by Saat's folly—'"

"Friend Corenn, I don't understand," Bowbaq interrupted. "What does it mean? Who are all these people?"

"It's only the end of the journal," Corenn reminded him. "The explanations must be in the pages we lost."

"It's like that right up until the end," Lana confirmed. "It seems that our ancestors weren't alone in Jal'dara."

The Maz waited for more questions, then began reading again.

We would have been put in danger sooner or later by Saat's folly, with consequences much more serious than the sorcerer's death. However, despite the scorn we felt for him, we tried to come to his rescue, and three men died. Three men chosen by their people to represent them to the young gods.

I don't feel much regret for Vanamel; the prince, in my humble opinion, deserved his fate. But I cried for Ssa-Vez and for Fer't the

Solenese, two wise and honorable men who had gained our confidence and were an integral part of the group.

Nol cried with us when only eight returned, after twelve descended into Karu. He confided in us his regret that his neutrality prevented him from interfering. But we had been witness to his powerlessness so often that we could not hold it against him. He was He Who Teaches, and that was the extent of his power.

The children, still placid, circled around us. Like always, and despite our seething emotions, we tried not to influence them, instead letting them watch us, touch us, and listening to their incomprehensible babble, hoping that one of them would speak directly to us, as they had done to Tiramis, Fer't, Moboq . . . and Saat.

One of the oldest suddenly noticed the bloody bandage around Arkane's stump. The courageous king tried to smile, but his other injury, to his head, turned it into a grimace.

Rafa suffered from his burns and occasionally sighed in pain. Each time, the children turned and stared at him, worried.

Two smaller ones grabbed Tiramis by the hand, but the Mother was oblivious and did not respond with a caress, as she had done before. The courageous Yon set the Kaulienne down on the soft grass and patted the shoulders of the young gods, as if consoling them. It wasn't enough.

None of them were smiling now. The smallest started to cry, soon followed by all their elders. The gods were crying. A disaster for mankind.

"You have to leave," Nol announced. "The Harmony is broken."

He was only saying what we already knew. Staying would have disastrous consequences.

Arkane needed to be healed. Even in Jal'dara, an injury like his was serious. I can't imagine what would have happened if the king had died at the feet of the growing gods.

Nol brought us directly to the portal. At the time, it surprised me, but what ceremony could I have expected? The children would rapidly forget us, or at least we hoped so. And we had no one else to say good-bye to, other than the valley's doyen.

As Nol approached the archway, the portal activated. The whistling, the light, the fog. We tended to forget that Nol himself is an Eternal Guardian for Dara's portal.

The fog in the portal's vision soon lifted, revealing the titanic trees in Oo's forest.

"And the Wyvern?" Pal'b'ree the Wallatte protested, as Nol pointed to the other side.

"In your world, it's the Season of the Earth," the doyen assured him. "She is probably sleeping."

"Wasn't she supposed to be doing that last time?" the Eastian retorted before walking under the arch.

He didn't even say good-bye to us, we who had saved his life. His only worry was to escape the rebellious Guardian that had decimated the emissaries from the east three days before the Day of the Owl. Of eight sages sent by the barbarians, only two made it to Jal'dara, and Fer't the Solene wouldn't be leaving.

"I had proposed to him to open the portal on Tuze," Nol commented as the vision of Oo faded. "Or the one in Walloranta, or Greloes. There was no reason he had to return to the Oo and the Wyvern."

"What did you tell him about the Season of the Earth?" Moboq asked for clarification.

"It started a few days ago, in your world. Time is sovereign over all things in the universe," the doyen explained. "But there are places where it is less active."

"What are you trying to say?" Duke Reyan asked, concerned. "How long have we been here exactly?"

"Six dékades. In your world, you understand. If you hadn't gone into Karu, I would have sent you back earlier. I am sorry."

We all glared at him in silence. Our stay had felt five times shorter.

Nol gestured and the arch's mist disappeared, revealing the dark cavern on Ji. It seemed like the right time to say something, but I couldn't find the words and instead walked through the door after a small wave and a final glance at the marvelous valley.

It stayed visible for a long time. But as we stood in the cave's cold water, we felt sufficiently melancholic to turn away and stop staring longingly at our lost paradise.

Then Duke Reyan walked at the front of the group toward the light. Once we had sufficient light, we fabricated a stretcher for Arkane. Tiramis was still in her trance when we reached the escorts, who had waited for us, though we were seventeen days late.

The rest is history. Our vow of silence caused us dishonor and grief, to varying degrees, but we put up with these evils without complaint. They were nothing compared to the torment the secrets brought us—they were nothing compared to the cruel curse we all now suffered under.

The power of Jal'dara had made us Gweloms, in only a few dékades. What would happen after several moons? Years? I can hardly think of it.

The idea of a long life was nothing compared to the almost certain loss of our fecundity. I think that we all hoped to fight the curse, the only way one can.

Except perhaps for Arkane. The king of Junine already had an heir, and contrary to us, had resigned himself to his fate calmly. If he was the first to disappear, I think it's because he didn't want to fight anymore. To him, death was a welcome peace. Arkane had embarked for Ji as the king of the Baronies; he came back with one arm, dishonored, and constantly worried. If we knew the same spiritual hardships, at least we were physically fit.

Whatever it was, after failing to reach the other Emaz, I concentrated my life on making descendants. I, who had been celibate my whole life, took Mièlane, one of my students, in Union. We left for Mestèbe, as far from the Holy City and my memories as possible. Never did my young wife learn the truth of this sad adventure; at least, not until now. I hope to Eurydis it will always be this way, that none will share my burden. To the Emaz who are my intended audience: leave her, and my children, in peace.

We lived together for five years before we finally had a boy. Perhaps the powers of Jal'dara had faded with time; perhaps the goddess had heard my prayers. I learned at our next reunion that Tiramis and Yon had also been blessed with child. We celebrated these events as anyone would, though our joy was sullied by Arkane's death, which came that same year.

Luckily, our sterility was only partial. In their own turn, Reyan, Moboq, and Rafa had their own heirs. How can I explain, after all those years of anguish, the overpowering joy we felt at each of these births? More than personal joy to see our lines continue, we rejoiced to give humanity a chance for the Age of Ys and Nol's Harmony, even if it is thousands of years from now.

If Vanamel and Pal'b'ree hadn't descended into Karu, if they hadn't met the Undines, we would have been ignorant of our responsibility. And it would have been better that way. The burden of Jal'dara's secrets was already heavy enough to bear, but since we did know, we couldn't help but rejoice, seeing the second generation expand and grow.

Our only fear, now, is that they will also be Gweloms. Our children, will they be able to have their own?

I suppose I won't benefit from a long life after all. I won't ever see my grandchildren, if there are any. Can our heirs prosper in ignorance of these evils? Will they respect the Moral of Eurydis and the memories of their ancestors?

We will never return to Jal'dara. But we show our sons and daughters the portal, which every time resonates from our presence, on each Day of the Owl. We do it to show the child gods how much we love them. And how similar we are to them.

"I didn't understand much of that," Bowbaq admitted when Lana set the pages down. "A Gwelom? What's that? A sort of sickness?"

"I think," Corenn tried to explain, "that Maz Achem called anything that had been altered by Jal'dara a Gwelom. But we understand only a part of what it does to humans. We don't really know what those powers are . . ."

Seeing her friends' bemused expressions, Corenn could tell that her explanation hadn't clarified Achem's nebulous tale.

"More simply: anything that stays in Jal'dara long enough is influenced by the place and becomes a Gwelom. For a human, this translates to a longer life and a partial loss of fecundity. The principle of this change, what Achem calls gwele, escapes us . . ."

"And that's where you are proposing to bring us!" Rey said, jumping up from the ground. "Who wants to become one of these damned Gweloms?"

"Our ancestors were," Grigán reminded him. "Didn't you hear? That didn't stop them from having children."

"Who says we'll have the same luck?" the actor argued. "I hate the idea of being modified by any form of magic, that's all."

"We simply have to keep our stay short," Corenn countered. "The effects should be kept to a minimum."

"*Should*," the actor repeated cynically. "Not to mention that every day spent in this 'paradise' counts for five here."

"At least we understand why there have always been so few heirs," Lana said sadly. "Surely we are already Gweloms."

The only child in her family, the Maz thought of her father, and her grandfather, who had only two boys, despite his desire for a large family. During five years of Union, she had never had a child. The heirs carried part of their ancestors' curse in their flesh.

"Could Saat be hunting us for that?" Yan proposed timidly.

"What do you mean?"

"I'm not sure. To be Gweloms makes us peculiar. Saat might know something on the subject, something we don't."

"We don't know so many things," Lana said sadly, thinking of the journal's lost pages.

Corenn skimmed the pages on which the Maz had transcribed the journal. It was rich with information and she didn't want to miss anything.

"Achem mentions a second responsibility," she said. "Something about allowing humanity to reach the Age of Ys."

"He must mean the knowledge about how gods are made," Grigán disagreed. "That's what he tried to tell the Grand Temple."

"No, no! He makes the distinction clear: *the burden of Jal'dara's secrets was already heavy enough to bear.* That's what motivates Saat. It's this mystery we have to solve."

"What do our births have to do with the Age of Ys?" Rey interjected. "Lana, correct me if I'm wrong, but isn't Eurydis supposed to start it herself?"

"Exactly, Rey. It's said that the goddess will come for the third time to this world, to help humanity take the last step. But only the last one. Mankind must first finish the universal quest for the Moral. Perhaps one of the heirs is destined to bring her word. Like Comelk in his time?"

"Those are just words." Grigán waved her off with a disdainful swipe. "That doesn't explain why Saat is so focused on our extermination. Even if our births contributed, by some mystery I don't understand, to the coming of the Age of Ys, what does that have to do with Saat?"

The warrior had hit the nail on the head. His intervention brought the conversation back to their immediate problems.

"Perhaps it's about vengeance," Bowbaq proposed. "Our ancestors thought he was dead when they left Jal'dara without him. Maybe he feels abandoned or betrayed."

"He wouldn't go through all this trouble for vengeance," Corenn disagreed. "Did he hate his companions so much that he hunts the fourth generation of their descendants? That would be the sign of a deep madness. And, to the contrary, Saat seems to possess all his mental faculties."

"But why then? *Why is he our enemy?*" Grigán asked.

"That's what we have always wanted to know. We can't respond to this question until we meet Saat. Or Nol."

Corenn turned to Grigán, inviting him to share his decision, but the warrior didn't respond.

"He is with the Wallattes," Rey reminded them. "That might have something to do with the Eastians who were in Jal'dara."

"We always thought there had been only ten emissaries," Lana commented.

"We should have thought of that," Corenn said. "Now it seems obvious that if Nol sought out representatives from every kingdom, he would have invited the Eastians as well."

"What could they have done there?" the Maz asked reflexively. "Nol certainly had good reasons to bring them all there. But what were they?"

"Have you ever heard of He Who *Teaches*?" Yan asked.

"Never. If Nol is a god, as he seems to be, his name is rarely invoked in the Holy City."

"Like Reexyyl," Grigán added, "and the Undulating Drake, and the Wyvern of Oo. And all the Eternal Guardians whose names we don't even know. They are all gods."

Yan's mind wandered briefly. Only two moons earlier, he hadn't even believed in magic. Since then, he had learned to use it, and every step of their voyage brought him more proof of the supernatural. What if all the legends were true, at least partially? Dragons, elves, chimeras, griffins, the Fey, ogres, hydras, unicorns, and so many other extraordinary creatures . . . Did they all exist, somewhere in this world, which had become so rich and fantastic?

If mankind can create gods, can't we make monsters as well? Yan thought. The Eternal Guardians were probably born out of the nightmares of early man, materialized versions of their primal terror. Yan wanted to share his thoughts, but didn't dare interrupt Rey and Corenn's intense discussion.

"Lady Corenn, you know how much I normally respect your suggestions," the actor explained. "But this time, I can't agree with you. What kind of chance do we really have to get through that portal, supposing we can even find it? Very little. Practically none. The only thing we know about it is that there is a murderous monster waiting for us there."

"Saat is another," Léti retorted, "and smarter."

"Saat is mortal," Rey responded. "What do we know about this Wyvern? And can we count on it to open the gate?"

"It did so on the Day of the Bear, a century ago," Corenn explained. "According to Achem, it should still resonate from Pal'b'ree's passing, like the one on Ji."

"And if that is insufficient? Like on Ji?"

"The portal's power grows when the Guardian is close. We just have to touch it..."

"Nothing could be easier!" the actor said, reaching the end of his patience. "And how do you plan to convince it to share its divine touch? You know, the only thing mortals need to get the portal to function?"

"Perhaps we can touch it ourselves," Léti proposed. "And then we run for Jal'dara."

"My dear friends, excuse me, but I don't share your optimism. I won't bet my life on it, to borrow Grigán's favorite expression!"

The divine touch, Yan thought, Usul's unusual gift. "You won't know until the moment is right," he had said.

"I have been touched by a divine," the young man announced, trembling with emotion. "Usul touched me."

He had already told them the story, but like him, his companions had forgotten, thinking the god had been lying. Now the strange gesture showed its value.

"Why did he do that?" Grigán asked. "By the very act, he interfered with the future himself."

"Usul has never wanted to be a passive observer," Lana said, as excited as the others. "Only, he has no power outside of his cave; he can only act on his visitors."

"He is terribly bored," Yan confirmed, pensive. "If he helped us, it's only to better entertain himself, to add some uncertainty to his terrible game."

"Whatever his reasons," Corenn concluded, "we should thank him. Rey, are you convinced now?"

The actor thought for a long moment, an uneasy expression on his face. Too many elements of this project were out of his control, and that did not please him.

"Grigán, what do you think?" he finally asked, standing at the warrior's side. "Don't you think this is too risky?"

Grigán looked up from the fire where he had been staring, thinking. He had never felt so indecisive. In his opinion, both plans were equally dangerous. There was no obvious choice.

But if the warrior decided to seek Saat, it would mean that he would have to leave Corenn behind, and this argument swayed him.

"We will go to Oo," he said finally. "If that doesn't help us, I will find Saat. Alone."

They all agreed, relieved and worried at the same time. Yan spent the rest of the night wondering if they had taken a wrong turn. *Usul must be enjoying himself!*

They had only nine days left before the Day of the Bear, barely enough to reach Oo in time. Oo was in the Solene Federation, and they had to both travel cautiously and allow for some time to find the portal.

Yan had little knowledge on the subject; if the manuscript from the Deep Tower had indicated a few landmarks, it was silent when it came to the exact placement of the portal in relation to these milestones. The heirs knew they had to find the ruins of a keep in the forest described as the Forest of Titans. The portal couldn't be far from there. They just had to hope that it wasn't as well hidden as the one on Ji.

Rey followed the group from behind, showing his disagreement with being dragged into an adventure he thought was by all accounts too risky. Sulking, he let his rebellious side show. One night, he even threatened to leave them if the experience in Jal'dara was fruitless. They all reacted to his declaration as if he were joking, and at the time the actor didn't correct them, but the next morning he spoke with Lana, begging the Maz to accompany him, or at least to wait for him somewhere.

"But where would we go, Reyan?" she asked. "We can't hide anywhere, and Saat can see us wherever we go!"

"I plan to go visit the sorcerer first," the actor confided. "I rarely let others fix my problems. Grigán wants to go alone, fine. I'll do the same. We'll see who gets to Wallos first," he finished, with a smile.

"Reyan, it's not a competition!" Lana responded, panicked. "I beg of you, promise me you won't decide anything until we meet Nol."

"For you, I promise. No decision before the Oo country. But then we will have nothing left to discover, Lana. We can't keep running across the world while Saat gathers his army.

"I would give my life for any one of you, but not in vain. The solution is not in our current quest. It's in taking action. I would be happy if you all followed me, but I won't change my mind, even if I have to leave alone. And that's exactly what Grigán feels too," said Rey.

His words troubled the Maz more deeply than Rey had wanted. He might have been right, but the idea of leaving Grigán, Corenn, Bowbaq, Yan, and Léti brought tears to her eyes. The thought of Reyan's departure seemed just as tragic.

On their fifth day of travel, as they approached the Col'w'yr, the river marking the Thalite Kingdom's border, Lana followed through with her promise to her father and burned Achem's journal. They all watched the little ceremony and sympathized with Lana's dismay, not knowing that there was another cause. For her, burning the journal was a symbol that the heirs were going to split up.

Grigán's and Rey's wishes were the first signs of an inevitable rift. Soon they would all take their own paths.

Grigán had been doubly vigilant as they crossed the Thalite lands, and, extraordinarily, they had avoided contact with any natives. They had seen smoke from faraway hearths, hamlets in the distance, villages, and even villagers, but they had kept their distance. The nearby war played in their favor; the heirs were able to avoid contact with the Thalittes because they in turn wanted to avoid the Wallattes, who had invaded their territory.

Now only four days remained before the Day of the Bear, and the heirs couldn't afford to lose more time with detours and furtive riding. The ease with which they forded the Col'w'yr encouraged the warrior to accelerate the pace, and the Solene Federation seemed to have been spared from the wars to the west.

Continuing their trek, they noticed how advanced the Upper Kingdoms were compared to the Eastian Kingdoms. The trails here were poorly marked and completely unkempt, very few buildings were constructed with stone, and every village had an outer wall built of sharpened logs, showing that war reigned in this region.

The Eastians, like the people of the Lower Kingdoms, were always at war, but these conflicts rarely reached the level of nations. Most often, battles were between two neighboring villages or, more rarely, neighboring provinces. To bring all of these people together under one banner, as Saat had done, was an exceptional achievement.

If the sorcerer had united them with force, wouldn't he use the same powers to bring his army victory in the coming battle? The Goranese confidence of defending the Warrior's Vale bordered on arrogance, Grigán thought. Having himself lived in the Grand Empire, Saat would know every weakness and would penetrate the Vale. Or perhaps he had another plan in mind? What could it be?

The warrior could only guess, as they encountered no new information. But the idea haunted him until they reached Oo. From there, he had other things to worry about.

They entered the Forest of Titans on the eve of the Day of the Bear, which was a feat in and of itself. That Grigán could guide them there with only the help of his compass and his memories of glimpsed maps was a testament to his abilities, and they all thanked him. Reaching the forest wasn't their end goal, though; the most difficult part was yet to come.

"We have to find the door before tomorrow night," Corenn reminded them. "If Achem is right, the passage will open from the resonance of Pal'b'ree's passage a century ago."

"And if it doesn't?" Rey asked, for the tenth time.

"Then we will have to call the Guardian and hope that she doesn't hibernate for all of the cold season, as Nol led Achem to believe."

"Hope that she isn't waiting for us!" the actor corrected, grimacing.

They started looking for the portal immediately, entering the shaded forest at random. The Forest of Titans earned its name from the trees, which stretched thirty yards into the air, rendering anything at their base tiny and awestruck.

Most of the trees were barkors, which Bowbaq recognized from the White Country, but there were also other varieties. Apart from lénostores, atar birches, and the resonating alters, which supplied the wood for vigolas, they could see dozens of others that they didn't recognize. It had been this way since the Warrior's Vale; even nature seemed to be somehow different from what they knew in the Upper Kingdoms. Yan wouldn't have been surprised to see a flying margolin.

The forest's ceiling was rich with vegetation and leaves, but the ground was almost completely devoid of plant life. Except for a few types of mushrooms and an omnipresent moss, the trees kept out any plants shorter than fifteen feet tall. Above that, the branches and winter leaves mixed to form a canvas, which was held together by a parasitic ivy that flowed through the entire forest. When they were well into the forest, the heirs could practically feel the weight of the vegetation towering over them.

"Even when it rains, the soil must stay dry," Bowbaq commented, as he tried to see the sky.

"It must be teeming with life up there," Yan added. "Insects, birds ... Ifio would love it here." Of course, he had no intention of abandoning the mimastin, nor would Ifio let him.

"Look at the size of this trunk!" Rey said, pointing to an enormous barkor. "You could build a house inside it."

"Maybe that's what the Wyvern did," Léti said. "What do you think she looks like?"

"Like Grigán," Rey responded without hesitating. "More beautiful, and with a mustache."

"Ha, ha. Very funny," Grigán said, annoyed.

But Léti's remark had given Corenn an idea.

"What could the portal look like?" she asked the group. "The one on Ji is in a cavern, but this landscape has no caves. The Sohonne Arch is made of stone ... Perhaps the portal here is carved into a tree?"

"That seems unlikely to me." Grigán rejected the idea. "The ones we know so far are supposed to endure forever."

"The barkors live for a very, very long time," Bowbaq said, happy that he could help. "And they become so hard and dry when they die that you can only destroy them by burning them."

Rey commented, "If there were ever a fire here, the dry vines covering all the trees would burn so hot that not a twig would escape!"

"Don't forget that the portals are magical," Corenn continued, "built by divine hands. Given that, they must posses a certain resistance. Or, at least, a protection . . ."

"The Guardian," Lana finished for her. "The Wyvern must ensure that no fire spreads to the portal. Or even, throughout all of Oo."

Luckily, the heirs hadn't yet lit a torch or a lantern, despite the feeble light that trickled through the thick canvas of leaves.

"At least now we know how to coax it out of its hiding place," Grigán said.

"As long as we don't have to make friends with it, yes," the actor cynically responded.

"If the portal is in a tree, we should find it quickly," Léti said excitedly. "It must be one of the largest ones in the forest!"

"Unfortunately, we can't see from here," Corenn said looking at the chaotic canopy. "These trees are too high to be climbed."

"Not for Ifio," Yan offered timidly, already certain how the Mother would respond to his idea.

"That's out of the question. You can't risk your mind for a simple piece of knowledge! Read her mind if it pleases you, but no more of this deep mind connection."

The young man nodded, disappointed, but relieved. The experience of stealing a body was so trying that he would prefer to avoid it.

"I don't think climbing would be so hard," Rey said. "The ivy makes for a great stairway, and the branches can handle my weight. We brought some rope, I think?"

The actor stopped his horse and dismounted, before loosening some of the straps on his horse. Feeling vaguely concerned, Yan handed him the rope he had used to descend into Usul's cavern. Though he wasn't superstitious, two moons of travel had taught Yan to listen to these feelings of premonition. Grigán must have learned at least as much after his twenty years of travel.

"Reyan, you can't climb up there alone!" Lana said.

"In every inn where we have stayed, I dreamed you would say something like that to me," the actor joked. "But you had to wait until now."

They all dismounted and watched their friend prepare for his climb. He tied a few knots, after passing the rope under his armpit.

"Don't kill Saat without me!" he said as he started to climb. Six yards higher, he disappeared from view behind the living mass of leaves, vines, and branches.

As he had predicted, the climb was easy, not dissimilar to the climbs he had made to escape the Kercyan house in Lorelia. At least this time he wouldn't find his cousin's corpse, he thought bitterly.

Though he liked to be the center of attention, he wasn't rash, and he attached the rope to the tree every five or six yards. Working this way slowed his climb, but at least he wouldn't fall to his death if he slipped.

He continued to speak to his companions as he climbed, but the conversation ceased when they could no longer hear him. Rey needed his breath to climb; though there were ample holds and support, he still had to climb straight up.

Nearly forty-five feet high, when he had thought he would be leaving the oppressive labyrinth of plants, he was surprised to find that instead it thickened. Soon, he faced a real dead end of foliage, which he got through with great difficulty, using his dagger to cut away the vines.

Life began above this level. The ivy formed an irregular carpet, housing insect colonies, birds, rodents, and even a few reptiles, which fled when Rey entered their world.

The actor forced back his repulsion and continued to climb, every step setting off a flurry of activity. The most nauseating surprise was the snakes, small and scared, but apt to stay camouflaged in the dense vegetation. A close second was the largest insects he had ever seen, which flew right at his face whenever he scared them. After a frenetic flurry of cutting and cursing, Rey finally cleared a worthy vantage point for himself.

Everywhere he looked, the forest was devoid of humanity. No smoke, no construction. The trees were very tall, and he couldn't be sure, but somewhere out there, there should be the ruins of a keep. And close to there, the portal to Jal'dara.

Unfortunately, many trees were notable for their enormous size. Desperate, Rey mentally noted where the closest, largest trees were.

That's when he felt a sharp stab of pain in his calf.

A snake was attached to his leg, its jaws clamped shut. Not one of the camouflaged little snakes from earlier, but a long reptile, as thick as his arm, with a strange ring around its nose, staring at him with cold eyes.

Risking a fatal tumble and gritting his teeth against the pain, Rey leaned over and stabbed the animal in the head. If he hadn't been wearing boots, the animal would have reached his bones.

Horribly mutilated by the blade, the serpent wrapped its body around the actor's legs, despite his best efforts to escape. That's when Reyan heard the rustling.

A single glance was enough to make a decision. All around him, more of the strange snakes slithered toward him. Rey could see at least five, but there could have been thirty.

He jumped off the branch and fell the equivalent of two stories before being brutally caught by the rope. Scratched, bruised, and with the snake still wrapped around his leg, he grabbed the rope and slid down as fast as possible, not bothering to check if it would hold him.

His terrified friends saw Rey fall out of the sky. Grigán immediately stabbed the serpent behind its ring, and Léti forced open its mouth, using her dagger as a lever. Luckily, the reptile was already dead. Only a reflex held his bite.

Rey pulled off his boat and groaned, while the rodents and insects he had brought down with him scurried back up the tree.

The wound was deep, considering it had reached through his leather boot. Deep enough to pierce his skin and draw blood from the actor's calf.

"A snake with teeth!" Bowbaq said, surprised, as he examined the dead reptile. "What a strange thing!"

"It's almost a kind of eel," Yan added, before joining his friends around the injured Rey.

Corenn examined his wound. The skin color looked normal, and the reptile had no fangs; there was hope that it wasn't venomous.

"It's fine, Corenn," the Lorelien thanked her. "I think I was mostly just scared," he confessed. "Don't worry."

As Lana wrapped his wound, he stared at the thick layer of plant life above them. How many snakes were up there? How many other dangers were hiding in those trees?

The first giant barkors they came across had nothing they hoped for. Rey's accident had lost them valuable time, and night was falling quickly in the shadowy world beneath the trees. They decided to continue their search the next day, hoping a new start would bring better luck.

Despite the cold that crept into the night, Corenn wouldn't allow them to start a fire, or even a lantern. If there was any chance that fire brought out the Wyvern, they would do all they could not to confront it.

No one fell asleep until late that night, and only then because their fatigue was as strong as their fear. They huddled close together in the darkness, without the stars to light the night. The forest bustled with noise: growls, cracks, pattering paws, smacking jaws, and insects singing.

"This could be our last night in this world," Yan whispered, as much to himself as to Léti.

"Why did you say that?" the young woman mumbled. "We won't die. Not before we grow old."

"No, I mean tomorrow night, we could be in Jal'dara. We are going to see *gods*, Léti."

"You already saw one," she said soberly.

"Yes, but . . ."

He didn't finish. After all, he was the only one who understood what such an encounter felt like. In the birthplace of gods, it must be tenfold stronger.

More tired at dawn than when they had gone to sleep, the heirs began their search anew, aware that today's hunt would decide their entire future.

It had been a dékade since they had spoken to anyone outside of the group. Now the Oo country, deserted and monotone, silent and loud at the same time, made them deeply conscious of their solitude. In this forest, only a strange half-light separated night and day, and the heirs felt like they were walking in a dream.

Similar to the day before, they walked toward the cluster of trees Rey had spotted. But failure stacked up and pessimism began to spread, more so because it became so difficult to locate themselves as they moved farther from their original location.

Midday came and went without any better results. They ate quickly and returned to their search, knowing that the next few decidays were all they had left.

"The portal will light up like the one on Ji," Léti reminded them, as the idea came to her. "Perhaps we should post someone in a tree to look for it?"

"No one will climb up there again, unless I ask for it," Grigán said.

"Supposing we see it, we might not have the time to reach it, anyway," Corenn added.

Time passed, and still they found nothing. If they hadn't had Grigán and his compass, they surely would have gotten lost. The forest was so large.

In the fifth deciday, as they anxiously watched the sun drop toward the horizon, the vines above them bustled loudly. By the time the heirs stopped to listen, the sound was gone.

They kept quiet for a moment, everyone trying to see or hear something in the branches, but the Oo country had settled into its peaceful quiet.

"We probably scared an animal," Corenn suggested.

They started their search again, still curious what kind of animal could make so much noise. The ivy mass was solid and had supported the weight of a human. It was disturbing to think of such a large animal living above their heads.

"The keep!" Bowbaq cried out suddenly. "It's there! I found the ruins!"

They guided their horses over to his. The giant, with Ifio still perched on his shoulders, smiled like a child. In fact, they could all easily perceive the gray form of a crumbling tower, abandoned for centuries.

"The portal is close," Lana said enthusiastically. "We are *so close*!"

"Don't get too excited," Grigán tempered, despite his own desire to join his companions in their joy. "Now we have to be even more careful. Don't forget that something may be waiting for us."

The heirs quieted, but the excited mood and their joyful smiles said enough.

"We shouldn't lose this landmark," Grigán continued. "We are going to search in larger and larger circles around this area, until we find the portal."

"You don't want to go see the keep?" Rey said, surprised.

"I do, but the Wyvern could live there, and that's enough to kill my curiosity."

Slightly frustrated that they couldn't explore the ruins, the heirs did as the warrior said. As Léti grabbed her rapier, Yan did the same with his broadsword, and Rey soon followed suit.

The first circle kept them nervous and joyful at the same time. By the second, they had lost all joy and were only nervous. By the third, they had lost their view of the ruins, and were guided only by Grigán's compass.

Yan started to wonder if his memory of the Rominian script were inexact, and if the portal really was close to the keep's ruins. And how should they interpret "close"? Maybe his companions were nursing similar doubts. If so, they didn't say anything. Not yet.

They discovered the portal together, at the same time. It couldn't have been any other way; it was that imposing. That they hadn't seen it earlier was only because it was surrounded by a group of centuries-old lénostores.

The portal was carved into a barkor that was at least forty yards tall. The portal itself, which the ever-present ivy declined to approach, was more than twenty yards tall, and eight wide. Larger than a house.

Grigán walked through it on his horse, touching the Ethèque symbols deeply carved into the dry bark. They were the same as on Ji, and in Sohonne. The Oo portal was the third the warrior had seen. Perhaps he would finally cross through.

The others dismounted and approached the monument respectfully. Lana, who had never before had a material connection to their ancestors' adventure, cried under the pressure of many emotions.

"It would obviously take a long time to burn this," Rey commented, as he wrapped his arms around the Maz.

"What do we do now, friend Corenn?" Bowbaq asked.

"We wait for nightfall," the Mother answered without hesitating. "We prepare ourselves."

And we pray, she said to herself. Because if the Guardian came, they would lose much more than a dékade.

No one was hungry, so they skipped their last meal. Yet the interruption might have helped them pass the time, because they found it nearly excruciating to wait. Time felt slow, very slow, until the sun finally dipped below the horizon.

The wait was difficult for all, but more than for anyone else, the slow passage of time weighed heavily on Yan. The young man knew that the expedition's success depended on him. If he had misunderstood Usul's gift, or how the portals worked, or if it simply didn't open tonight, crushing their hopes . . .

His companions all had their weapons in hand; even Bowbaq carried his mace with him every time he moved. Corenn had accepted a dagger from Grigán, and Lana held Rey's crossbow.

Yan carried his broadsword and its sheath at his hip, but he knew it would be useless against the Guardian, who was probably as large and terrifying as the Leviathan described by Achem.

They jumped at even the smallest sounds, but more often than not, it was simply the horses roaming in the forest, munching on moss and branches low enough to eat, walking farther and farther away. If the heirs crossed the portal, they wouldn't need horses anymore, and if they didn't, they would have plenty of time to find them.

They had left their baggage near the portal, but knew they would abandon it if they had to flee the Wyvern. As such, they all carried their most prized possessions with them. It was a strange spectacle to see Grigán armed from head to foot, or Lana carrying her copy of *The Book of the Wise One* while pacing in front of the portal.

The night's cold soon pushed them to huddle together, as they had the night before. This time they were standing, and no one wanted to sleep.

"We could at least light a little fire," Rey suggested, his teeth chattering. "It wouldn't kill anyone."

"I'm not sure of that," the warrior responded. "We have to wait."

Standing, frozen in the darkness, Yan noticed once again how strange his life had become. He had never thought he would travel east of the Curtain, let alone be standing here in the heart of the Eastian Kingdoms, waiting for a magical door to open to another world.

"I heard something," Léti warned them suddenly.

Corenn turned around to look at the portal, but nothing happened. They heard no whistling sound, which would accompany the opening of the portal.

"No, no!" the young Kaulienne explained. "I heard something *in the trees!*"

Their horses had heard the same thing. They froze, then burst into a gallop in the next instant, commanded by the most basic animal instinct: to survive.

Grigán grabbed his bow and nocked an arrow toward the sky. Curiously, the ivy had avoided the divine barkor, except at the highest branches, but the surrounding trees were crawling in the stuff, just like the rest of the forest.

In the following silence, they could hear their own heartbeats, but only briefly. The leaves shook, branches cracked, and they knew a large animal was moving toward them.

"The Guardian," Léti whispered.

"Silence!" Grigán said sternly.

He was looking for where the monster would approach and, in the profound blackness, he had only his hearing to aid him.

A branch cracked, to their left. Then another, in front of them. Then to their right, an instant later. Another in front? *She can't move that fast*, the warrior thought. *Maybe there are many of them?*

Listening more closely, the sounds from above were uniform and spread out at the same time. He came up with another theory.

"A *snake*!" Grigán announced in a low voice. "The Guardian has the form of a damn snake!"

His companions shivered, alarmed at the image of a monstrous, undulating snake approaching from above the ivy. The gigantic creature was the queen of this forest. The trees could support her weight because her thirty-foot-long body was spread along many branches.

They listened, appalled, to the abominable slithering as the sound grew.

The Wyvern was headed for them.

"Grigán, we could light a fire now," Rey proposed.

A whistling sound burst into the night, and became a deafening racket. Behind them, a small luminous point appeared in the middle of the portal, illuminating Bowbaq, who worked with a piece of flint.

A spark flew from his hands and fell into the small pile of dry branches they had gathered.

The light in the portal grew to its peak and blinded them with its brightness. The gigantic trees in front of them shivered like grass in the wind.

A small flame grew under the giant's breath.

The light from the portal was replaced by a darker mist. Yan approached as close as possible, a knot in his throat.

Grigán kept his eyes on the forest as he released the tension in his bow, set aside his unused arrow, and nocked a new arrow to the string.

The small flame gave birth to others, larger and more voracious. Bowbaq nourished them with sticks, trembling with fear and cold, entirely focused on his mission.

The portal's mist dissipated, leaving behind an image of a mountainous landscape. It was night there as well.

Grigán dipped his modified arrow into the flames, and it took.

The forest exploded. The Guardian appeared. The heirs took a step back, holding back cries of terror. Yan forced himself to concentrate on the portal. Rey almost dropped his rapier.

They saw a serpent that looked exactly like the one that had attacked the actor. Exactly, except for the size. This one was thirty times larger.

The monster opened its mouth and spit like a furious cat. It seemed as if it would try to swallow them in one bite, though it was still fifteen yards away.

The landscape behind the portal clarified. Jal'dara. Yan recognized it immediately, filling with emotion.

The Wyvern slithered to the ground and raised its head six feet high. The rest of its body disappeared into the trees. It was titanic, Corenn thought. And furious.

The monster flared its crest and spit again. Then it slithered toward them, much faster.

"Yan, go!" Lana implored.

Yan put his hand in front of his face and gazed at the other world between his fingers. It seemed so close. If he hadn't felt the strange sensation of passing his hand through water, the illusion would have been perfect.

He pushed his hand forward and felt nothing. In the deceiving darkness, he wondered if he were still too far from the arch. So he took a slow step forward, and entered Jal'dara.

Grigán pointed his fiery arrow at the monster for a long moment, but mortal weapons did not scare the Guardian. As such, the warrior lifted his bow to shoot the arrow into the trees; it traced a luminescent arc before landing in the vines overhead.

The Wyvern stopped and watched the arrow's trajectory. Then it slithered toward Grigán, angrier than ever.

The warrior rapidly nocked another flaming arrow, handed to him by Corenn, and launched it, and then another. Léti lit as many fires as she could in the dry forest. The heirs stopped at the warrior's signal. As they had planned, Rey doused their own fire with a gourd full of water.

The Wyvern was only five yards away. It raised up to a third of its height, dominating the mortals. They walked away, slowly. The Guardian looked at them distractedly, but its attention was focused on the growing fires around the forest.

It took a last look at the heirs, then at the landscape beneath the portal, and turned back to the forest, hurrying to fight the fire that threatened Oo.

"Yan's gone!" Léti shouted.

The heirs gathered around the ancient barkor and gazed at the birthplace of gods. As they always had, they felt an unexplainable amazement, an enthusiastic fascination. They stared in awe at this landscape, which, despite its beauty, looked much like their own.

Yan came back into their view, smiling and excited. He had a companion.

"Welcome," Nol declared, offering his hand through the portal. "Welcome to your home."

SHORT ANECDOTAL ENCYCLOPEDIA OF THE KNOWN WORLD

Alt—The largest river in the known world. Its headwaters are located in the highest of the Curtain Mountains. It crosses the Ithare Kingdom and the Grand Empire before reaching its delta in the Ocean of Mirrors.

A Goranese legend claims that when the time has come, the dead will float down the river in gigantic phantom boats and take revenge upon those who have committed atrocities toward their living kin. Every once in a while, someone claims they've seen the vanguard of the dark army. Some harbors even refuse all embarkations after nightfall.

Apogee—The moment when the sun is at its highest point: noon, in our world. It's commonly accepted that the end of the third deciday marks the apogee.

Arque—Native of the Arkary Kingdom. It's also the main language spoken in this land.

Bells (of Leem)—At one point in time, Leem experienced such a crime wave that the city seemed to be completely overrun by thieves, pillagers, arsonists, and murderers of all shapes and colors. Although the city doubled the guards' night rounds, and then tripled them, the criminals remained untouchable, since they were too well organized.

The provost at the time then came up with the idea of installing a bell in the house of each of the most prominent people in the city. When these important people were threatened by or witness to a crime, they could ring the bell and the city guard would come right away. Most of the time it wasn't quickly enough, with the villains fleeing the scene the moment the first strike sounded. But it was still better than before.

More modest citizens followed this example, and soon there were quite a few artisans and merchants who had equipped their shops with a bell. After a few years, there were so many bells in Leem that crime nearly disappeared.

Unfortunately, the criminals found a countermeasure: setting fire to each house that dared to ring its bell, as an act of vengeance and as a warning.

Today, there are still more than six hundred houses in Leem fitted with bells, but now the bronze only rings during the occasional festivity.

Brosda—A divinity whose cult is especially widespread in the Kaul Matriarchy. Brosda is the son of Xéfalis, and Echora's reflection.

Brothers (of the night)—What the members of the Grand Guild call themselves, as do members of any guild of thugs in general. Some of them even go as far as renaming their new members, creating fake "families," etc.

Calendar—The one used in the Upper Kingdoms is the Ithare calendar. It contains 338 days, which are divided into thirty-four dékades and four seasons. The year begins with the Day of Water, which also marks the first day of spring. There are two dékades that contain only nine days instead of the usual ten: those preceding the Day of the Earth and the Day of Fire. Each day on the calendar begins with the sunrise.

Every day, as well as every dékade, carries a meaningful name originating from the cult of the goddess Eurydis; the moralist priests of the Wise One brought their nomenclature to the furthest reaches of the known world. But time and use brought about changes of varying degrees depending on the region. The Day of the Dog, for example, which the Grand Empire doesn't observe with any particular importance, was renamed the Day of the Wolf in the area around Tolensk, and corresponds to a feast day that all the locals really look forward to. Similarly, the Dékade of Fairs, kicked off by the Day of the Merchant, is well-known and will ever be so to the Loreliens, whereas it represents nothing to the Mémissiens.

Few know all the days of the calendar, and even fewer know what they represent for the cult of Eurydis—priests aside, of course. In the Upper Kingdoms, they use it very naturally, as they would talk of the day or the night, yet a lot of people are completely unaware of its religious origin.

Other calendars are used in the known world; they arise out of royal decrees, from other cults besides that of Eurydis, or quite simply out of tribal tradition. Many of them are based on the lunar cycle, like the ancient Roman calendar: thirteen cycles of twenty-six days.

Centiday—A unit of time of Goranese origin representing one-tenth of a deciday: approximately fourteen earthly minutes.

Council of Mothers—The main governing body of the Kaul Matriarchy. Each of the villages has such a council, presided over by the elected Mother and advised by the Ancestress.

Curtain—The Curtain is the mountain chain that separates the Grand Empire of Goran and the Ithare Kingdom from the countries to the east.

Dékade (pronounced "day-cahd")—Ten days. A division specific to the Eurydian calendar. The days of each dékade are named in chronological order. The first day is prime, the last is term. The other days, from second to ninth, are: dès, terce, quart, quint, sixt, septime, octes, and nones.

The dékades of Earth and Fire, which only contain nine days, don't have an "octes" day. In these dékades, the calendar skips directly from septime to nones. The Maz have provided a religious explanation: The omission of octes symbolizes the victory of Eurydis over Xétame's eight dragons.

Deciday—A unit of time of Goranese origin representing one-tenth of a day: approximately two hours and twenty-five minutes in our world. The first deciday begins with the sunrise, the instant at which the tenth deciday of the previous day ends. The apogee generally falls around the end of the third deciday.

This unit of time is used crudely by the ignorant, but a lot more precisely by the learned people in all nations, who do not use a common sundial for reference, but rather consult calculations indicating the position at which the sun rises relative to the city of Goran, and make adjustments depending on the season. This is also the only method that enables one to discern precisely when the change between the night decidays, from the seventh to the eighth, occurs.

Dona—First and foremost, Dona is the goddess of merchants. The daughter of Wug and Ivie, legend has it that Dona created gold so that she could cover herself with it and thereby exceed her cousin Isée's beauty. She then gifted humans with her creation so that those like her, upon whom destiny endowed a less favorable lot, could outshine others with their intelligence, with the possession of this precious metal acting as a testimony.

Unfortunately for Dona, the young god Hamsa, whom she had chosen as referee, renewed his admiration for Isée. Dona then resolved to disregard the singular opinion and became renowned for her parade of lovers. And so she also became the goddess of pleasure.

There's a Lorelien custom that requires a merchant who has just made a lucrative deal to give an offering to a stranger, and more specifically a young, impoverished-looking woman. They call the offering "Dona's share." Unfortunately, the custom is dying out, since the members of the cult feel that the share they routinely offer to their temples is in itself a sufficient display of piety.

No successful merchant would ever forget to glorify Dona with his gifts, if only to preserve the affection of a few "priestesses" who are particularly devout to the goddess of pleasure.

Eastian—A Levantine. A native of the lands that lie to the east of the Curtain Mountains.

Emaz—The chief figureheads and high leaders of the Grand Temple of Eurydis; in other words, the heads of the entire cult. There are thirty-four Emaz. Each Emaz reserves the power to pass on his or her title to a chosen Maz.

Erjak—An Arque title given to an individual who has the ability to communicate with animals from mind to mind.

Eurydis—The chief deity in the Upper Kingdoms. The cult of Eurydis has spread to even the most remote areas of the known world, at the instigation of Ithare "moralists."

The legend of the Goddess has forever been tied to the history of the Holy City. During the sixth Eon, the Ithare people—who didn't yet carry this name—were merely a colorful grouping of more or less nomadic tribes, assembled at the foot of Mount Fleuri, one of the old summits of the Curtain Mountains. It is said that the people first came together thanks to the vision of one man, King Li'ut of the Iths, who wanted to create a powerful new nation by bringing together all of the independent clans residing east of the Alt River.

King Li'ut dedicated his entire life to this dream, but the building of the city of Ith—the Holy City, as it is now more commonly called—took more time than he had. With Li'ut gone, ancestral divisions sprang up again, and stronger than ever: Without Li'ut's art of diplomacy, the beautiful dream would crumble.

It is then that the Goddess is reported to have visited Li'ut's youngest son, instructing him to finish the immense work his father had begun. Comelk—as he was named—thanked the Goddess for her confidence, but explained that given the severity of the tribal quarrels, he didn't believe he could succeed. Eurydis then asked him to bring all of the clan chiefs before her, which Comelk promptly did.

Eurydis spoke to each one of them, demanding that they follow the path of wisdom. Everyone listened respectfully, for as barbaric and unruly as they were, their superstitions and traditions made them fear divine power.

Once Eurydis had left them, the chiefs spoke for a very long time, consulting the elders and the oracles. All problems were brought to the table, and all of them were resolved. They swore to keep peace forever, under the name of the Ithare Alliance.

Years passed, and little by little Ith became a city of reputable size, and eventually a truly grand city. At the time, Romine alone could still rival the young kingdom's capital. The tribes mixed among themselves, and the old quarrels became nothing more than a memory of the past. Ith had everything in its favor to become the leading power in the world . . . which it became, but not as it should have.

Blinded by their new power, which was so easily obtained, the descendants of the first tribes started to boast of their superiority over the rest of the known world. Eventually, a few wanted to demonstrate it. The Ithares launched small-scale war raids, and later small border disputes, which finally escalated to full-scale conquest campaigns that progressively became more frequent and deadlier.

At the end of the eighth Eon, they had made themselves masters of all the territory stretching from the Curtain Mountains in the east to the Vélanèse River in the west, and from the Median Sea in the south to the Crek region in the north. The Ithares behaved like genuine conquerors: They pillaged, burned, and ravaged shamelessly, massacring thousands...

One day, as the war chiefs gathered once again to consider an invasion into Thalitte territory, Eurydis appeared for the second time.

It is said that she came in the form of a young girl, hardly twelve years old, the way she is most often depicted to this day. Still, many of the seasoned warriors present thought they might die of fear, the Goddess's ire was so great.

She didn't speak, feeling that a piercing look was sufficient. She simply bored her gaze into the eyes of every one of the powerful individuals in the Ithare Empire, as it was called at the time. The war chiefs understood her warning, immediately gave up all their plans for conquest, and made every resolution possible to put an end to the battles and the occupation of foreign lands. Each of them felt personally responsible for the major changes that needed to be brought to the Ithare way of life.

The next generation of Ithare people turned toward religion. At first, they experienced great tragedies. Their former victims, such as the young Goranese people, in turn became the executioners. The Ithare territory shrunk back to about what it was to start with: Ith and its surrounding area, and the Maz Nen Harbor.

But the years went by, and the Ithares launched into a new form of conquest, one that was surely more in line with what the goddess had in mind: The Maz left in all directions to the most distant reaches of the known world, with the aim of bringing the "Eurydis Ethic" to all the people of the known world. These excursions were very beneficial to the less evolved peoples, since the Ithares also brought their civilization with them: the calendar, writing, arts, and skills... everything they had learned over the course of their past conquests.

Some theorists are now proclaiming the third appearance of the Goddess. She will come again, of course, since she has appeared twice already. But the main question the Ithares ask themselves is this: What will be the next path to follow?

Gisland River—River that partially draws the border between the Kaul Matriarchy and Lorelia.

Grand Guild—This term designates the loose collective of practically all the criminal organizations in the Upper Kingdoms. There is no formal structure or hierarchy to the Grand Guild; it is more like an agreement among gangs that guarantees the respect of one another's territory and activities, just like the kingdomwide and citywide guilds.

Despite their numerous internal quarrels, the groups sometimes manage to agree to conduct an operation together, notably with contraband.

The Grand Guild does not officially deal in hired killings, but more often in extortion, kidnapping, fraud, contraband, and of course any form of stealing. However, it should be noted that any newcomer organization that doesn't respect the agreements doesn't last long.

Grand House—This is the seat of power of the Kaul Matriarchy, where the Mothers hold their council. Their living quarters are also located here, as well as their study chambers. Anyone can come to the Grand House to express their grievances; fifteen or so Mothers are permanently present to accommodate them. At various times during the year, the study and council rooms of the Grand House are open to any curious visitors.

Holy City—Another name for Ith, the capital of the Ithare Kingdom. This term is most often used to describe the religious quarter, an enclave with its own walls, laws, and citizens, constituting a veritable city within the city.

Ithare dice—A very popular game throughout the entire known world. While its origin remains uncertain, it is nevertheless known that it spread at the same time as the Ithare Empire, during the seventh and eighth Eons, and was quickly adopted by all of the conquered territories.

The Ithare die has six sides, with four depicting the elements Water, Fire, Earth, and Wind. The two remaining sides represent a double or triple of one of the four elements. There are four kinds of dice: one for Wind, generally white; one for Fire, red; one for Earth, green; and one for Water, blue.

The number of dice used in a game varies depending on the rules of the chosen game and any specific arrangements decided upon between participants. While a set of four dice—a soldier—is generally all that's needed, it isn't uncommon to see games requiring several dozen dice. The star, the prophet, the emperor, the two brothers, and the guéjac are the most popular variations of the game. However, there are many more.

Jez—A native of Jezeba.

Kauli—The native language of the Kaul Matriarchy.

Kaulien(ne)—A native of the Kaul Matriarchy. Kaulienne indicates a female, while Kaulien indicates a male.

Kurdalène—This Lorelien king is celebrated for having fought long and hard against the Züu during his reign. The cult of the goddess of justice, Zuïa, through threats, extortion, and murder, then exercised such strong influence on the kingdom's nobles and bourgeois that the king couldn't make the slightest decision without the endorsement of the Züu.

At his wit's end, one day Kurdalène decided to put an end to it, and from then on he dedicated all his energy to the annihilation of the cult—at least in Lorelia.

He survived for almost two years cloistered in a wing of his palace, surrounded by handpicked guards, before the Züu finally assassinated him.

Lermian (kings of)—Five centuries ago, Lermian was still the capital of a rich kingdom that had nothing to envy in the nascent Grand Empire, or in the expanding Lorelien land. The royal family had controlled the throne for eleven generations, and the dynasty didn't seem anywhere close to dying off, since Orosélème, the monarch at the time, had three sons and two daughters with his wife, Fédéris.

Lermian had endured the Rominian invasions, the domination of the Ithare, and later on the Goranese expansion, all with relative ease. It seemed that she would just as easily resist Blédévon, the king of Lorelia, and his attempts to exert his influence. Blédévon wanted to incorporate Lermian, which was practically an island within his own kingdom, into his realm. But it wasn't in his interest to launch an assault against Lermian's walls, since the city acted as a buffer zone between his kingdom and the Goranese border; Orosélème was well aware and teased the Lorelien king with games of intimidation, promises, and intrigue.

Lermian could have become—more than it is today—a leading city of the Upper Kingdoms if misfortune hadn't struck its rulers. Orosélème died from food poisoning; his oldest son had been on the throne for only six days before perishing in a fall from the city's high walls. The younger son reigned for a little more than eight dékades before he just vanished. Since the last son was too young to rule, the prince consort was given the title of regent, but not one year later he had to be relieved of this title because he went mad after falling off his horse. The husband of the second princess refused the honor of ruling the kingdom, choosing a life of exile with his wife. Queen Fédéris asked her councilors to elect one of their own to be regent. Only one came forward, but he perished just a few days later, stabbed to death in the street by thieves.

After that, no one wanted to volunteer to be regent. The queen, feeling unable to rule alone, finally accepted the deal King Blédévon offered her, making Lermian a simple duchy of Lorelia. In return, the merchant kingdom offered the protection of its army.

The curse that weighed on Orosélème's dynasty seemed to stop there; Queen Fédéris and her last son escaped death.

Rumors spread that the deaths were a series of assassinations; some even said that Blédévon was behind it all. But the theorist of the Lorelien court managed to dispel any doubt by revealing that it was the will of the gods to join the two kingdoms under one crown.

From this tragic episode sprang the popular expression "as dead as the kings of Lermian."

Lesser Kingdoms—Another name for the Baronies.

Lorelien Fairs—One of the oldest Lorelien traditions. During the tenth dékade, from the Day of the Merchant to the Day of the Engraver, the entry and exit of all goods into and out of the city—whose trade is authorized by the kingdom's laws—are tax free.

Obviously, this is the time of the year when the majority of occasional traders, faraway artisans, foreigners, and rare-goods sellers decide to find buyers.

The fairs draw in a lot of people. In fact, about a third of the participants don't come for business at all, but to simply enjoy the numerous attractions that come along with the fairs—street shows, games, banquets, and more. Some of them are generously paid for by the Crown, which sees it as an opportunity to affirm its prestige.

Anyhow, the kingdom's coffers hardly lose out in the deal: Each seller has to pay a three-terce fee before he can set up even the smallest stand in the street. The process is tightly monitored and violators are severely punished: no more and no less than the immediate confiscation of the entirety of the violator's goods.

Fairs also take place in the other large Lorelien cities, Bénelia, Lermian, and Pont. Here the fairs enjoy a relative local success, but they remain insignificant in comparison to the capital's fairs.

Louvelle—River marking the border between the Baronies and the Lower Kingdoms.

Lower Kingdoms—This term designates either the territories stretching south of the Louvelle or the land collectively formed by these same territories *and* the Baronies.

Margolin—A medium-sized rodent. Adults can grow up to two feet long. There are several species: the copper, the screamer, and the glutton, among others.

Margolins are well-known in the south and central areas of the Upper Kingdoms, and thrive just as well on the plains as in the forests or along riverbanks. Generally considered to be pests because of their rapid proliferation, their occasional aggression, and their unpleasant-tasting flesh, they are sought after only for their skins, which artisans use for all sorts of furs, bags, and leathers.

Maz—Honorary title used primarily by the cult of Eurydis, but other religions have borrowed the title as well.

The title can only be transferred—with exactly one exception—from a Maz to one of his or her novices who, as shown by work and devotion, deserves the position. The Grand Temple must approve the transmission, which takes effect either immediately or at the death of the granter, depending on the arrangement. A rule forbids any Maz from passing on his or her title to a family member.

The one exception involves the spontaneous "elevation" of a novice as a thank-you for a service deemed particularly noteworthy. The title is often bestowed posthumously—and therefore cannot be transmitted—as a sign of gratitude for a lifetime of service to the cult. The Emaz reserve the exclusive power to elevate novices in this way.

The tangible advantages of a Maz are not defined, for they vary greatly according to the particular priest's "career." Some have many responsibilities in the cult's main temples; others are entrusted with the occasional apprenticeship of a few novices, and still others are never called upon.

The number of living Maz is unknown, except by the archivists of the Grand Temple, who keep a continuous count. Many priests in foreign lands grant themselves the title without actually earning it, which doesn't help the estimates. But legend has it that the Maz were originally only 338, as many as there are days in the year; similarly, there are as many Emaz as there are dékades.

Mèche—A small river that is completely contained within the borders of the Kaul Matriarchy, whose capital sits on her banks. A tributary of the Gisland River.

Milliday—A unit of time of Goranese origin representing one-tenth of a centiday: approximately one minute and twenty-six earthly seconds. Most people consider it useless to measure anything that takes less than a milliday; however, the unit is itself fractioned into "divisions," representing about eight seconds, and then "beats," which are less than a second.

Mishra—The cult of Mishra is at least as old as the Great Sohonne Arch. She was the Goranese people's chief goddess before the Ithare army finally overcame Goran's defenses, sometime during the eighth Eon. She reclaimed her role as chief goddess of the Goranese after the Ithares completely abandoned their warrior ways for religion. In the period that followed, the city of Goran progressively became the empire of Goran, then the Grand Empire, and Mishra's cult developed at the same time.

Mishra is the goddess of just causes and of freedom. Anyone outside of Goran can appropriate her. And so it has happened that the people conquered by the Grand Empire have called upon the goddess for help, just as their conquerors did.

She has no known divine parentage; a few theologians present her as Hamsa's sister. There are very few Grand Temples dedicated to her—apart from Goran's impressive Freedom Palace, of course—but there are many followers who individually revere miniature idols of the goddess or her symbol, the bear.

Moralist—The moralist priests use the writings and narratives from all religions and combine them to find the morals that are most common and important: pity, tolerance, knowledge, honesty, respect, justice, etc.

They are often teachers and philosophers who humbly limit their task to the education of a small community. The most recognized of moralist cults is that of the goddess Eurydis.

Niab—A Kauli term. The niab is a deep-sea fish that only comes to the surface at night. Kaulien fishermen use a large dark-colored cloth to lure the fish by stretching it out on the surface of the water between several boats, thereby fabricating artificial darkness. Then all they have to do is dive in and "pick" them like fruit, since the fish enters into a state of drowsiness near the surface.

From this, the term "niab" is used as an insult for someone who is gullible, or acts without thinking.

Odrel—Divinity whose cult is widespread in the Upper Kingdoms. According to legend, Odrel is the second son of Echora and Olibar.

After a lifetime of work, a single Odrel priest managed to assemble more than five hundred stories that centered on the god of sadness, as he is sometimes called. None of the stories finish well. The most famous story by far is the one that tells of Odrel's complicated love affair with a shepherdess. It ends with the dramatic death of the woman and their three children, and Odrel's agonizing realization that he can't follow them into death, the only thing in the world beyond his reach.

The priest-historian finishes his work with these words: "No one has experienced such misfortune as Odrel. It's surely because of this that all the ill-fated, unlucky, and destitute; those who carry the burden of mourning, regrets, and of memories; those who have known injustice, despair, disgrace, misery, all of life's trials; all have come, do come, and will come one day to seek comfort beside Odrel. He's the only god capable of understanding them, because he's the only one who himself inspires pity."

Old Country—Another name for the Romine Kingdom.

Queen moon—A small, smooth seashell, almost perfectly round in shape. Precious because of its rarity, the shell exists as three known types: the white, the most common; the blue, less common; and finally, the multicolored, a rarity. At one time, the last two varieties were used as money in some isolated parts of the Kaul Matriarchy. Elders may still accept a few shells in a transaction.

In fact, the seashell is still represented on every coin minted by the Treasury of the Matriarchy, and the Treasury adopted its name for its official currency, the queen, which exists in denominations of one, three, ten, thirty, and one hundred. The hundred-queen coins, as large as a hand, are not in general circulation, and are only used as a guarantee in transactions with the Matriarchy and other kingdoms.

Ramgrith—Native of the Griteh Kingdom. Also the primary language of this kingdom.

Ramzü—The language of the Züu.

Terce—The terce is Lorelia's official currency. There is a difference between the silver terce, which is most commonly used, and the gold terce, which is minted with an image of the king's head. Gold terces are known to have a level of purity unrivaled by similar coins. The denomination of official currency is the tice; one silver terce is worth twelve tices.

Theorists—A caste of priests devoted to all of the gods in general or, less frequently, to a few, or even just one. The theorists work to reveal the will of the gods through divine omens. Although the Grand Temples view them rather dimly, the royal courts and lords prize them, and they often act as astrologists and advisors.

Three-Steps Guild—Name given to the circle of prostitutes in Lorelia. The name originates from the fact that this "business" used to be confined to the part of town known as the lower city. These merchants of charm were so numerous that the pimps, tired of arguments that frequently devolved into fights, finally gave each one of them a portion of the street measuring exactly three steps.

Some pimps have held on to this tradition, even though the majority of prostitutes now gather in the harbor neighborhood, which is much larger.

Upper Kingdoms—Term used to designate the group of kingdoms comprised of Lorelia, the Grand Empire of Goran, and the Ithare Kingdom, and sometimes Romine. In the Lower Kingdoms, however, the term is used to indicate *all* of the countries north of the Median Sea, meaning the kingdoms listed above, with the addition of the Kaul Matriarchy and Arkary.

Vélanèse River—A Lorelien river. The town of Pont was built at its headwaters.

White Country—Another name for the Arkary Kingdom.

Wise One—Name sometimes given to the goddess Eurydis.

Zuïa/Züu/Zü—Called the goddess of justice by her followers, Zuïa is the goddess of the Züu assassins. A single follower of Zuïa is called a Zü, with the plural form being Züu.

ABOUT THE AUTHOR

A native of France and a lifelong fantasy enthusiast who numbers Jack Vance, Fritz Leiber, and Michael Moorcock among his heroes, Pierre Grimbert has been awarded the Prix Ozone for best French-language fantasy novel, and the Prix Julia Verlanger, for best science fiction novel in any language. He is the author of thirteen much-beloved novels of the Ji mythos, including the series The Secret of Ji, The Children of Ji, and The Guardians of Ji. He lives in northern France with his wife, Audrey Françaix (also a writer), and four children.

ABOUT THE TRANSLATOR

Matt Ross lives in Durham, North Carolina, with his wife, Nicole. He has been translating French since 2009, and enjoying fantasy novels since he first read The Lord of the Rings in 1995, while at a basketball camp in Kansas.